Evans to Betsy

Also by Rhys Bowen
in Large Print:

Evan Can Wait

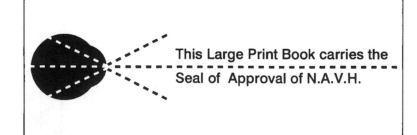

This Large Print Book carries the
Seal of Approval of N.A.V.H.

Evans to Betsy
A Constable Evans Mystery

Rhys Bowen

Thorndike Press • Waterville, Maine

Published in 2002 by arrangement with St. Martin's Press, LLC.

Thorndike Press Large Print Core Series.

The tree indicium is a trademark of Thorndike Press.

The text of this Large Print edition is unabridged.
Other aspects of the book may vary from the original edition.

Set in 16 pt. Plantin.

Printed in the United States on permanent paper.

Library of Congress Cataloging-in-Publication Data

Bowen, Rhys.
    Evans to Betsy : a Constable Evans mystery / Rhys
    Bowen.
        p. cm.
    ISBN 0-7862-4903-X (lg. print : hc : alk. paper)
    1. Evans, Evan (Fictitious character) — Fiction.   2. Police
— Wales — Fiction.   3. Druids and Druidism — Fiction.
4. Wales — Fiction.   5. Large type books.   I. Title.
PR6052.O848 E95 2002b
823′.914—dc21   2002035871

This book is dedicated to my many friends in the mystery community, with special thanks, for their support and encouragement, to certain ladies known to drink a lot of tea, tell dubious jokes, wear purple thingies, and give great hugs.

And with thanks, as always, to John, Clare, and Jane — my wonderful family critique group.

The spectacular property called Portmerion, which was the inspiration for the Sacred Grove in this book, has been many things during its existence, ranging from private home to set for the BBC's cult classic *The Prisoner* to fabulous hotel. It has never been, and probably never will be, a New Age center or Druid temple.

The book *The Way of the Druid* only exists in my imagination. The information it contains was gleaned from various books and Web sites on Druidism, to which Rhiannon's own brand of creativity has been added. It is therefore not to be considered accurate.

Glossary of Welsh Words

Cannwyll Corff — candle of death, pronounced *canwheel corf.*

Cwm Rhondda — the Rhondda Valley, place and title of hymn tune. Pronounced *Coom Rontha.*

Derin Corff — bird of death, pronounced as written.

Diolch yn fawr — thank you very much. Pronounced *dee-olch en vower.*

Escob annwyl — literally, "dear bishop." Good heavens! Pronounced *escobe ann-wheel.*

Iyched da — good health, cheers, pronounced *yachy dah.*

Llanfair — name of Welsh town, pronounced *Chlan-veyer.*

Maredudd ap Owain — pronounced like the modern spelling of the name, Meredith Bowen.

Nain — grandmother, pronounced *nine.*

Or gore — all right. Pronounced *or goray.*

Plisman — Welsh spelling of *policeman.*

Ysgol gyfun — Welsh secondary school. Pronounced *u-skol guffin.*

Note: There are many towns in Wales called Llanfair, including the town with the longest name in Britain. My Llanfair is fictitious. I chose the name because it is so generic.

We Are at One with the Dark Earth.
We Are at One with the Mother
With the Oak Tree and the Yew
With the Deep Pools and the Wells
With the Rushing Streams and the Crags
With the Meadows and the Woods
With the Sky and the Sun
With the Stag and the Eagle
With the Dolphin and the Whale
With the Creeping Things That Live in Darkness.
The life force of the universe flows through all of us.
Awen, life force, essence, spirit,
Awen flows through us.
We are one with the universe.

— Rhiannon, ***The Way of the Druid***

Chapter 1

"Llanfair." The driver read out the battered sign beside the road. "I thought this might be a good place to start." He changed down a gear and the Jag slowed with a discontented growl. A village appeared ahead — a mere cluster of cottages, nestled under the steep, green walls of the mountain pass.

The woman in the passenger seat leaned forward to peer through the windscreen. It was hard to tell her exact age — the long straight hair and lack of makeup, coupled with the jeans and T-shirt, made her look, at first glance, like a teenager, but a closer inspection put her in her thirties. She studied the gray stone cottages, the sheep on the high hillsides, the mountain stream dancing over rocks as it passed under the old stone bridge. "It's worth a try," she said. "Certainly remote enough. No supermarket, no video store, and no satellite dishes on the roofs. And it's got the proverbial pub where jolly locals meet."

The Jag slowed to a crawl as they approached the square black-and-white-timbered building. A swinging pub sign outside announced it to be the Red Dragon. "I don't see too many jolly locals around right now," he said. "The place looks deserted.

Where is everybody?"

"Perhaps it's the Welsh version of *Brigadoon*. They only come out once every hundred years." She laughed. "Oh, wait a second. Here's somebody." A young girl with wild blond curls had come out of the pub. She began hopefully wiping off the outdoor tables, although the sky was heavy with the promise of rain. A loud yell from across the street made her look up. There was a row of shops directly opposite the pub. G. Evans, Cyggyd (with the word "Butcher" underneath in very small letters), R. Evans, Dairy Products, and then, preventing an Evans monopoly, T. Harris, General Store (and Sub Post Office).

A large, florid man in a blood-spattered apron had come out of the butcher's shop, and was now shouting and waving a cleaver. The two occupants of the car looked at each other uncertainly as the cleaver-waving and shouting continued.

"Jolly locals?" He gave a nervous chuckle.

The young girl appeared to be unfazed by the tirade. She tossed her mane of blond hair and yelled something back and the butcher burst out laughing. He waved the cleaver good-naturedly and went back into his shop. The young girl glanced at the Jag, then gave the last table a halfhearted wipe before going back into the pub.

"What the hell was that all about?" the

woman in the car asked. "Was that Welsh they were speaking?"

"I don't suppose it was Russian, honey. We are in the middle of Wales."

"But I didn't realize people actually spoke Welsh! I thought it was one of those ancient languages you study at Berkeley. You might have warned me. I could have taken a crash language course. It's going to make things more difficult."

He put out his hand and patted her knee. "It will be fine. They all speak English too, you know. Now why don't you hop out and test the waters, huh?"

"You want me to get hacked to death by a cleaver? Do you suppose they're all violent up here in the mountains? I'd imagine there's a lot of inbreeding."

"There's only one way to find out." He grinned as he gave her a gentle nudge. "And this was your idea, remember."

"Our idea. We planned it together."

He looked at her for a long moment. "I have missed you, Emmy."

"Me too. I didn't think it would take so long. I'm damned jealous, you know."

"You don't have to be."

An elderly man in a cloth cap and tweed jacket came down the street at a fast pace and disappeared into the pub. A couple of women walked past, deep in conversation, with shopping baskets on their arms. They

11

wore the British uniform for uncertain weather — plastic macks and head scarves over gray permed hair. They paused to give the car an interested glance before settling at the bus stop.

"I should get out of here," the man said. "I shouldn't be noticed. There's a big hotel higher up the pass — you can't miss it. It looks like a damned great Swiss chalet — ugly as hell. I'll wait for you up there, okay?"

"All right. Give me about an hour." She opened the door and was met by a fresh, stiff breeze. "Gee, it's freezing up here. I'll need to buy thermal underwear if we decide that this place will do."

"Start at the pub," he suggested. "At least we know somebody's there."

She nodded. "Good idea. I could use a drink." Her thin, serious face broke into a smile. "Wish me luck."

"Good luck," he said. "This is a crazy idea, Emmy. It damned well better work."

Chapter 2

The big car moved up the street. Emmy pushed her long dark hair out of her face as she opened the heavy oak door and went into the Red Dragon pub.

She stepped into a warm and inviting room. A long, polished oak bar ran almost the whole length of one wall, and the matching beam above it was decorated with horse brasses. A fire was burning in a huge fireplace at the far end. The girl with the wild blond hair was standing behind the bar, talking to the old man and a couple of young men in mud-spattered work overalls. The low murmur of conversation in Welsh ceased the moment the stranger was noticed.

"Can I help you, miss?" the girl asked in lilting English.

Emmy joined the men at the bar. "Sure. What beer do folks drink around here?"

"That would be Robinson's," the girl answered. "Although some like their Guinness or a Brains, even though it comes from South Wales. I don't know why we stock it, personally."

"Weak as water," the old man muttered.

"Okay. I'll take a half-pint of Robinson's then."

The barmaid glanced at the men. She was

looking distinctly uncomfortable. "I'm sorry, but ladies usually drink in the lounge, if you don't mind. Why don't you go through and I'll take your order."

"Okay." Emmy managed a smile. This wasn't an occasion for making waves. "Would you mind directing me to the lounge?"

"It's through that doorway."

Emmy went through the open archway and found herself in a much colder room dotted with several polished wood tables and leather-upholstered chairs. There was a fireplace in this room too, but the fire wasn't alight. Along one wall there was a long oak bar. Emmy was amused to realize it was the back of the same bar where the men were standing. The girl with the hair had turned to face her.

"Found it all right, did you then?"

"Is this some sort of law in Wales?" Emmy asked. "The women in one bar and the men in the other, I mean."

"Oh, no," the barmaid said. "Not the law exactly. It's just the way it's always been, isn't it? And the men don't feel they can chat properly when there are ladies present. They might use bad language or want to tell a joke."

Emmy smiled at the quaintness. "So the ladies sit alone in here and discuss knitting patterns?"

"To tell you the truth, the ladies don't

come to the pub very often on their own. And if they're with their man, why then they all sit together in the lounge." She turned back to the elderly man leaning on the bar. "Isn't that right, Charlie? I was saying that women don't come to the pub much on their own."

"They don't come much at all," Charlie replied, "seeing as we're usually here around the time when they have to be home, cooking our dinners. Besides, most women don't like the taste of beer. My Mair says she'd rather drink medicine."

The barmaid had finished drawing the half-pint and put it in front of Emmy. "That will be one pound, miss, if you don't mind."

Emmy got out the coin and put it on the counter. "Thanks. Well, cheers then. How do you say 'cheers' in Welsh?"

"Iyched da," Charlie and the other men said in chorus.

"Yacky dah?" Emmy tried it, stumbling over the pronunciation, and making them all laugh.

"We shouldn't leave her all alone in that cold old lounge," one of the young men suggested. "It wouldn't do any harm to have her come and drink with us."

Emmy noted the muscles bulging through the threadbare T-shirt and the unruly dark hair. *Not bad,* she decided. *This assignment may have hidden perks.*

15

"Harry wouldn't like it," the barmaid said firmly. "Besides, she wouldn't want to hear the kind of language you use sometimes, Barry-the-Bucket — it would make her blush, the kind of things you say."

"Me? When do I ever say something that makes you blush, Betsy *fach?*"

"Well, I'm used to it, aren't I? I have to put up with you all the time."

She turned back to Emmy with an apologetic smile. "Don't mind him, miss."

"What did you call him?" Emmy asked, fascinated.

"Barry-the-Bucket, on account of he drives the bulldozer with that big scooper thing in the front."

"Barry-the-Bucket. I like that."

The men were now all leaning on the bar, watching Emmy with interest as she took a long swig of her beer. She was tempted to drain the glass in one go, as she had learned to do in college, but it was important that she create the right image. She took one swig, put the glass down, and smiled at them. "It's good," she said. "Nice and full-bodied."

"You like beer, then, do you?" Barry asked her. "Do they drink beer in America? It is America you come from, isn't it?"

"That's right. Pennsylvania. And we drink quite a bit of beer, although you'd probably find it too weak and cold."

"That very pale stuff, fizzy like lemonade. I had some once. Bud — wasn't it?"

Barry turned to his mate, who nodded agreement.

"Here on holiday, are you, miss?" Charlie asked.

Emmy noted with amusement that apparently it was okay if the men talked to her through the bar — rather like a convent with a grille, she decided. "Actually, I'm here to do research," she said. "I'm a grad student at the University of Pennsylvania, doing a Ph.D. in psychology, and my thesis is on psychic ability."

"Fancy!" The barmaid gave the men an impressed glance.

Emmy had worked on the speech long enough and now the words flowed out easily. He'd be pleased with how it was going so far. "I'm over here because Celts were famous for their psychic abilities. If there are any pure-blooded Celts left, it would have to be in an area like this. So I'm here to look for anyone with psychic power."

"Like reading the tea leaves, that kind of thing, you mean?" The barmaid leaned forward, eagerly.

"Yeah, that kind of thing. Seeing the future, having prophetic dreams, sensing danger — the ancient Druids supposedly possessed all of those abilities."

"Pity my old *nain* passed away a couple of

years ago," the barmaid said.

"Nine what?" Emmy was puzzled. She knew that nine was a significant number in Celtic mythology, but . . .

"*Nain* — oh sorry, I mean my grandmother. *Nain*'s how we say it in Welsh. I get mixed up sometimes."

"So your grandma was psychic?"

"Oh, indeed she was, wasn't she, Charlie?" Betsy turned to the older man. "She even saw the Derin Corff a couple of times, or was it the Cannwyll Corff?"

"What are they?" Emmy got out her notebook and started scribbling.

"Well, the Derin Corff is the bird of death and the Cannwyll Corff is the candle of death. They're the same really — you see them when somebody's about to die."

"Fascinating," Emmy said. "And your grandma saw them?"

"Oh, she did. I remember she came home late one night and she said to us, 'Huw Lloyd won't last the night. There was the Derin Corff perched on his shed roof.' "

"That was probably only the Lloyd's old rooster," Barry-the-Bucket commented, chuckling.

"You be quiet, Barry," Betsy said and slapped his hand. "Whatever it was, she was right. Huw was gone by morning. And so was the thing she saw on the rooftop." She shuddered. "It still gives me goose bumps to think of it. And she was a dab hand at reading the tea leaves too, was my *nain*."

"Did she ever tell you that you'd go out with a good-looking bloke from the village this Saturday night?" Barry asked, leaning across the counter until his face was close to hers.

"Yes, but Constable Evans hasn't asked me yet," Betsy replied smoothly. "Even though I've given him enough hints."

The older man chuckled. "She's the match of you, boyo."

"And she's wasting her time mooning over Evan Evans," Barry replied with a sniff.

"I don't see why." Betsy's gaze was challenging.

"You know very well why. You let Bronwen Price get a hold on him, didn't you? You'll not shake him loose from her now."

"We'll have to see about that, won't we?" Betsy smoothed down her tight sweater. "I'm going to get my chance someday, and then I'll show him what he's been missing — even if I do have to push Bronwen-Bloody-Price off a mountain first!"

The men laughed and so did Betsy. Then she seemed to remember Emmy standing alone at the other bar and turned back to her. "Sorry, miss. Don't mind them. Always teasing me, they are, because I've got my heart set on our local policeman."

"Nothing wrong with that," Emmy said.

"So tell me about your grandma seeing the future, Betsy. That is your name, isn't it?"

"That's right, miss. Betsy Edwards."

"Hi, Betsy, I'm Emmy." She held out her hand and Betsy took it awkwardly. "So go on about your grandma."

"Well, she was well known in the village for having the sight, wasn't she, Charlie?"

"She was," Charlie agreed. "If she dreamed something was going to happen, then it did."

"Wonderful." Emmy beamed at them. "You haven't inherited her talent by any chance?"

"Me?" Betsy blushed. "Oh no, I don't think so. Although . . ."

"Yes?"

"I do sometimes know the phone's about to ring just before it does. Stuff like that."

"There you are. You probably have the psychic ability but you've never tried to use your powers yet."

"Her 'powers.'" Barry-the-Bucket nudged his mate.

"You be quiet, Barry," Betsy said. "We're having a serious conversation here. So you think I might have inherited my granny's gift of the sight, do you?"

"It often goes in families," Emmy said. "Through the female line. You're not a seventh child, by any chance, are you?"

"No, I'm an only child. And my mother was an only child too."

"Perfect," Emmy said. "That's the strongest

connection of all. Only daughter to only daughter. Couldn't be better."

"You really think?" Betsy stammered. "My, but that would be wonderful, wouldn't it? Imagine if I could really see the future!"

"You could let your dad know what horse was going to win in the two-thirty at Doncaster." Barry dug his silent mate in the side again.

"If you have powers like that, you have to use them for good," Betsy said solemnly. "Not for winning horse races."

Emmy was flicking the pages of her notebook. "Look, let me take your name and phone number, okay? I'd like to get together with you and do some testing, if you're willing."

"Testing?" Betsy looked at Charlie uneasily.

"We have to test psychic ability in a controlled environment. . . ."

"I wouldn't want to go to any hospital," Betsy said.

"Oh, nothing like that." Emmy smiled. "I'm going to be working at a place called the Sacred Grove. Do you know it?"

"I can't say that I do," Betsy said. "Is it in Wales?"

"That big place on the coast near Porthmadog, isn't it?" Charlie interrupted.

"Used to be a private estate, built by that crazy English lord. Tiggy, or something, isn't that the name?" Barry asked.

"It's Bland-Tyghe," Charlie said, "and it's

21

pronounced 'tie,' you ignorant burke."

Barry grinned. "They're all round the bend, aren't they? Didn't the old man used to walk through the village in his pajamas, spouting poetry?"

"Didn't I read that his daughter has turned it into some kind of hospital or sanitarium?" Charlie said.

"Loony bin, more likely," Barry commented. "You want to watch out, Betsy. If they take you in there, they might never let you out again."

"I'm not going to any loony bin," Betsy said anxiously.

"No, you've got it all wrong," Emmy interrupted hastily. "It's a New Age center."

"New age center?" Charlie asked. "Like an old folks' home, you mean?"

"New Age," Emmy repeated. Really, these people were just perfect. Totally clueless. "They're into all kinds of cool stuff — alternative healing, psychic research. That kind of thing. I haven't been there yet, but I've been in contact with them and they sound like they've got great facilities and staff." She smiled hopefully at Betsy. "I've only just arrived in the area. I need to get settled in and then maybe you and I can go take a look down there. See if it's the kind of thing you'd like to do, okay?"

"Okay," Betsy said. "I don't mind going to take a look."

"I'd better get going," Emmy said. "I've got a lot to do. I need to scout out all the other villages for people with psychic ability, and I need to find myself a place to stay. The hotel's too expensive. You don't know of any good b-and-bs that don't charge an arm and a leg, do you?"

"We don't go in for tourism too much up here," Charlie said. "There's the holiday cottages up on what used to be Morgan's farm, but they're not cheap, I hear."

"I'd rather just find a room somewhere, and someone to cook me breakfast," Emmy said. "I imagine I'll be working pretty hard."

"I know a room that's going to be empty," Betsy said suddenly. She gave the men an excited glance. "Well, there is, isn't there? If Evan Evans moves into that cottage, Mrs. Williams will have a room free."

"Has he really decided to move out?" Charlie asked. "I know he was thinking about it, but he might change his mind at the last moment, seeing as how Mrs. Williams looked after him so well."

"If he says he's going to do it, he will," Betsy said firmly. "Anyway, we'll ask him next time he comes in."

"Fantastic," Emmy said. "I've got your phone number, so I'll call back and see. That would be so convenient if I could get a room in Llanfair." She pronounced it *Lan-fair*.

The other occupants of the bar smiled.

"What?" Emmy demanded.

"It's called *Chlan-veyer*," Betsy said. "That's how we say it. But don't worry about it," she added. "No foreigners can get it right."

"Chlan-veyer," Emmy repeated. "I'll get it right next time. You'll have to clue me in, Betsy."

"Okay, miss."

"Call me Emmy." She gave another warm smile. "I'll be in touch, Betsy."

She had just come through the archway into the main bar when the door opened and the butcher came in, now without his blood-spattered apron. He looked around the room and his gaze fastened on Emmy. As he let out a torrent in Welsh, Emmy moved hastily out of the way. She had forgotten about this cleaver-wielding maniac, who might make living in this village hazardous.

Betsy answered him back in Welsh and he relaxed as he came up to the bar.

"Sorry, miss," Betsy said, "but Evans-the-Meat is a little out of sorts this morning. A little matter of a bet we had over the football match last night. He was betting on Manchester United but Liverpool won, like I said it would."

"A football match?" Emmy couldn't help smiling.

"Mr. Evans thought the ref was unfair. He gave their best player a red card when it wasn't a foul," Betsy said. "But now he's going to pay up like the gentleman he is."

Evans-the-Meat gave a sheepish smile. "It breaks my heart to see a quality team like Manchester United beaten by a load of louts like Liverpool, that's all. Oh, well, nothing we can do about it now, is there? So you'd better make it a pint of Robinson's then, Betsy *fach*."

Emmy slipped out of the pub as Betsy poured the beer. She hurried up the village street, past the rows of identical gray cottages, each with a brightly painted front door, shining brass letter box, and white scrubbed front step. Some had boxes of spring flowers growing outside — splashes of yellow daffodils and blue hyacinths against the gray stone. *All very nice and bright and quaint,* she thought. *Cut off from the real world.* Wouldn't he laugh when she told him they hadn't even heard of New Age!

She passed a schoolyard with a school building beyond it. Through an open window she heard the sound of young voices chanting. It sounded suspiciously like times tables, although it was in Welsh, of course. Beyond the school were the last buildings in the village — two chapels. They stood across the street, mirror images of each other in solid gray stone. Each of them had a notice board outside, announcing them to be Capel Bethel and Capel Beulah. Each notice board had a biblical text on it. One said, "Whoever asketh, receiveth," while the other stated, "Not everyone who says Lord, Lord will enter into the kingdom."

Emmy smiled to herself as she walked past. They really were clueless up here in the boonies. Presumably they hadn't even realized that the two biblical passages contradicted each other.

The hotel he told her about dominated the crown of the pass. It was, as he described it, a hideous giant chalet, complete with gingerbread trim and geraniums in boxes — completely out of place on a bleak Welsh mountainside. The discreet stone sign had the words "Everest Inn" carved in gold letters. The car park beyond was dotted with expensive cars so that the Jag didn't look out of place. She walked up to the car and got in.

He looked up expectantly. "Well?"

She pushed back her hair and a big smile spread across her face. "We hit pay dirt in one. She'll be just perfect."

Chapter 3

Excerpt from the book
The Way of the Druid,
by Rhiannon

Who Are the Druids?

To many outsiders the word Druid *conjures up a white-robed, bearded gentleman offering a sacrifice on Midsummer Night at Stone Henge. However, this picture does not represent the truth. Stone Henge was built long before the first Celts set foot in Britain and there have always existed Druid priestesses as well as priests. And while Druids did offer sacrifices, they were not blood hungry.*

Who then were the Druids? In the golden age of Celtic spirituality, they were a priestly ruling class, advising warlords, predicting the future. They were the keepers of the ritual but far more than priests. They were involved in politics as well as sacrificial ritual, prophesy, and control of the supernatural world. They were the teachers, the keepers of the oral tradition. They were the philosophers, shamans, physicians, and judges. They were feared and venerated.

Julius Caesar wrote of them, "They have

the right to pass judgment and to decide rewards and punishments."

We know from ancient writings that Druids underwent a twenty-year course of study before they became fully fledged priests.

There were three subcasts to the order of Druids:

> *Bards, who were the poets, singers, musicians, genealogists, and historians;*
>
> *Ovates, who were the diviners and read the omens;*
>
> *Druids, who were the priests and judges.*

Caesar also wrote: "they know much about the stars and celestial motions and about the essential nature of things, and the powers and authority of the immortal gods, and these things they teach to their pupils."

In many ways they were similar to the Hindu Brahmins and the Chaldean astronomers of Babylon. They were then, as they are now, the bridges between the two worlds — seen and unseen.

"Please don't cry, Mrs. Williams." Constable Evan Evans reached out awkwardly and patted his landlady's large shoulder. This gesture only made the generously built woman sob into her handkerchief even more loudly.

"I feel like I'm losing a son," she said. "The son I never had, you were."

"It's not like I'm going far. Just across the

28

street, isn't it? And you'll be able to see me every day. I might even drop in for a cup of tea and a chat."

"But it won't be the same."

"Come on now." He put a tentative arm around as much of her shoulders as he could reach. "It's time I moved on, isn't it? I can't go on being spoiled by you all my life. I've got to learn to stand on my own two feet."

Mrs. Williams made a supreme effort to collect herself. A big shuddering sigh went through her body. "I suppose so," she said. "I knew it would have to come someday."

"Believe me, I'm not completely thrilled about it either," Evan said. He bent to pick up a cardboard box of possessions from the floor of his room. "Cooking for myself after eating your good food for over a year — that's going to take some getting used to. I'll probably be as thin as a rake within a month."

"You could come back here for your dinner anytime you wanted. You know that," Mrs. Williams said.

"I know." He smiled at her fondly. "But that's not the point, is it? Bronwen won't make any commitment until I've had a taste of living on my own." He hoisted the box onto one shoulder and started down the stairs. "She's perfectly right, of course. I went from my mother's cooking to yours. I've never really lived alone before. How can I hope to be a husband and father someday if I don't know how to look after myself?"

"So you've made up your mind? You're thinking of marrying Bronwen Price and settling down then, is it?" Mrs. Williams's tears were forgotten. She hurried down the stairs behind him. "We all knew you were courting her, of course, but . . ."

"I'm thinking about it," he said. "I've turned thirty, haven't I? About time I settled down."

"You could do worse, I suppose," Mrs. Williams said grudgingly.

"Worse? I don't think I could do much better. She's a lovely girl, isn't she?"

"I won't deny that. A nice-enough girl. Sensible too. But a little too serious, if you ask me. A man needs some fun in his life. He needs to go dancing from time to time. Let his hair down a little after a hard day's work."

"Are you saying I should be dating Betsy then?" He knew perfectly well what she was hinting. She had dropped the same hint, none too subtly, at regular intervals since he moved in.

"Betsy Edwards? Betsy-the-Bar? Escob annwyl! Indeed, I am not suggesting a thing like that. Betsy's too flighty to make any man a decent wife. What you need is someone who is a good homemaker and knows how to have fun too."

30

She reached around Evan to open the front door for him. A swirl of cold wind flapped the pages of a book on top of the pile. "Now, I know you haven't liked to ask out our Sharon while you were living with me. I can understand that. A young man likes some privacy in his romantic dealings. He can't go courting when the girl's grandmother is supervising. But now you'll be living on your own, why don't you take her out — with my blessing? Then you'll see — a lovely little cook, Sharon's turning out to be, and a lovely little dancer too."

Evan was glad his back was turned to his landlady so that she missed the involuntary wince. Sharon, Mrs. Williams's granddaughter, giggled like a schoolgirl at everything he said, and she was too enthusiastic, all over him, constantly pawing at him. It was like fending off a Saint Bernard puppy.

"I'm sure she'll make some man very happy, Mrs. Williams," he said, "but you know me. I'm a quiet sort of bloke. I don't go in much for dancing and that kind of thing. Bronwen suits me quite nicely, thank you."

He stepped out into the blustery day, holding onto the objects on top of the pile that the wind threatened to snatch away. It was supposed to be spring, he thought gloomily, and yet there was another dusting of snow on top of Mount Snowdon last night. He glanced up at the mountain as he crossed the street, but the peak was hidden under a heavy blanket of dark cloud. On the other side of the street was a long row of terraced gray stone cottages, typical of any mining village. Evan put down the box outside the door of number 28. The only thing that distinguished it from numbers 26 and 30 was that it had a red front door. Such splashes of outlandish color were frowned upon in rural Wales. The last inhabitant, a widow called Mrs. Howells, had always been considered flighty on account of the red front door. She hadn't shown any other signs of exhibitionism during her fifteen years of tenure, but the local women were still apt to speak of her as "Mrs. Howells Number Twenty-eight, you know, the flighty one with the red door."

Now she had gone to live with her daughter in Cardiff, of all places — another sign that her judgment was slightly off. Evan had heard through the grapevine that the cottage would be vacant and he had jumped to take it. Not that there would have been too many others waiting to fight over it. The population of Llanfair, like that of most other Welsh villages, was aging and shrinking. No work since the slate mines closed and no prospects for young people apart from waiting tables and making beds at nearby hotels.

He fitted his key into the lock, turned, and pushed the door open. He picked up the box and stepped inside, conscious of the damp-cold feel of an empty house. It was so different from the warm friendliness of Mrs. Williams's front hall that he looked back longingly across the street. He wondered how long it would be before he could turn this place into a home. So far he had a couple of saucepans and some mismatched china, courtesy of Bronwen, a vinyl-topped table, two chairs from the discount hardware emporium in Bangor, and a single bed. Hardly a promising start.

Evan carried the box through to the back room, which would serve as his living/dining room, and put it on the floor. The brown, pockmarked linoleum made the room feel even colder and gloomier. A rug would be one of his first purchases. Maybe he'd go down to Bangor or Llandudno this afternoon and do a rapid tour of the thrift shops. With his police constable's salary he couldn't afford to buy the kind of furniture he'd like all at once. He reminded himself this was just a temporary measure. With any luck the permits would come through for him to rebuild the old shepherd's cottage in the national park above the village. This was his dream and he had been waiting patiently for several months with no word from the national parks people. When he finished building his own cottage, then he could start furnishing it the way he wanted — he corrected himself — the way Bronwen would want it. She had already expressed her willingness to live there, although she hadn't mentioned anything about marriage. Neither had he, for that matter. It was still a hole in the ice around which they skated cautiously.

He wished that Bronwen were here to help him. But his department was on a cost-cutting drive and had started scheduling him to work every other weekend. This meant he was doing this on a Tuesday, when Bronwen was teaching at the village school. Evan took out a lamp, looked around the room for somewhere to put it, then stood it, for want of anywhere better, on the mantelpiece. He was just heading back to Mrs. Williams's when the front door opened and Bronwen burst in.

"Haven't got very far yet, have you?" She stood in the doorway, looking around disapprovingly. She was wearing a navy fisherman's sweater that made her eyes look almost the same color, and her cheeks were pink from walking in the wind. Strands of ash blond hair had escaped from her long braid and blown across her face.

"What are you doing here?" Evan asked, his face lighting up. "You haven't abandoned your pupils to come and see me, have you?"

Bronwen grinned. "It's lunchtime and I've

got two volunteer mothers on lunch duty, so I thought I'd pop over and see how you were doing." She pushed back her wisps of hair as she surveyed the room. "Oh, dear. I hadn't remembered it as quite so dreary."

"That's because last time you saw it it was full of Mrs. Howells's furniture. And this floor was hidden under a rug," Evan said. "I think a rug better be one of my first purchases, don't you? As well as pots and pans, chairs and tables, a wardrobe, chests of drawers — oh, and food."

"They've given you a raise then, have they?"

"I thought I'd go down to Bangor this afternoon and have a look at the charity shops. It's the only way I'll get this place furnished."

Bronwen nodded. "And you don't want to spend a lot on stuff that might not fit in the cottage someday."

"If the permission ever comes through." Evan sighed. "There's some old codger on the board who thinks that all national park property should be allowed to return to wilderness."

Bronwen came across and wrapped her arms around his neck. "It will come through. Just be patient. And in the meantime you'll be gaining valuable experience at survival techniques."

"You make it sound as if I'm about to

35

cross Antarctica on foot." Evan chuckled. "Of course, with my cooking, I may die of starvation pretty rapidly."

"Get away with you." Bronwen released him and gave him a playful slap. "You know very well that you'll be eating at my place half the time, and Mrs. Williams will be popping round every day with a little something she's baked, just to make sure . . ."

"She already invited me to dinner any night I felt like it," Evan said. "But I'm going to be strong and resist temptation. And no take-aways and frozen meals either. I've got that cookbook you gave me for Christmas and I'm going to learn to cook. You'll see."

"I'm very proud of you," she said. "I shall expect to be invited to dinner in the —"

She was interrupted by the beep of Evan's pager. He took it from his belt and grimaced. "Oh, no, that's all I need. HQ on the phone for me."

"That's not fair," Bronwen said angrily. "First they take away half your weekends and give you two useless weekdays off instead, and then they phone you on your days off too."

"I am a policeman, Bron," he said. "It goes with the job. If there's some sort of emergency, days off don't count."

"But I hardly ever see you these days," she said. "I'm busy marking papers all week and you're working all weekend. I had to do that lovely hike over Glyder Fach by myself."

"We could always solve that," Evan said, slipping an arm around her. "I could give up trying to make this place habitable and come and live with you instead."

"Oh, yes, that would go down very well with the locals, wouldn't it!" Bronwen laughed. "Imagine what fodder that would give the two ministers for their Sunday sermons. Besides," she reached up and stroked his cheek, "we're doing this for a purpose, aren't we?" She gave him a hasty peck on the cheek. "Got to go," she said. "If I don't get back, those kids will be running wild."

Evan followed her out and watched her run up the street before he made his way down the hill to his little sub-police station.

"Oh, Constable Evans. Glad we found you," Megan, the dispatcher, came on the phone. "Sorry to be disturbing you on your day off, but the chief inspector would like a word with you and he's off to Birmingham for a conference in the morning. It's all about this reorganization he's planning. He's come up with a solution to making you more — upwardly mobile, shall we say."

"Is he there to speak to me now?"

"He'd like you to come down so that he can speak to you in person. Is that all right? I know it's your day off, but . . ."

"I'll be there in half an hour," Evan said.

He put the phone down and went out to

his old clunker of a car. It started on the third attempt. Community policemen were not equipped with police cars. Mobile units were sent as backup from Caernarfon when needed, so the car was his own — had been his own for many years now. "Upwardly mobile" — what could that mean? And she had sounded so enigmatic when she said it, too. Did she know something he didn't — a promotion maybe? His transfer at last to the plainclothes division? He put his foot down and the engine growled in protest as he drove out of the car park.

"Ah, Evans. Good man." It was Chief Inspector Meredith's standard method of greeting, unless one had done something wrong, in which case it was just "Ah, Evans," with the "good man" part omitted. So he knew he wasn't in trouble.

"Glad you got here so quickly." This was also part of the standard welcome. "Pull up a pew."

The chief inspector was in his customary rolled-up shirtsleeves and Evan noted that the room was pleasantly warm. No cost-cutting attempts with the central heating going on here.

"So how are things up at Llanfair?" The chief inspector pronounced it awkwardly, not able to get his tongue around the double *l*, like all non-Welsh speakers. He was from

North Wales, but from the coastal city of Llandudno, which had always considered itself gentrified and where Welsh-speaking was a rarity.

"Oh, about the same as usual, sir." Evan perched himself on the hard wooden visitor's chair and wished the chief inspector would cut the small talk and get to the point. The anticipation was killing him.

"No bodies for a while? You must be getting bored." He laughed — a polite little *ha ha*. Evan smiled and wisely kept silent. He knew that his apparent knack for solving murder cases had not always gone down well with the top brass. In fact, he sometimes wondered if his track record was what had prevented him from being selected for detective training.

"I expect it's pretty quiet up there in Llanfair at this time of year, isn't it? No tourists around yet to get lost or stranded or lose their keys."

"That's right, sir."

The chief inspector leaned forward in his chair. "Look here, Evans. You probably know that we've been given a directive from Colwyn Bay to cut departmental costs considerably. One of the suggestions, of course, was to do away with the smaller outstations and consolidate our personnel at headquarters."

"I thought that had been tried before, sir,

before I got here. I thought they discovered that having an officer on the spot was a great crime deterrent." (*As if anyone with any sense hasn't already figured that out,* he thought.)

"True, but then the population out in the villages is shrinking all the time, isn't it? In a few years they will only exist for the tourists — a sort of Walt Disney re-creation of Wales as it used to be. Bed-and-breakfasts, craft shops, ye olde blacksmiths — that kind of thing."

"Not for a while yet," Evan said. "We must have at least a couple of hundred people in Llanfair and we're one of the smaller villages." He looked directly at the chief inspector. A sinking feeling was growing in his stomach. He had rushed here, filled with expectancy, dreaming of possibilities. He didn't like the way the conversation was going. "You're not thinking of closing the Llanfair station, are you?"

"Not for the moment. However, I can't afford to keep officers where they are not fully utilized. I know you have periods when you're busy up there. I know there have actually been some major incidents since you joined our force and your presence has been most —" Evan thought he would say, "instrumental," but instead he said, "— useful in solving them quickly. Then, on the other hand," he picked up a logbook, "there are days when you seem to do little more than answer phone calls and make cups of tea."

"It's not quite as bad as that, sir," Evan said. "I catch up on my paperwork when there's nothing to do. And I imagine there are days down here when you're not exactly run off your feet either."

The chief inspector managed a smile. Evan couldn't stand the suspense any longer. "So what are you planning to do with me?" he blurted out.

"Expand your territory," Chief Inspector Meredith said. "At the moment you are confined to an area you can cover on foot. I know you're a fine climber and you've been able to get up to accidents on the mountains, but the response time is naturally slow. We're going to make your job easier by issuing you a motorbike."

"A motorbike?" Evan couldn't have been more surprised, or disappointed. "I've never actually ridden a motorbike, sir."

"No problem. There will be training, of course. And that way we can justify keeping the Llanfair substation open. You'll be able to patrol the territory from Llanberis on one side to Beddgelert on the other and the most frequently used mountain paths as well. Everyone carries cell phones these days. If we get a call from a climber or hiker in distress, you'll be able to whiz straight up to them." He beamed as if he was giving Evan a wonderful present.

"So — uh — when do I get this — motor-bike?" Evan asked. He tried not to let his feelings show in his voice. He had never actually wanted a motorbike, even when his teenage friends were pleading with their parents to get one. They had always looked cold and uncomfortable. He saw no point in getting the rain in his face when he could be safely inside a car. Now he pictured himself riding up mountains in rainstorms in search of stranded tourists. It wasn't a pleasant prospect.

"It's already over at the motor shop, being checked out," the chief inspector said. "There are five of you constables who are being turned into mobile units, so we have to find time to schedule each of you for training. Go and look at the master schedule in dispatch and see when you can fit in a training session. We want it done as soon as possible, so you can be out and about before the tourists show up en masse."

Evan got to his feet. "Will that be all, sir?"

The chief inspector stretched, leaning back in his chair, extending his arms, and cracking his knuckles. "Yes, that's about it. Off you go then. And no doing wheelies when we're not looking!" He chuckled again.

Evan started for the door then turned back. "About my request, sir. My transfer to plainclothes. Any idea what chance I've got?"

"None at the moment with all the cost cutting going on, I'm afraid," Chief Inspector Meredith said. "Plainclothes is having to pare down to the bare bones, just as we are. And I'm in no hurry to lose a good man, either."

Evan came out into the hallway and made for the front door. He didn't even feel like stopping at the cafeteria for a chat and a cup of tea. Megan, the cheerful carthorse of a dispatcher, poked her head through the window as he passed. "Seen the chief, have you? Did you like my little joke? Upwardly mobile, get it?"

"Very funny," Evan said, and pushed the swing door open.

Chapter 4

It had started to rain, the fine Welsh misty rain that locals sometimes described as a "soft day." You didn't notice it as much, Evan thought, but it soaked you just as thoroughly as the heavy stuff. He didn't even bother to turn up his collar to keep it out. It matched his mood. Megan's laughter rang through his head.

He swung away from his car and instead walked through the car park to the maintenance sheds beyond where the new motorbike would be waiting. Might as well get it over with and take a look at it. He couldn't understand why he had such a negative feeling about motorbikes. He had never owned one. None of the friends of his youth had ever owned one either. So why was he so sure he'd hate riding one? It wasn't the cold and rain in his face that was worrying him. Anyone bred in the Welsh mountains was used to cold and rain in their faces. He'd had plenty of experience of it in his life waiting for school buses or playing rugby. And he never even minded the weather when he was hiking or climbing. It had to be something more than that. . . . Evan racked his brains. He had never been a speed freak, but then he'd never been too worried by

44

speed either. An image came into his head of a motorbike leaning over at an impossible angle as it rounded a sharp curve. When had he ever seen . . .

Then all at once it came back to him. He was on holiday with his parents on the Isle of Mann and they had gone to watch the motorcycle grand prix race held there every year. Evan couldn't have been more than five or six at the time. He remembered climbing up on the fence to see over. The bikes had flashed past, engines screaming, going so fast that they were a blur of bright color. He'd thought it was the most exciting thing he'd ever seen. He couldn't wait to get home to his new two-wheeler and pretend that it was a motorbike. Then it had happened — one of the bikes took the bend too fast. It was leaning at an impossible angle, the rider's head only inches from the tarmac. It had been raining and the surface was slick. Suddenly the motorbike was over and sliding into the other bikes. There was a horrible crunch of metal and then a great ball of flame shot up. Evan didn't think that anyone had actually been killed, but the image was still sharp and clear in his mind. He heard his mother saying, "Promise me you'll never ride one of those dreadful things. Promise me." And he had promised.

She had made him make similar promises about anything that frightened her, and extracted similar promises from his father too. But it hadn't done any good. His father had promised, over and over, that he would be careful and yet he had fallen in a hail of bullets one night, trying to intercept a drug transaction.

Evan hoped his mother had forgotten about the grand prix incident, but he didn't think she would have. He'd have to remember not to mention the motorbike in their weekly phone conversations.

His new machine, with four others, was standing in the garage, next to a dismantled squad car. It didn't look nearly as big or impressive as Evan had feared. It was a lightweight contraption with big, knobbly tires. He let out a sigh of relief.

A head poked out from under the squad car and Dai, the mechanic, emerged. "Hello, Constable. It's Evans, isn't it? Come for your bike then?"

"I just came to take a look at it today. I'm supposed to sign up for training before I'm allowed to ride it."

"Oh, there's nothing to it," Dai said, grinning. "Any ten-year-old could ride this bike. It couldn't go fast if it tried. Made for off road, really, like all the farmers have around here for rounding up their sheep. See the big tires. You'll be able to take it up to the top of Snowdon if you've a mind to. Ever ridden one before?" Evan shook his head. "Go on then. Hop on and get a feel for it. I'll run you through the basic controls. After that there's nothing to it. You could take it out for a spin today if you wanted."

Evan climbed onto the bike. It was small and compact, a pony not a race horse. "You switch on here," Dai said, "and your throttle is there on your handlebar. Go on, try it."

As the machine sputtered into life, Evan was conscious of two figures standing in the garage doorway.

"Would you take a look at that, Glynis?" Sergeant Watkins said, grinning to his partner. "It's King of the Road. Don't tell me that Hell's Angels have invaded the motor pool."

"Give it a break, Sarge." Evan smiled, hastily switching off the engine and climbing off the bike. "Did you hear I've been assigned one of these things?"

"I heard something about it, yes," Sergeant Watkins said. "Not a bad idea, really. You'll be able to respond more quickly when some stupid Englishwoman drops her purse down a mountain, won't you, boyo?"

"I think it looks like fun." Glynis Davies, the young detective constable, gave him one of her dazzling smiles.

Not as much fun as doing your job, Evan thought. *The job I applied for but you got.* He tried to push the thought from his mind. He knew it wasn't her fault that she'd received the promotion before him. She was smart and able; also a woman at a time when they'd been directed to hire more female detectives. But it still rankled.

"Are you allowed to carry passengers?" she asked.

"I've no idea what I'm allowed to do yet. I only heard about it a few minutes ago."

"If you are, I'm first in line for a ride," she said. She glanced across at Sergeant Watkins. "Have you heard the other news yet?" Evan thought he noticed Watkins give her a warning look, but she didn't stop. "Our chief is taking early retirement."

"The D.C.I.?"

"That's right. And guess who is going to take his place?"

"Not D.I. Hughes?" Evan sounded incredulous. "You're not serious. That man couldn't detect a fried egg sitting on top of his toast."

"He knows the right people," Watkins said, "and he was the only choice, really, unless they brought someone across from Colwyn Bay."

Evan nodded. Why should he worry? It wasn't as if the change of power at the top of the plainclothes ladder affected him.

"So they'll be doing without a D.I. then, will they?" he asked.

Watkins's face turned bright red. It was the first time Evan had ever seen him blush.

"Sergeant Watkins is being sent for training," Glynis said proudly. "He's in line to be promoted to inspector."

"That's wonderful, Sarge," Evan said, giving his hand a hearty shake. "Congratulations."

"Let's wait until it actually happens, shall we?" Watkins muttered. "With all these cost-cutting measures, they'll probably decide they can't afford to promote me." He turned to Dai, the mechanic. "That's why we're down here. Cost-cutting measures again. They're resurrecting old cars that should have been sent to the scrap heap years ago and we've been assigned this beauty. I take it it's not going anywhere for a while, Dai?"

"You can say that again, Sergeant," Dai said. "A proper mess, if you ask me. It's going to cost them a fortune in new parts to get it back on the road. And you should see the rust in the chassis. You'll be lucky if it doesn't fall to pieces while you're driving."

"Thanks a lot. Very encouraging," Watkins said. "Looks like we might have to ask Evans for a ride on the back of his motorbike after all."

"You're out of luck. I'm not taking it anywhere yet. I've got to sign up for training sessions first."

"Training sessions?" Watkins chuckled. "What are they going to do — start you out with training wheels? Our Tiffany could ride

49

that thing. You should have seen her at the go-cart track at Rhyl the other day. Proper little speed queen she is. Am I glad she can't get her driving license until she's eighteen!" He put a hand on Evan's shoulder. "We might as well get a cup of tea in the cafeteria then. Coming, boyo?"

"All right, why not?" Evan left the work-shop with them and crossed the wet parking lot.

"Isn't it supposed to be your day off today?" Glynis asked him. "I was planning to come up to see you, but then I looked at the duty roster and saw you were off."

"I was supposed to be, but the chief in-spector called me down here to tell me the wonderful news in person."

"Wonderful news?" Glynis asked innocently.

"About my motorbike."

"I gather you're not too thrilled," Watkins commented.

"I thought it might have been better news," Evan said.

Watkins nodded. "It will come."

"So what did you want to see me about, Glynis?" Evan asked, steering the conversa-tion to safer areas.

"You know about youth hostels and things, don't you?" she said. "I thought you could help me. I've got to put up flyers in all the local youth hostels. We're trying to locate a missing girl."

"Staying at a local youth hostel?"

Glynis shook her head. "No idea. She's an American college student, doing some kind of course at Oxford University. The course finished before Christmas. She called her parents and said she'd like to stay on over here and do some traveling before she went home. She promised she'd be home by Easter, in time for her spring term at university over there. Her parents haven't heard anything since February and she didn't show up for Easter. They're worried sick, naturally, and they've come over to look for her."

"What makes them think she's been around here?"

"Her last postcard said she was going to Wales. That's all they've got to go on."

"I see." Evan frowned. "Tough order. She could be anywhere. I presume there are other police looking into this too?"

Glynis nodded. "The police in Oxford, obviously, and the Met as well. She stayed at a friend's flat in London over the Christmas holidays."

"I'll be happy to put up flyers for you at the youth hostels," Evan said. "She was an outdoorsy type of girl, was she? Might have come here to hike or climb?"

"No, she wasn't. That's the strange thing," Glynis said. "Very quiet, studious, socially conscious, played the violin. But a good sense of humor. The last postcard she wrote

51

to her parents said, 'Gone to Wales. Got a date with a Druid.' "

"And that's all you've got to go on?"

Glynis nodded. "Not much, is it?"

"And if she's been wandering around since Christmas, she could be long gone by now. We'd be lucky to find anyone at a youth hostel who remembered her. These kids wander around for a month at the most then disappear again."

"That's exactly what Rebecca's done — disappeared," Glynis said. "She never showed up at her friend's flat to collect the rest of her stuff."

"Doesn't sound too good, does it?" Evan said. "The flyers have a picture of her on them, do they?"

"Yes, but not a very good one. I'm hoping for a better one when we meet the parents. They're due up here in a few days, working their way from the North of Wales to the South, leaving no stone unturned."

"Poor people," Evan said. "I've always thought that must be the very worst thing — not knowing. People can take bad news as long as they know the truth."

Glynis nodded. "You're right. I'll bring Mr. and Mrs. Riesen up to meet you when they get here. You always know the right things to say."

"All right." Evan smiled. She was a nice girl. If she wasn't dating the chief constable's nephew and he didn't have Bronwen in his life, he might well . . . he stopped short as they got to the police station door. "I've just remembered," he said. "I don't think I'd better stop for tea with you. I'm moving house today. I've got a ton of things still to do and I wanted to go round the charity shops before they shut. I've got to furnish the place somehow."

"So you finally did it?" Watkins grinned. "You cut the cord and moved away from your landlady. Well, good for you, boyo. Now you'll find out what life is really like. It will be beans on toast and washing your own shirts like the rest of us."

"I'll have you know that I plan to become a gourmet chef," Evan said. He tried not to smile when Watkins nudged Glynis. "No, seriously. I've got a fancy cookbook that Bronwen gave me and I'm going to teach myself to cook properly."

"We'll expect a dinner invitation, won't we, Glynis?" Watkins said.

"Absolutely." Glynis Davies's large brown eyes held his.

It was with some regret that he watched them go through to the cafeteria. In spite of everything he had to admit that he still found her fascinating.

Chapter 5

A few days later Evan headed out of Caernarfon on the new bike. He had passed the course, ridden around cones without knocking them down, and knew how to start and stop. He was ready to become a motorcycle cop. He grinned to himself at the term, imagining himself involved in the kind of high-speed chases that always seemed to happen in places like Los Angeles. The only high-speed chase around Llanfair would be with a sheep that had wandered onto the road.

He left the last of the urban sprawl behind him and let out the throttle as the bike began to climb the pass. The engine gave a satisfying roar. The first of the zigzag bends approached. He was supposed to lean into it, but it seemed such an improbable thing to do. He felt gravity pulling at him, leaned, and smiled to himself as the bike hugged the curve. Very satisfying. Maybe this wasn't going to be so bad after all. He couldn't wait to try it off road, but after several days of steady rain, he'd better let the hillsides dry out a little first.

Llanfair appeared ahead of him, nestled between green slopes. It was late afternoon and the village was bathed in sharp, slanting sunlight, making the gray stone of the cottages glow pink. The stream that flowed from the mountains was almost spilling over its banks, passing under the stone bridge with a thunderous roar and sending up droplets of spray to dance in the sunlight. Everything always looked its best after rain. All fresh and new. Just the sort of evening for a brisk hike. Instead, he had to finish painting the living room. Evan sighed. He had found a bright and cheerful rug for the living room, but it wasn't enough to lift the gloomy, damp feeling, which even a roaring fire couldn't drive away. The brown wallpaper on the walls hadn't helped, so in a fit of enthusiasm that first night, he had started to tear it down. It had peeled off in satisfying strips and now he was left with bare walls. So he had started to paint the whole thing sparkling white. Only after he'd done a couple of walls did he realize that the whole cottage hadn't been painted in half a century. Everything looked dirty and dingy in comparison. The ceiling needed painting too, and after the living room the front hall, the kitchen, the stairs . . . he had let himself in for a major project. For the first time he appreciated Sergeant Watkins's constant complaints of weekends being filled with do-it-yourself projects.

He felt daunted by the whole prospect as he pulled into the police station yard. He was about to dismount when there was a shriek and someone sprinted across the street, arms waving.

"Constable Evans!"

It was young Terry Jenkins, the local tearaway who had been mixed up in one of Evan's former cases. His face was lit up with excitement. "Is that your bike? Did you just get it?" He stroked the chrome handlebars lovingly as if the bike were a living thing. "It's beautiful, isn't it? Will it do a ton?"

Evan laughed. "Nothing like a ton, Terry. It's not meant to go fast. It's just so that I can get around my beat more easily."

"I bet it can go pretty fast if you really try. And with those tires, you could do motor cross — you know how they come flying over the hill — whee — airborne!"

"It's a police bike, Terry," Evan said, grateful he wasn't going to have to show off his nonexistent motor cross talents. "I won't be doing any stunts."

"Pity." Terry's face fell. "Still, you'll have to go fast if you're chasing a crook, won't you? Like that guy in the red sports car that time."

"I don't think anything like that is going to happen around here for a while." Evan put his hand on the boy's shoulder. "Come on, help me wheel the bike under cover in case it rains."

After a disappointed Terry had gone home, Evan let himself into number 28. It still felt

cold and inhospitable and he thought longingly of the smell of cooking that had greeted
him when he opened Mrs. Williams's front
door. Now if there was going to be any
cooking smell, he'd have to produce it. And
after last night's effort he wasn't so sure the
result would be edible. He had tried making
a steak-and-kidney pie. He had followed the
recipe faithfully, but the steak and kidney
had ended up as unidentifiable shriveled
morsels and the pastry crust needed a chisel
to puncture it. Maybe he was being too am-
bitious, he decided. Maybe he should stick to
egg and chips until he knew his way around
a kitchen.

He took out a couple of eggs and started
to peel a mound of potatoes. It took a while
to cut them up, so he started heating a block
of lard in a saucepan. Then he realized he
should have lit the fire in the living room
first if he wanted it to be habitable by meal-
time. He went through and coaxed newspa-
pers and kindling to life. They started
smoking merrily, instantly filling the room
with the smell of burning. He'd let them get
going well before he put on coal. As he returned to the kitchen, he saw where the
smell of burning was coming from. Smoke
was billowing from the saucepan and as he
approached, it sent up a great sheet of flame
with a *whoosh*. Evan grabbed a saucepan lid
and managed to drop it over the pan.

"*Pfew*, that was close," he muttered, pushing back his hair from his face with a sooty hand. "Smoke alarm," he wrote on the growing list on the fridge.

He had renewed admiration for Mrs. Williams, who could turn out a whole meal without apparent effort. It seemed pointless to start over with new fat and he had gone off the idea of chips anyhow. Scrambled eggs then. They were edible, if a little rubbery, but he was still ravenous. None of the cans in the pantry looked appetizing. There was nothing for it but to admit defeat and go over to the pub for bangers or a meat pie. Besides, he needed to get away from the smell.

Having checked that the fire now glowing anemically in the fireplace wasn't about to burn the house down, he put on his raincoat and crossed the street to the Red Dragon. Inside, it was as warm and welcoming as ever, the big fire glowing in the grate and the air heavy with smoke and conversation. Evan pushed his way to the bar. Instead of Betsy's welcoming smile, Harry-the-Pub's bald head poked up over the counter.

"What do you want then?" he demanded.

"And good evening to you too, Harry *bach*." Evan looked at the men standing around the bar for some explanation of what was wrong. "I'd like the usual Guinness and something to eat if it's not too much trouble."

"It is too much trouble," Harry said. "Guinness you can have. Food's not on to-night."

"Why, what happened? Where's Betsy?"

"You tell me," Harry snapped as he drew Evan's pint of Guinness. "She was due to work at five, wasn't she? Where the devil is she?"

"It's not like her to be late," Evan said. "Have you phoned her place?"

"Yes, and there's no answer. Her dad says she went off with some woman this morning."

"Some woman?"

"I know who that would be." Evans-the-Meat put down his empty glass and indicated that he'd like it refilled. "That foreigner who was in here the other day."

"English person, you mean?" Harry asked.

"No, American, Betsy said she was. Over here studying."

Evan's ears pricked up. "American girl, studying over here? Her name wasn't Rebecca, was it?"

"How would I know?" Evans-the-Meat demanded. "And I don't think I'd call her a girl either. Mutton dressed up as lamb, if you ask me."

"So what was Betsy doing with her?" Harry asked, smoothly refilling the pint and putting it down in front of the butcher.

"I'm not really sure. I only came in at the

end of it. A lot of nonsense about Betsy having special powers and second sight, from what she said."

"Always was daft in the head, that girl," Harry commented. "She'd believe anything you told her."

"Still, I hope she hasn't come to any harm." Evan looked around uneasily. "Where was this American supposed to be studying? At Bangor?"

Evans-the-Meat shrugged. "Ask Barry-the-Bucket. He was there. He might know."

Heads turned to where Barry was chatting with his friends in the corner by the fire. "Hey, Barry, boyo," Evans-the-Meat called. "You were there, weren't you? When that American woman came into the pub and talked to Betsy."

Barry left his corner and came across to the bar. "I was," he said. "Real brainy type with all kinds of degrees. Not a bad looker either — bit on the scrawny side but she'd be okay with some fattening up. I bet she's the kind that eats nothing but nuts and rice."

"So where do you think Betsy might have gone with her?"

"That place she was going to be studying. You know, that estate down on the coast built by the crazy lord Tiggy. What do they call it now? That's right. The Sacred Grove. That's what she called it. From what she said the lot that own it now are even crazier than

60

that old lord — she was going to find out if Betsy had the second sight."

"Like reading tea leaves, you mean?" Harry asked.

"I'd imagine so. Seeing into the future, anyway. This woman told Betsy that Celts used to have the ability and she thought Betsy might still have it, seeing that her old *nain* used to see the Derin Corff."

Harry let out a chuckle. "Well, if that isn't one of the daftest things I've ever heard. And Betsy believed her, did she? She would. But she's got no more knowledge of the future than the chickens in my back garden, and they're the daftest creatures on God's earth. If she could see into the future, she'd have helped me pick the right horse in the Grand National, wouldn't she? And I wouldn't have lost my ten quid."

And she'd have foreseen that old Colonel Arbuthnot was going to be murdered that night he left the pub, Evan thought. If ever there was a moment for second sight, that would have had to be it. Betsy was so anxious to be noticed that she'd say and do anything.

"I can tell you haven't got the second sight of the Celt, Harry," Barry-the-Bucket said, banging his glass down on the counter, "or you'd have seen that I was dying of thirst, waiting for a refill."

Harry opened his mouth to answer this when the door opened and Betsy stepped in,

61

her blond curls windswept but her eyes sparkling with triumph.

"Sorry I'm late, Harry," she said, pushing through the crowd of men to reach the bar, "but I want you to know that you're talking to someone who may be a real live psychic."

"So your psychic ability didn't tell you that you were late then? You didn't pick up the negative vibrations in the air from me being ticked off at you?"

Betsy gave him a dazzling smile as she opened the swing section of the bar and came through, taking off her coat as she walked. "I thought you'd understand, just this once. This is a special day in my life, Harry. You won't believe the things that I've seen today. It's like another world down there."

"You were abducted by aliens, were you?" Barry leaned on the bar, grinning at her.

"You have no idea, Barry-the-Bucket," Betsy said. "If you saw what I've seen today, your eyes would pop right out of your head. It's like another world."

"Well, go on then, tell me what I'm thinking if you're a real psychic," Barry teased.

"If your aura is anything to go by, it's the sort of thoughts a gentleman shouldn't have, as usual," Betsy said.

"My aura? What aura?"

"Emmy says we all have an aura around

us," Betsy said. "And we psychics can learn to see it. Everyone is surrounded by lovely colored light. Some people have gold auras, some have pink, some have mauve — and you, Barry-the-Bucket, have a dirty brown aura."

"I never heard such a load of rubbish," Harry said. "Where on earth have you been that they've filled your head with ideas like that?"

"It's not rubbish. You wouldn't understand, not being psychic like me," Betsy said. "The Sacred Grove is full of people who can see auras and heal with crystals, and who worship the trees — all kinds of wonderful stuff. It's the most amazing place. It's like this beautiful village you'd see on television, not like somewhere in Wales at all. Pools and fountains and spas, and the guests each have their own little houses. Like another world."

"You've said that about ten times already. So stop talking and start pulling. These gentlemen are dying of thirst and poor Constable Evans is going to go hungry because you weren't here to put pies in the oven."

Betsy turned her blue Barbie-doll eyes on him in horror. "You haven't had any dinner? You poor thing. I knew it was a bad idea moving in on your own without a woman to look after you."

"Betsy, I'm perfectly capable . . ." Evan began, conscious of all the eyes on him. "It's just that I haven't had time to get my kitchen properly stocked yet."

"He can't do a thing without his soufflé dishes!" Evans-the-Meat nudgcd Charlie Hopkins, who had just come in. "We all expect to be invited to dinner when you've become a gourmet cook, you know."

"I don't know why everyone thinks my living on my own is doomed to failure," Evan said. "I can handle myself in most situations, you know."

"Betsy is dying for you to handle *her* in a few situations, aren't you, Betsy *fach?*" Charlie Hopkins asked, his body shaking with a silent laugh.

"I'd know how to handle *him,* that's for sure," Betsy responded. "And I'd start off by feeding him right." She gave Evan her most encouraging smile. "Hold on a second and I'll pop a meat pie in the microwave. Will that do, do you think?"

"Lovely. Thanks."

"I give him a week," Charlie Hopkins said to Evans-the-Milk, who had just come up to the bar. "Then he'll be back with Mrs. Williams again."

"Oh, but he can't do that!" Betsy exclaimed.

"Why not?"

"Because she's already let his room."

There was an instant hush. It wasn't often that something happened in Llanfair without the news being spread within seconds.

"Let his room?" Evans-the-Milk said. "There are no tourists at this time of year, surely."

"It's not a tourist," Betsy said. "It's my friend Emmy. You know, the American lady from the university who I told you about. She needed a cheap place to stay because she'll be here for a while doing her research. She wants to find out how many Celtic people still have ESP. That's extrasensory perspication, in case you didn't know, Barry-the-Bucket." She added triumphantly, "And I'm her first subject and what do you know? She gave me one test and I scored right off the chart."

"Off the wall, if you ask me," Harry muttered.

"So I've got to go back for further testing. I met the owner of the place today and he's going to test me himself."

"Bland-Tiggy or what he's called? I thought the old lord died long ago and it was his daughter who owns it now."

"It's pronounce *Bland-Tie,* not *Tiggy.* You lot are so ignorant," Betsy said crushingly. "And Lady Annabel Bland-Tyghe does still own the place, but she's married to an American man called Randy and he's a very famous psychic over there and he's going to make this place just as famous. I met him today. Ooh, he was lovely, just. Like a film

65

star — long blond hair right over his shoulders. . . ."

"A bloke?" Barry asked. "With long blond hair?"

"That's right."

"Sounds like a proper pansy to me." Barry looked around at the other men for agreement.

"Ooh, he's not at all. He's ever so sexy-looking — just like those men you see on the covers of romance novels — you know, rippling muscles and open shirtfront. Too bad he's married and to an old woman like her too. He's going to be testing me tomorrow."

"Hang about," Harry said. "What's all this about tomorrow? It's Saturday tomorrow. I'll need you here all day."

"Oh, but Harry . . ." Betsy turned her big eyes on him, pleading.

"I can't have you going running off just when you feel like it. You've got a job to do here, young lady, and Saturday isn't your day off."

"Not just this once, seeing as how it's so important?"

"No, not just this once. Tell your psychic friends they can wait for Monday and your day off. And if they were really bloody psychic, they'd already know that Monday is your day off! And before you start pouting, go and collect the empties. I'm running out of glasses back here."

"Old spoilsport," Betsy muttered as she pushed past the men at the bar.

She was just passing the front door with a tray full of glasses when it opened and a woman came in. Betsy looked up and gave a shriek of delight. "Emmy! You're here. How lovely to see you! Everybody!" She raised her voice. "This is Emmy I've been telling you about. The one who has just moved in with Mrs. Williams."

The woman smiled shyly, pushing a curtain of dark hair back from her face. "Boy, what a dinner I've just had!" she said. "Can that woman cook, or can she cook? I owe you big-time, Betsy, for finding me that place to live. Those lamb chops tonight — boy, am I glad I stopped being a vegetarian. I am in hog heaven!"

Evan swallowed hard as disturbing visions of Mrs. Williams's lamb chops danced before his eyes — nicely brown on the outside and just pink enough in the middle, probably accompanied by fluffy mashed potatoes and cauliflower in a parsley sauce. He remembered that Betsy hadn't served him the warmed-over meat pie yet.

"Come on in, Emmy, and meet everyone," Betsy said, clearing a path for her through the crowd with her tray.

"I wasn't sure whether to come or not, seeing that women aren't really welcome in the pub."

"Not really welcome — who's been telling you that?" Harry demanded. "Of course they're welcome. We've a lovely lounge with comfortable chairs and tables all ready and waiting. Show her the way through then, Betsy."

"Oh, don't make her go in there on her own," Betsy said. "It's terrible cold and unfriendly in there tonight and she's the only one. It's up to us to make her feel welcome in the village."

"Rules are rules," Harry said in Welsh, "and we're not breaking them for any foreigners."

"You really are being an old grumpy tonight," Betsy said, also in Welsh.

"On account of my being run off my feet because the hired help didn't turn up on time," Harry said.

"Come on through to the ladies' lounge then, Emmy," Betsy said in English. "Harry here is a stickler for his rules, I'm afraid."

"That's okay. I find it delightfully quaint," Emmy said. "It's nice to know that there still are parts of the world where tradition is important." She approached the bar from the lounge side and leaned on it looking through at the sea of male faces watching her. "So has Betsy told you the news? Aren't you excited about having a genuine psychic in your midst?"

"Genuine psychic, my foot," Harry said,

putting a pint in front of Emmy none too gently. "If she's a genuine psychic, then I'm the duke of Edinburgh."

"No, I'm sure we're onto something here," Emmy said. "Of course, she hasn't learned how to harness her psychic ability yet but it's there all right. I can't wait for the director to see her tomorrow. He's a famous psychic in the States. Anyone who is anyone consults him, y'know. He used to have his own TV show."

"No wonder he looks so lovely," Betsy said as she ducked through into the bar area and popped up close to Emmy. "I said he looked like a film star, didn't I?"

"He's one of the best-known psychics in the world," Emmy went on. "I'm so happy that he's agreed to help me with my research. He's really excited about finding local people with untapped powers. I know it's going to blow his mind when he meets Betsy tomorrow and feels all of that untapped energy bursting out of her."

"I won't be able to meet him tomorrow," Betsy said, with a catch in her voice.

"Don't tell me you're chickening out, Betsy?"

"No, but Harry here won't let me have the day off. He's making it hard for me."

"She has a job and that comes first," Harry said. "She's bloody lucky to find a job around here. Most young people have to move away, don't they?"

The American woman touched Betsy's arm and leaned close to her. "Look, Betsy. If this is going to be a problem, maybe I've got a way out. I happen to know that they're hiring extra help at the Sacred Grove, ready for the summer season. If you like, I could speak to the owners about finding you a job there. Then you'd be on the spot so that we could do further testing and help you to bring out your hidden talents."

Betsy's eyes were shining. "Me, miss? You think they'd hire me down there?"

"Sure they would. The place is already booking solid for the summer and they need the same kind of staff as a five-star hotel. You've already worked in the hospitality industry so you've got a head start. Let me ask the owners in the morning and see what they say."

"You hear that, Evan?" Betsy looked round at him. "Did you hear what Emmy was saying? She thinks she can get me a job at the place where they're testing me. Imagine that — me among all the healers and priestesses and everything. You just watch how psychic I get when I'm surrounded by all those good vibrations."

"You're not seriously thinking of leaving Harry and going to work down there with foreigners, are you?" Evans-the-Meat had also overheard the conversation.

70

"Why shouldn't I? Grumpy old man," Betsy said. "Do you think I haven't been dying to find something better than this? I've got dreams and ambitions, you know. If they'll have me, I'll be out of here in the morning and Harry can like it or lump it!"

Chapter 6

Excerpt from *The Way of the Druid,* by Rhiannon

The History of Druidism

The Druid religion extends back into the mists of time. It is not known whether the Celts brought Druidism with them when they migrated from their homeland around the Black Sea to populate and dominate much of Europe, or whether Druidism evolved only among the western Celts — those in Britain and northern France. It is in those areas that we have found the physical evidence of Druids — the carved statues of the gods, the stones with charms inscribed on them, the priestly torques, the ritual objects placed in wells and lakes.

It is in Wales and Ireland that we feel their presence most strongly.

In any case we know that Druidism was flourishing in the British Isles when the Roman armies invaded with Julius Caesar in 55 B.C.E.

It is also shortsighted to speak of Druidism as being a thing of the past, recently resurrected. In Ireland and Wales, among the true

Celts, Druidism has never died out. It has been subdued, Christianized, but it still lurks at the base of every Celtic psyche.

Druidism has suffered from what today would be described as bad press. The only historical accounts of Druid worship still extant come from Roman sources. The conqueror justifying the act of conquest. Julius Caesar, Pliny the Younger, and other notable Romans describe the Druids as savage barbarians, prone to unspeakable sacrifices and torture of prisoners, holding mysterious and terrible ceremonies in oak groves. These same Romans failed to mention that captured Britons, many of them Druids, or adherents of the Druid religion, were shipped off to Rome to provide spectacle in the arenas by fighting gladiators or lions.

Tacitus writes: "The graves devoted to Monas barbarous superstitions he demolished. For it was their religion to drench their altars in the blood of prisoners and to consult their gods by means of human entrails."

What few facts we can glean from these Roman distortions tell us that the Druids were indeed formidable foes. When the Romans reached the Isle of Mon (which the English call Anglesey), they were confronted by a horde of blue-painted Celts, both men and women, brandishing weapons and howling so fiercely that the mighty Roman army was unnerved and the soldiers could not be *persuaded to cross the strait to do battle. Eventually, when reinforcements arrived and the Celts were hopelessly outnumbered, the Romans advanced and there was a fierce battle before the Celtic army was wiped out.*

Wales became a Roman province. Christianity arrived in the fourth century. Druidism was suppressed but never completely wiped out. The Christian missionaries cleverly incorporated the most important Druid feasts into the church year, so that the winter solstice, with its garlands of holly and ivy, its burning of a great log, and its feast to brighten the shortest day, has become Christmas.

Beltane, with its lighting of the new fire, its sprigs of flowers, and celebration of spring awakening, has been incorporated into Easter. And Samhuinn, that most mystical of days, on October 31st, when the door between this world and the otherworld is open so that spirits may pass freely between, has now become the children's festival of Halloween.

Evan opened his eyes and blinked in a blinding white light. For a second or two his heart raced, and he sat up, wondering what was happening to him. Then he realized it was only the sun, streaming in through his as-yet-uncurtained bedroom window. It was the first sunny day since he had moved and he hadn't realized that the window faced due east, allowing the morning sun to come streaming in. That strength of sunlight must also mean that it was quite late. He groped for his watch on the packing case that was presently standing in for a bedside table. Eight-fifteen. He rarely slept as late as that. Mrs. Williams had made sure that he never overslept and the tempting smell of bacon cooking had been enough to wake him. Then he remembered that it was Saturday. On weekends Mrs. Williams would serve him a full Welsh breakfast — bacon, sausage, fried bread — the works! Evan swung his feet onto the cold linoleum and sighed.

At least it was a sunny Saturday for a change. Maybe Bronwen would like to go for a hike, or they could drive down to the Llyn Peninsula and do some bird-watching. Spring was the best season for the seabirds. Then he remembered something else. This was his weekend to work. He took a lukewarm bath, not having learned yet how to coax the water heater into producing hot water for more than a couple of minutes, shaved, and made himself toast and tea. At least the stove had a grill element that worked. As he carried the toast through to the vinyl table, he heard a sound — the pop-popping noise of a revving motorbike. Evan jumped up and rushed outside. Surely he'd remembered to lock the lean-to where he was keeping the motorbike? And surely nobody could start it without the key? He imagined what D.C.I. Meredith would say if he had to call in and report the bike stolen after one day. He rushed outside in time to see a lanky figure wobbling down the hill on the bike, a large bag on his back. As Evan watched in horror, the bike picked up speed and the man gave a yell and jumped off, just before the bike ran into the gatepost of the Red Dragon and fell over, its engine still roaring

Evan rushed to pick the man up. It was Evans-the-Post, his large mailbag still over his shoulder. "You blithering idiot!" Evan yelled. "What did you think you were doing?"

Evans-the-Post staggered to his feet and started brushing himself off. "Is the bike wrecked?" he asked. "I bloody well hope so."

"You hope my bike is wrecked? Are you out of your mind, man?"

"I told them I wouldn't be able to handle it, didn't I?" Evans-the-Post went on, his large, mournful eyes staring at the prone motorbike. "I kept telling them. 'I'm not good with mechanical things,' I kept on saying, but they wouldn't listen. 'Directive from the postmaster general,' — that's what they told me. 'Rural postmen have to be motorized.' "

Evan was beginning to get the gist of what the postman was saying. "Wait a minute — are you saying that this is *your* bike?"

"Not mine. No, indeed. Belongs to the post office, doesn't it? And they're welcome to it. Telling me I'm not productive enough just delivering the letters to this village. Been doing it for twelve years now, haven't I? Never missed a day sick and they're not satisfied. And they think I should be taking the mail out to all the farms too — and right over to Capel Curig. The nerve of it."

Evan went ahead of him, picked up the bike, and switched off the engine. "You're lucky," he said. "It doesn't seem much the worse for wear. You'd have been in big trouble if you'd wrecked their bike, wouldn't you?"

"Do you think they'd have fired me?" The basset-hound eyes fixed on Evan. "They wouldn't fire me, would they?"

"They could," Evan said. "You're just going to have to get used to that thing, you know. I've been given one too, and I'm not too thrilled about it either."

"Ah, but it will help you catch crooks, won't it?" He grinned like a ten-year-old. "Tell you what — I'll learn to ride mine better and we'll have a race someday."

"You'd better start off going up hill." Evan helped him onto the saddle and adjusted his mailbag for him. "That way you won't go so fast."

"Or gore, plisman," Evans-the-Post said. "All right. If you say so. I think I'll go up to the youth hostel first. They always get a lot of letters with interesting foreign stamps on them. There's one from America today. It's from this girl's boyfriend. He says he's coming out to join her. Won't she be surprised, eh?"

"Dilwyn — how many times have I told you you're not supposed to read the mail?" Evan said.

"There's no harm to it. Not when it's postcards." Evans-the-Post sounded hurt. "Postcards are meant for everyone to read, or they'd be in an envelope, like letters."

Evan turned for home, then checked himself. "I've just had an idea," he said, touching the postman's shoulder. "How would you like to help the police? If you have to deliver any mail to a girl called Rebecca Riesen, will you come and tell me about it?"

"Is she a crook on the run?" Evans-the-Post's long, lugubrious face lit up.

"No, she's a missing American student. I've been around all the youth hostels to see if she's stayed there. So far no luck."

"Rebecca Riesen. Right you are," Evans-the-Post said importantly. "Off I go then." And he set off up the hill, the bike still wobbling dangerously under its heavy load.

Evan went back to cold tea and cold toast, then went to open up the police station. His bike was where he left it the night before and he chuckled when he thought of his encounter with Evans-the-Post. If only all post-men read every piece of mail like Dilwyn Evans, maybe they'd have tracked down the missing girl by now, and solved a few crimes too!

As he came out of the lean-to, a white Ford Fiesta drove past, slowed, and honked at Evan. Betsy wound down the window and put her head out. "Guess what, Evan — I've got the job! Emmy called them this morning and they said they could use me right away, so Emmy's driving me down there. Imagine me, working with famous people and swimming pools!"

"Have you told Harry?" Evan asked her. "It's not really right to walk out on him and leave him stuck, is it?"

Betsy's face fell. "I wouldn't have done it if he hadn't been such a grumpy old devil," she said. "He's never done a thing to praise or encourage me, all this time. And I'm the one who brings in the customers for him. Let him see how full the bar is when there's no pretty girl to gape at, that's what I say."

"I still don't like it, Betsy. And I don't think it's like you, either."

"I've got to take my chances in life, haven't I? You were the one who told me to follow my dreams, remember? Well, now I've got a real opportunity. If my powers are as strong as Emmy thinks they are, maybe I'll turn into a proper psychic someday, like Randy,

79

and people will watch me on TV." She leaned out of the window as the car sped up again. "Wish me luck, Evan."

Evan watched her white hand fluttering in a wave as the car disappeared down the pass. Poor Betsy, always dreaming of big things. He did wish her luck. He hoped this turned out to be the break she wanted, but he didn't have good feelings about this Sacred Grove place. Not that he knew anything about it, but he was inclined to think that all these so-called spiritual healers and psychic types were a lot of bosh. Of course, naïve people like Betsy were easily impressed. She was so thrilled to be among — he paused as he remembered her actual word — "priestesses," she had said. Hadn't the American girl written about a date with Druids? Then he remembered that Druids used to worship in sacred groves.

He went inside and called headquarters.

"Constable Davies, it's Evans here, from Llanfair." *Better keep things on a strictly professional level.* "Any developments on your missing girl yet?"

"Oh, hello, Evan. No, nothing at all yet. Thanks for putting up the flyers in the youth hostels for me. I feel so bad that her parents are coming and I've got nothing positive to tell them."

"Listen, Glynis, I've had a thought," he said. "What do you know about that new healing center near Porthmadog?"

"Oh, yes, I've heard about it. Ever so posh, isn't it? Five-star rates to have your aura read?" She chuckled.

"It's called the Sacred Grove," Evan said. "And someone from our village who has just been there spoke of priestesses."

"Priestesses?"

"Yes. So I wondered if it might be a place where we'd find Druids."

"How very interesting. Look, you don't think you could go and check it out for me, do you? Sergeant Watkins has started on his course this weekend, so I've got all his work dumped on me. Stolen property at the flea market again. I'm supposed to stake it out."

"I'd be happy to go down there for you. I've been told to get out and practice on my new bike."

"You want an excuse to play with your new toy." Glynis laughed, then checked herself as if this might have overstepped a boundary. "But seriously, I'd be really grateful if you went and had a look. Have you got one of the flyers left?"

"I put one up on the board outside the station here," he said.

"Brilliant! You could show it around and see if anyone there has seen her."

"All right. I'll do that."

"Thanks. I owe you a pint."

Evan put down the phone. It was hard not

to like Glynis. At least he had an excuse to check out this Sacred Grove for himself and keep an eye on Betsy, too.

Chapter 7

The sky was the clear blue that only comes after rain. There was a softness in the breeze, too, with wafts of blossom, hinting that summer really might not be too far-off. The wind in Evan's face felt good as he negotiated the Nantgwynant Pass. Down below him Llyn Gwynant sparkled in the morning sunlight. There were primroses growing beside the road and the fields were full of frisky lambs, jumping and dancing as if their limbs contained no bones.

Evan forced his eyes back to the road as the first of the hairpin bends approached. He knew too well how easy it was for a vehicle to misjudge the turns here. He had seen it happen. The bike, which had behaved itself perfectly on the ride up to Llanfair from Caernarfon, now felt as if it might run away with him on the steep descent. Trying to regulate his speed and remembering to lean into each of the bends, Evan found that he was sweating with concentration by the time he rode over the stone bridge and into Beddgelert. The attractive village was all decked out for the first spring tourists — tubs and wheelbarrows planted with spring flowers gave the place a festive air. A coach was parked outside the Goat Inn and tourists were already heading off to find Gelert's Grave or morning coffee.

Then the village was left behind. The road narrowed through the dark Aberglaslyn Pass. The roar of water from the river on his left echoed from the high rock walls that blocked out the sunlight and gave the place a chill, eerie feel. Even in a car he had found the place creepy. Now he was even more glad than ever to emerge on to the flat, green fields before Porthmadog. He skirted the town, then crossed the estuary by the narrow causeway they called the Cob, accompanied on his right by the little steam engine that went up the mountain to the old slate quarries at Blenau Ffestiniog.

On the other side the road wound through dappled oak woodland, then started to rise again. After a mile or so he came to impressive gateposts, each topped with a stone lion, its paw resting on a shielded crest. A discreet sign beside the gateway, carved from local granite, read, THE SACRED GROVE, CENTER FOR HEALING ARTS AND CELTIC SPIRITUALITY. As he passed through the gates and out of the sunlight, the wind in his face became colder. Over the crest of a little hill, and suddenly the most improbable of sights — an Italian-style bell tower, decorated with blue-and-white mosaic tiles rising from the green woodland. And beyond it the sparkle of the ocean. He rounded a corner and found the road ahead of him barred by a security gate. He looked around then spotted an intercom box on the left of the gate. He pressed it.

"Yes?" a male voice barked. "Can I help you?"

"It's Constable Evans, North Wales Police, here on official business."

"Hold on a minute."

A long pause. Then the gate slowly opened. As soon as Evan had ridden through, it swung shut again with a loud clang. He could make out the roofs of buildings nestled among the trees. He came to a glass-fronted booth and a man in guard's uniform slid open a window. "Leave your bike here, will you? They don't allow motor vehicles any further. Disturbs their concentration." He looked Evan up and down. "North Wales Police, is it? Who did you come to see then?"

"I've come to ask questions about a missing person," Evan said. "Maybe I should start with the owners."

"I'll ring through and have you escorted down."

"That's all right. I expect I can find my own way," Evan said.

The man gave him an unfriendly stare as he picked up the phone. "Someone will be up in a minute," he said. "Wait here, please."

Evan waited. He noticed there were several monitors in the booth and that the man was checking surveillance cameras. *A lot of security for a place that is supposed to be a center of healing and tranquility,* he thought. He looked up as he heard footsteps approaching on the gravel. A slim young man wearing a large dark sweatshirt and scruffy cords came into view. He was slightly built, and walked with the awkward, gangly gait of someone who hasn't quite grown into his body yet. As he came closer, Evan noticed that the sweatshirt had the Sacred Grove logo on it — an old oak tree with roots entwined into a Celtic knot around it.

"Hello," he said. "C-can I help you?" He peered at Evan shyly through round wire-rimmed glasses.

Evan was surprised to find that the voice wasn't local Welsh but betrayed a recent stint at an English public school.

"North Wales Police. I'd like to speak to the owners, please," Evan said.

"I think you've come to the wrong place. We haven't reported any 'incidents,' as you would say, and I don't think we have any c-criminals on the premises either." Evan sensed an uneasiness behind the banter. He suspected that the boy was shy by nature, but had picked up the upper-class innate arrogance when dealing with authority.

"It's about a missing person."

"Nobody's missing from here." The young man grinned. "Everyone was p-present and accounted for at breakfast, I can assure you."

Evan sensed that the boy might have been sent to hedge. "This person might have stayed here a couple of months ago. Now if you'd just take me to the owner."

"All right. This way then. I think Annabel's in her study."

"And you are?" Evan asked.

"I'm Michael. General dogsbody."

He set off at a brisk pace. Evan found to his astonishment that he was walking down a narrow cobbled street lined with pink-and-white stucco cottages, tiled porticos, old archways, and battlements. It was as if he had been teleported to a mixture of the Italian Riviera, medieval Germany, and Disneyland.

"Bloody 'ell," he exclaimed as the cobbled street came out above an area of reflecting pools and lawns. Rows of Greek columns lined the path. The lawns were bordered with statues. The pools were adorned with spurting mythical beasts.

"Yes, it does rather knock your socks off the first time you see it, doesn't it?" Michael said. "The old man who built it was quite crackers, of course. But in a lovable kind of way. He created this fantasy around him. Was still working on it when he dropped dead."

"His daughter owns it now, does she?" Evan asked. "That would be Lady Annabel?"

"She and her husband," Michael said flatly. "Co-owners."

Evan picked up his tone. "Her husband?"

"Her third husband. The American wonder boy. Randy Wunderlich."

"Wunderlich?" Evan gave him an amused glance. He wondered if the boy was having him on.

Michael returned the grin. "His name really is Wunderlich. Isn't that convenient? I bet it started out as plain old Smith. Randy Wunderlich, world-famous psychic and almost young enough to be her son. She married him last year."

He cut up a flight of steps, past a medieval church, and under another archway. Evan found himself outside a very different building, this one with the simple elegance of the Georgian period, and genuine too. This was obviously the original stately home around which the fantasy land had been built. Michael led him in through a set of gracious double doors. "This is our main building. Offices, admin. The guests, when there are any, stay in the cottages."

Evan shot him a glance. "I thought the place was heavily booked."

"Not yet," Michael said. "Cold, gloomy weather doesn't encourage meditation and dancing in the dew. We're hoping it will pick up in the summer."

They were in a tiled entrance hall with a

grand chandelier over a curved dark wood staircase. "Wait here, please," Michael said. "I'll go and see if Annabel is receiving visitors. What did you say your name was?"

"I didn't," Evan said, "but it's Constable Evans."

"Right-oh. B-back in a jiffy." The boy disappeared down a hallway, then returned almost immediately. "She'll see you now."

It was like being summoned to a royal presence. Lady Annabel was seated at a large desk. She had been reading but took off her glasses hastily as Evan was ushered in. "Thank you, sweetie," she said to Michael. "Now please go and see if those idiots have got the loo in number eighteen unclogged."

"You give me all the fun jobs." Michael pushed his hair back from his forehead as he left.

"Now, Constable. Exactly how can I help you?" The voice was deep and very uppercrust. Lady Annabel must have been quite a beauty in her time but youthful curves had now given way to fat. Her rich auburn hair was impeccably styled around a large face with an extra chin or two. Her chubby hands were decorated with a lot of rings and she had a floating, flowered silk scarf at her neck. Spoiled rich girl gone to seed was written all over her.

"Sorry to trouble you, ma'am." Did you say "Your Ladyship" these days? It sounded very feudal. "We've had a report of a missing girl, so we're going around all the likely places in the area. She's an American college student and it's just possible that she came here earlier this spring."

Lady Annabel's eyes twinkled with amusement. "A college student? I think it's hardly likely that she stayed here. We are what's known as exclusive, which means expensive. Most of our guests are either famous or old or both. There wouldn't be much here for a young person."

"Maybe I could take a look at your guest book," Evan said. "Just to make sure."

"Of course. Come through to registration." She led him to the other side of the building, where there was a hotel-style foyer, complete with front desk. "Show this gentleman the list of guests for the year, would you, Eirlys?" she said to the young girl sitting at the computer. "You don't need to go back to last year, do you?"

Evan shook his head. The girl handed him a Rolodex file. "What name was it? They're in alphabetical order."

"Riesen. Rebecca Riesen," he said. "And she probably would have come here in February or later."

"We weren't exactly overflowing with guests in February," the girl said and got a frown from Annabel. She helped Evan flip through the cards. "There's no Riesen here. Sorry."

"I can't imagine that she would have checked in under another name," Evan said. "Of course, if she had come here with somebody — a bloke — maybe they'd have checked in under his name."

"I don't recall any young couples. . . ." Annabel began.

"But you don't know his name?" the girl asked Evan. She gave him a shy but encouraging smile.

"Do you always work at the front desk?" Evan asked. She nodded. "So you'd be the one who checked guests in?"

"Usually."

Evan got out the flyer. "This is the girl we're looking for."

She studied it. "I didn't check her in. I'd have remembered."

"Sorry to have troubled you," Evan said. "I thought it was probably a long shot. We don't even know what part of Wales she went to. It's just that she said something about Druids in the last postcard she wrote to her parents."

"Druids?" Annabel's voice sounded sharp.

"I noticed this place mentions Celtic spirituality so I thought that maybe . . ." He looked hopefully at Eirlys.

"We have a resident priestess," Annabel said before Eirlys could answer. "She leads meditation sessions and guided imagery for our guests."

"And what about Druid ceremonies? Any of those?"

"At certain times of year she leads celebrations, yes."

"And are outsiders allowed into any of these — celebrations?"

"On certain occasions. She's hoping for a large gathering on Midsummer Night, and May Day is one too, I think. And she holds ceremonies outside of our community as well."

"May I please speak to her then?"

"Of course. I'll take you down to her myself."

"It's all right. I don't want to hold you up from what you were doing. Just give me directions. I'm sure I can find the way."

"I was planning to go down that way. I'm trying to locate my husband. He won't carry a beeper because he claims it disturbs the psychic vibrations he gets, but that's little use to the rest of us, who possess no psychic ability whatsoever."

She swept out through the revolving door, leaving Evan to follow in her wake. This time they took a paved back route, past a very modern-looking glass-fronted building. "The spa," Annabel said. "We run a full-service spa here. A massage therapist on duty twenty-four hours a day and experts in any kind of hands-on healing. Our aim is to soothe the body as well as the spirit."

It must be costing them a bomb to run this place, Evan thought. *All these experts to pay and buildings to maintain.* "So do a lot of people take advantage of getting their bodies and spirits soothed here?" he asked.

Again a brief frown of annoyance. "We only opened last year. It takes a while to build up a reputation and of course we are only catering to the most exclusive kind of guest. But things are beginning to pick up. Now that it's stopped bloody raining, that is." They were descending a graceful flight of curved steps with a carved stone railing beside them — another part of the old estate, he guessed. A clear view of a sparkling estuary opened up in front of them. On the other side were sloping green hills. Down below them, at the bottom of the steps, was another cluster of outlandish buildings, built around a little beach of yellow sand. A large swimming pool was built out over part of the beach.

"It's certainly a lovely spot," he said.

She nodded appreciatively. "I'm very fond of it. I'd do anything to keep it."

"It certainly keeps you fit, going up and down all these steps." As he said it, he realized this was rather a tactless remark, given Lady Annabel's generous curves, but she smiled and didn't seem to take offence.

"Actually I don't come down here too much. This is the area of spiritual healing and meditation. Spiritual healers are very touchy about being disturbed."

Evan blinked as he noticed a strange object among the buildings, dazzlingly bright with reflected sunlight.

"What's that?" he asked.

"That is our pyramid. A center of great healing energy."

Now Evan could see that it was, indeed, a pyramid, about the size of a small room, and made completely from beaten copper, decorated with Celtic knots.

"Copper is a wonderful conductor," Annabel said.

"Do you hold some kind of ceremony in it?" Evan asked. It was rather small, even for a chapel.

"Oh, no. You don't need a ceremony in a pyramid. You just *are* in a pyramid."

As Evan still looked confused, she went on. "You sit and let the energy of the crystals do its healing."

Evan forced himself not to smile. He was tempted to ask how many rich nutters were willing to pay big money to sit in a copper pyramid, but he thought better of it. Obviously Lady Annabel believed in this kind of stuff. Who knew — maybe it worked.

"Our meditation center is in here," she said and opened the door to a wonderful round room, with floor-to-ceiling windows looking out over the sea. Some of the windows were open and from outside came the cry of sea-gulls and the gentle hiss and slap of waves. The floor was polished wood but there were Persian rugs and large silk pillows strewn around.

"Very nice," Evan said.

"This is our contemplation room. We use it for group meditation. We also have smaller, more intimate rooms for past-life regression, guided imagery, psychic readings. I'll see if Rhiannon is available."

"Did somebody want me?" The voice was low and melodious. Evan stared at the woman who had emerged from the shadowy hallway. He couldn't have been more surprised. He was expecting flowing robes and large amulets. Instead, Rhiannon was wearing jeans and a black polo-neck sweater. It was hard to judge her exact age, but she had sensible, cropped gray hair and a face that had a weathered look of a life in the open air. Her figure, however, was as trim as a teenager's and stood in sharp contrast to Lady Annabel's flowing excess.

"Oh, Rhiannon, there you are. Splendid. I've brought someone to see you."

Rhiannon's eyes held Evan's. The power of her stare quite unnerved him. "Have you come to join us?" she asked. "You've felt us calling you?"

"Er — no, I'm on police business, actually," Evan mumbled, and felt himself blushing.

"The constable is looking for a missing girl," Annabel said. "American college student. It seems she might have been interested in Druids."

"Really?" Rhiannon looked amused. "A lot of Americans are drawn to us, it seems — which is understandable as so many Americans have Celtic ancestors — and so many of them seem to be searching for a spiritual purpose to their lives," she added.

Evan took out the flyer. "Lady Annabel thinks that the girl has never stayed here, but I understand that you hold ceremonies outside of this place. Is it possible that you've seen this girl at any of them?"

Rhiannon studied the flyer very carefully. Then she handed it back. "No, I can safely say that this girl has not been to any of our ceremonies."

"I'm sorry to have troubled you," Evan said.

"Oh, no," Rhiannon said. "You were summoned here."

"I was?" He looked confused.

"You belong with us, you know. You are one of us, even if you try to deny it."

Evan gave an embarrassed laugh. "Oh, I don't think so. I was brought up strictly chapel."

"I can tell a true Celt when I see one," Rhiannon said. "The Celtic religion is in your veins, boy. Your ancestors were worshipping here before Christianity was even thought of. You should at least come to one of our ceremonies. May Day is not far-off. Do come. You'd be amazed at what you will feel."

"Thanks, but . . . I don't think this is my cup of tea," Evan muttered. The woman's intensity was unnerving.

"It's not supposed to be a cup of tea," she said. "If you want a cup of tea, you go to your chapel. If you want the energy of the universe, you come here."

Evan shuffled his feet, wondering how he could make his escape without appearing too rude. "I — really ought to . . ."

"Just one minute." Rhiannon held up her hand. "What do you know about Druids?"

"I've seen the eisteddfod," Evan said. "They wear robes."

Rhiannon sniffed. "Stage Druids," she said. "Invented in the seventeenth century. Nothing to do with us or our religion. Promise me one thing." She darted into the darkness of the hall again and reappeared holding a slim book in her hand. "This will explain who we are and what we do. I wrote it myself. Promise me that you will read it and bring it back to me."

As she handed him the book, he felt a current of connection between them. He couldn't tell if it was just the static in that thick carpet or if there was really an electric charge when the book touched his hand.

"All right. I'll read it." Anything to get away.

"I'll be seeing you again soon," Rhiannon said. "Very soon."

Evan could feel her eyes watching him as he left the building.

Chapter 8

"She's an intense woman, isn't she?" he asked Annabel.

"A little too intense for her own good sometimes," Annabel said. "Now I just have to find my husband and — oh, here he is now."

A man was running up the steps from the beach. He was tanned, barefoot, wearing white pants and a flowing white shirt unbuttoned to his waist. His long blond hair blew out behind him like a halo.

"Hi, honey. What's the problem?" he asked, pausing to give her a peck on the cheek. "I was off jogging but I got a feeling that something was wrong." He looked inquiringly at Evan.

"The constable is looking for a missing girl," Annabel said.

"Then you've come to the right place," the man said, smiling. He held out his hand. "Randy Wunderlich. I've located plenty of missing people in my career. What can you tell me about her?"

"The constable thinks she might have stayed here," Annabel cut in before Evan could answer. "But I think we've established that she hasn't."

Randy put his fingers to his temples. "Wait

a minute. As you were talking, I got some
. . . something to do with water? Ocean?
Across the ocean?" he asked.

"She's from America," Evan said.

"Ah. Okay. That's a start. What do we
have to go on? Do you have anything belonging to the girl? Something I could touch
when I go into a trance?"

Evan thought that it was rather like giving
a bloodhound an old sock to smell and a ridiculous picture of Randy, sniffing out a trail,
sprang into his mind. "I've got this poster,"
he said, holding it up. "The photo's not very
good, and I'm afraid I can't tell you much.
She was studying over here, at Oxford, and
wrote to her parents saying she was heading
for Wales. She hasn't been heard from in
over two months now."

Randy barely glanced at the poster but put
his fingers to his temples again. "I'm not
picking up anything at the moment."

"I've already told the constable that she
hasn't been here," Annabel said. "And you're
probably not picking up anything because
she's gone back to America. 'Ocean,' you
said. The girl is across the ocean."

"Yeah. That could be it," Randy said.
"Sorry not to be more positive, Officer. I'll
keep on trying. If anything comes to me, I'll
be sure to let you know." He looked at
Annabel. "Did you want me, honey?"

"Yes, I did. We're supposed to be meeting

with Ben in —" she consulted her watch "— fifteen minutes. And you can't see him dressed like that."

"Just because he's a stuffed shirt doesn't mean that I have to be," Randy said. "He's an accountant. He's supposed to look like that. I'm a psychic and a well-known personality. He has to take me or leave me." He put an arm around her waist. "Come on. Race you up to the main house."

As he pushed her forward, Evan heard her mutter, "Sometimes I wish you'd grow up, Randy."

"But you married me for my youthful good looks," he chuckled, "as well as for getting your head straightened out."

Evan trailed behind them as they went up the steps. As they passed the spa building, Evan heard a shriek.

"Evan Evans — what are you doing here?"

Betsy and another girl were just emerging from the building with buckets and mops. They were both dressed in short green uniform dresses with the oak tree logo of the Sacred Grove on the breast pockets.

"Hello, Betsy," Evan said.

Randy turned back. "Hey — you two know each other? That's so cool."

"He's the constable in our village," Betsy said, her face bright red with embarrassment.

"Great. Terrific. So you've heard that you

might have a budding psychic living in your midst, have you, Constable?"

"Yes, I've heard all about it," Evan said.

"The grad student who discovered her is very excited by her preliminary results. She's asked me to test her on a more sophisticated level." He smiled at Betsy. "So you're all set for our session together this afternoon then, Betsy?" He gave Betsy a fake punch on the arm that was somehow very intimate.

"Oh, yes, sir," Betsy mumbled. "I'll be there, sir. And thank you for finding me a job here. It's wonderful."

"Glad you could join us," Randy said. "The more positive vibrations there are around this place, the better. We're going to make this place the psychic capital of the world, you see."

"Come on, Randy. Ben will be waiting." Annabel dragged at his arm.

Randy waved easily. "See you at four then. Don't be late."

"Thank you for coming, Constable." Annabel turned to Evan. "I'm so sorry we couldn't help you. And please excuse me if I don't show you out. We have an important meeting with our accountant. The main gate is through that archway to your right. I'll call Blaine to let him know you're leaving."

Then she and Randy hurried up the path. Betsy stood glaring at Evan, her hands on her hips.

"And just what are you doing here, I'd like to know?"

"Missing person report," Evan said, waving the flyer at her. "I thought this might be a good place to check out."

"Oh, yes, I believe that," she said. "You came here to spy on me, didn't you? Keeping an eye on me again."

"No, Betsy, I swear . . ."

"When will you learn that I can take care of myself?" Betsy demanded. "I'm a big girl, you know. If you were my boyfriend, I could understand that you wanted to run my life for me. But you're not, are you?"

"Betsy, I came here on official police business. But I'm glad to see you've come up in the world. You've traded a tray of glasses at Harry's for a bucket and mop."

Betsy tossed her curls defiantly. "That's all you know about it. I've got the cushiest job here you could ever want. I have to help out in the dining room for lunch and dinner and apart from that all I have to do is to check on the spa — you know, making sure there are fresh towels. That kind of thing. I just decided to help Bethan with the cleaning because I'd got nothing else to do. So you can tell Harry that I'm very, very content in my new job. They pay me very well and they don't work me to death."

"I'm glad you've landed on your feet," Evan said.

"I have to get back to cleaning the steam rooms," the other girl said to Betsy in Welsh. "See you later, Betsy."

"I'm coming, Bethan." Betsy smiled sheepishly at Evan. "Sorry if I yelled at you just then. I thought you'd come to convince me to come home again. I'm really happy here. Honestly I am. I can't imagine working at a lovelier place and they say all kinds of celebrities come here. I might meet someone famous!" Her eyes were shining. "Got to go then. See you around, Evan."

She ran back into the spa building. Evan continued on up the path and through the archway to the main exit. Something wasn't right here, he decided. The place seemed almost deserted and yet they'd hired Betsy to do very little work. If they had no customers, who paid all the staff it took to run this place?

Blaine was still unsmiling as he nodded to Evan and pressed the release button on the electronic gate.

Betsy found Bethan had gone into the steam room and was already wiping down the walls.

"Nice-looking bloke," she said as Betsy put down her pail and took out a sponge. "Friend of yours, is he?"

"That's right."

"Dating, are you?"

104

"If I had my way, we would be," Betsy said, giving the wall a savage scrub. "He seems to prefer the local schoolmarm, but I can't think why. She never tries to make the best of herself, you know — no fashionable clothes, and no makeup, and her hair in a plait. Dull as ditchwater, if you ask me. What can he possibly see in her?"

"It's always the way, isn't it?" Bethan said. "The good-looking blokes always seem to go for the plain women. I have the same trouble myself."

Betsy looked at Bethan's large, cowlike face with its mournful brown eyes and said nothing.

"You know it's a funny thing," Bethan went on, wiping the last of the wall with a grand flourish, "but I think I've seen that girl before. You know — the one on the poster he was carrying."

"You have — where?"

"She looks a lot like a girl who worked here earlier this year. She was only here for about a week, so I can't say I got to know her, but it does look a lot like her."

Chapter 9

Excerpt from *The Way of the Druid,* by Rhiannon

What Druids Believe

The ancient Celts perceived the presence of supernatural power in every part of the world. The sky, the sun, the dark places underground, every mountain, river, spring, marsh, tree, were endowed with divinity.

They believed in the concept of AWEN the liquid life force, essence, inspiration that flows through all living things.

They also worshipped the triple Goddess of the waxing, full, and waning moon and the Horned God of forest and animal powers. We, the heirs to the Druid religion, still hold these beliefs today. We see the Goddess as the fertile Earth Mother and the Horned God as the life-giving sun father.

We Druids feel more than a kinship with nature. We are part of nature. Nature is part of us.

We are a link between past and present.

We believe in the equality of all things and a balance between male and female.

We believe all life is sacred and worthy of

protection.

If we have a creed, it is "Do what thou wilt but harm none."

It was ten o'clock on a perfect spring Sunday morning as Evan wheeled the motorbike from his shed. Worshipers were filing up the village street, the older women in their hats and black lace-up shoes, the men in their stiff Sunday collars and dark suits, on their way to one of the two chapels. As they got close, they veered either to the left into Capel Bethel, or right into Capel Beulah, sometimes looking back across the street to give a disapproving stare to those going to the "wrong" chapel. They had also given a few disapproving stares to Evan, who was obviously going off on his bike when he should have been singing hymns.

The first hymns started, the lovely notes of the old hymn "Hyfrydol" echoing out from Capel Bethel, while Capel Beulah competed with "Cwm Rhondda." Evan stood for a moment and glanced up at the mountainsides. The first spring flowers were dotting the grass with splashes of yellow and white. Another great day to be climbing and instead he would be spending it down at the Sacred Grove. Betsy had reported her conversation to him the evening before and he had duly reported it to HQ. Now he was to meet

Glynis Davies in Caernarfon and drive her to talk to the people he had interviewed yesterday. He couldn't help seeing this as an insult. Now that there was a real mystery, he wasn't trusted enough to gather evidence without a member of the CID present. He reminded himself that this was just normal procedure. Glynis was not trying to pull rank, just do her job.

The hymns finished and from Capel Bethel came Reverend Parry Davies's powerful voice. "A great evil has come among us, my dear brethren. We Christians have fought for twenty centuries to stamp out the devil and pagan worship. Now it has sprung up again in our midst. It might call itself a center for healing and spirituality, but do you know what it really is? A place of devil worship — that's what it is! So-called Druids calling up evil spirits! Do we want this kind of corrupting evil in our midst, my dear brethren? What are we going to do about it?"

Evan smiled as he mounted his bike. So one of the ministers had heard the gossip about the Sacred Grove. He wondered what would happen when the other, more extreme minister also heard. And the other minister's wife — how would Lady Annabel fare against the power of a Mrs. Powell-Jones? He'd love to see that confrontation someday.

He started the engine and rode carefully down the pass.

"It looks rather fishy, doesn't it?" D.C. Glynis Davies sat beside Evan, who was driving the squad car. "I mean, why deny the girl had ever been there unless they had something to hide?"

"Exactly," Evan said. "Of course, the other girl, the one who spoke to Betsy, might be wrong. Betsy says she's not the brightest specimen in the world. And the photo on the flyer isn't exactly clear."

"I must say, I'm curious to see the place now," Glynis said.

"You won't believe your eyes." Evan chuckled. "It will make you realize that some people have more money than sense. It's a complete — well, I'd better let you see for yourself. You might like it."

"You don't, then?"

"I hate anything phony," Evan said. "Italian villages in Italy are all well and good. We've got some lovely Welsh buildings in Wales. Oh, it's pretty enough, but it doesn't feel real. And all this mumbo jumbo — pyramids and healing crystals and Druids. It's not right."

Glynis laughed. "There speaks the son of a true Welsh chapel. Crystals and healing ceremonies are all the thing these days."

"For people who are looking for something."

She nodded. "I suppose you're right. Have you never done any such soul-searching?"

Evan shook his head. "I've always had pretty much what I wanted, right here," he said. "Although there was a time, after my father died . . ." He paused, then shook his head more firmly. "Even then you'd not have found me sitting in any bloody pyramid."

They had reached the main gate and Evan pressed the buzzer.

"North Wales police again to see the owners," Evan said.

"They're busy today. I don't know if they can see you," Blaine's voice crackled through the intercom.

"Then they'd better unbusy themselves." Glynis leaned across to address the intercom. "Detective Constable Davies speaking. We've come on a very serious matter."

The gate swung open then shut again immediately. "The gate must be to keep their clients from escaping before they've paid the bill," Glynis quipped, then saw Evan's serious face. "What? Do you think there's something wrong with this place?"

"I don't know," he said. "There's something that doesn't add up. I can't put my finger on it yet."

"Interesting. I'll keep my eyes open."

Evan parked where he had left the motorcycle the day before. They declined Blaine's instructions to wait and set off down the cobbled main street.

"I see what you mean," Glynis said, laughing in amazement. "It's very Disneyland, isn't it? Quaint and pretty but strangely surreal."

They were just passing under the arch when Michael came running down the steps toward them. "Hey, just a minute. Oh, it's you, Constable."

"And this is Detective Glynis Davies." Evan indicated the young woman in the dark gray suit.

Michael looked momentarily startled. "Detective? Is there some sort of problem, C-constable?"

"There might be," Evan said. "Now, if you'd take us to Lady Annabel or Mr. Wunderlich straightaway."

"Lady Annabel is down at the spa, getting a massage," Michael said. "It's this way."

They went in through the glass doors of the spa building to a tiled atrium. A fountain was splashing against one wall, while soft piped music filled the background. The walls were tiled in an undersea motif with strands of wafting seaweed and schools of fish. It was so authentic that it felt like walking through an aquarium.

"If you wait here, I'll go and see if she's finished yet." He gave a half-apologetic grin. "She hates being disturbed when she's having a massage."

Evan and Glynis glanced at each other as Michael disappeared into the rear of the building.

"What the hell for?" they heard a sharp voice demand. "Oh, very well. Tell them I'll be right out."

Michael returned, his face pink with embarrassment. "She'll be right out. Take a seat."

A few moments later Annabel emerged, dressed in a large, fluffy white robe. Her hair was piled up on top of her head but her face was still perfectly made-up. "Thank you, Sergio. You're a gem," she called. "I feel like a new woman."

"Constable." She gave him a beaming smile. "What brings you back again so soon? Have you been converted to Rhiannon and her band?"

"Lady Annabel. This is Detective Constable Davies," Evan said. "She's the one who is looking into the missing American girl."

"But I thought we established yesterday that she hasn't ever stayed here." A frown of annoyance cracked the perfect makeup.

"Oh, yes, we know she was never a guest," Glynis said. "But you weren't entirely truthful with Constable Evans, were you?"

"In what way?"

"One of your staff recognized the girl. We understand that she used to work for you."

"A staff member?" Annabel sounded genuinely surprised. "I had no idea we hired college students. I thought the staff were all locals. I really don't have that much interaction — it is Mrs. Roberts, my housekeeper, who does the hiring and firing. Wait while I get dressed and I'll take you to see her. Michael, go and locate Mrs. Roberts for me, would you? This whole thing is most disagreeable."

Evan and Glynis waited again. "If the wonder boy is so psychic, then why didn't he know that she was working for him?" Evan muttered to Glynis, who grinned.

"I have to meet this wonder boy," she said. "If he's half as gorgeous as Betsy tells us, then . . ."

"I don't think your boyfriend would like it. Neither would Lady Annabel."

"I'm getting rather bored with that particular boyfriend, as it happens," Glynis said. Now, why exactly had she told him that? Evan wondered. At that moment Annabel reappeared, now dressed in a purple velour tracksuit.

"Right. Let's go and find Mrs. Roberts. I am most sorry that you had to come back here again, but you did only ask about guests, didn't you? I had no idea that staff might be concerned. . . ."

While she was talking, she started off at a great pace up the steps and into the main

113

house. For someone who carried excess weight, she was certainly light on her feet and full of energy, Evan noticed. Maybe there was something to this hocus-pocus after all.

Mrs. Roberts was found in a small, austere office behind the kitchens. She had the typical Welshwoman's face, one that has become the stereotype of the witch — long, thin, with pointed chin and high forehead. She got to her feet as they came in and she appraised Evan and Glynis critically.

"Mrs. Roberts is my wonderful housekeeper," Annabel said. "She's been with my family since the year dot. She can tell you anything you want to know. There's not much that escapes her eagle eye around here, is there, Mrs. R?"

Mrs. Roberts's face didn't even crack into a smile. She nodded. "What is it you're wanting?" she asked, looking directly at Evan.

"I'll leave you to it then," Annabel said. "I have guests arriving in half an hour. I don't want to greet them looking sweaty and unkempt like this." She went, leaving Mrs. Roberts still staring at Evan.

"Mrs. Roberts, I'm Detective Constable Glynis Davies." Glynis stepped forward to let her know that she was the one conducting the investigation. "We're here checking on a missing girl. An American college student. Her name is Rebecca Riesen and we understand from another member of your staff that she worked here earlier this spring."

"Rebecca?" The elderly woman frowned. "Yes, I do remember an American girl. She begged to be hired and then walked out within the week, but then I hear Americans are flighty — like the mistress's present husband. Wants one thing for his dinner and then changes his mind or leaves half of it. Flighty." She glanced around then asked, lowering her voice, "Do you have Welsh?"

"Constable Evans does," Glynis said. "I'm afraid mine is rusty."

"Pity."

"So what can you tell us about Rebecca?" Evan asked.

"Nothing much. She showed up in February, I think it was. She wanted a job and we were short a girl at the time. So many comings and goings these days. When Lady Annabel was growing up, we ran the place very nicely with a staff of four and a gardener. Now you never know who is who around here — masseurs and priestesses and God knows what. Change is never for the good, is it? And Lady Annabel never was one for making good decisions. Ever since she left her first husband, she's taken up with a succession of rotters." She smoothed down her dark skirt. "But getting back to this girl. She arrived. I put her to helping out in the kitchen and the laundry. General odd jobs,

115

you know. Then it hadn't been a week but one of the staff came and told me she'd upped and left. It seems the staff weren't too unhappy to see her go — somcthing of a God botherer, if you know what I mean. She didn't like the un-Christian things that were going on here and felt she had to do some converting."

"And you don't know where she went?"

"No idea. She just told one of the staff she was leaving, she'd had enough, and then she was gone. Didn't even stay long enough to collect her first week's paycheck. But then Americans are supposed to be rich, aren't they?"

"Is Mr. Wunderlich rich?" Evan asked.

"Famous TV star over there, so I've heard. But it's not right for me to go talking about my employers, is it? I think I've told you all I can."

"*Diolch yn fawr,* Mrs. Roberts," Evan said, breaking into Welsh. "Now I wonder if we could just have a word with the staff she worked with. I understand the girl Bethan was the one who recognized her picture."

"Bethan, yes. She might have been put to help Bethan. I'll have her sent up here."

"And the kitchens, you said. Could we go through there and ask some questions? She might have dropped a hint to someone where she was going when she left here."

"I suppose so." Mrs. Roberts walked ahead

of them into the dark hallway and then into the kitchens. The main kitchen was decidedly part of an old manor house, but nothing inside it was old — stainless-steel countertops, the biggest and best stoves and refrigerators lined the walls. No expense had been spared here. Evan stood watching while Glynis questioned the chefs and kitchen helpers. Most of them were from Spain or Italy, spoke only broken English, and couldn't even remember the girl.

When they got back to Mrs. Roberts's office, Bethan arrived, breathless.

"I was down at Meditation," she said. "I ran all the way up."

Glynis nodded to Evan. "Bethan," he said, "you said you remembered the American girl whose picture I showed you. Rebecca Riesen." He spoke in Welsh.

Bethan nodded.

"What can you tell me about her?"

"Very quiet, shy," Bethan answered, hanging her head as if she were answering a teacher in school. "Didn't say much. But nice enough. We folded linens together one day. That's when we had a little chat. She said she came from California and I said it must be wonderful and she said yes it was. That was about it."

"Did she say anything about Druids?" Evan asked. "Anything about being interested in Druids?"

"Druids? I'm sure she didn't. She was very religious. She told me it upset her what was going on here. 'A lot of pagans,' she said."

"So did she try and convert anybody?"

"Convert? How do you mean?" Bethan frowned as she looked up at Evan.

"Preaching at people?"

"I'm sure she didn't. Like I said, she was very quiet and shy. She only started talking to me because we were in the linen closet together. Otherwise, she pretty much kept to herself."

"So you don't know why she left? Do you think it was because the people here were pagans?"

"It could have been. I didn't realize she was gone until they told me. 'Where's the American girl?' I asked. 'Up and hopped it,' someone said. 'Just left a note.' "

"Well, at least we've established something positive," Glynis commented as they drove out of the compound. "We have the dates when she was here. Now, the next thing to check would be buses and trains out of Porthmadog. Damn, I didn't think to ask whether she had a car. Hardly likely to, being a college student, would you think?"

Evan shrugged. "You could check with the rental companies, but cars cost money. Did you say the family was rich?"

"Very ordinary. It was hard for them to come up with the cash to come over here

118

looking for her. She wasn't any spoiled little heiress, if that's what you're getting at." The car swung onto the main road and joined the line to cross the estuary. "By the way, thanks for agreeing to meet her parents when they arrive. You're the sort of person who knows what to say on occasions like this. I'm terribly awkward, I'm afraid. It's something I've got to learn."

"It's never easy," Evan said. "I've had to bring bad news quite a few times now and it doesn't get any easier."

"That's what Sergeant Watkins says." Glynis glanced up at him. "Look, do you want to go for a pint somewhere? I said I owed you one, didn't I?"

"I'll take you up on that sometime," Evan said, "but I have to get straight home tonight. I'm cooking dinner for my girlfriend."

"Oh." A definite pause. Then she said lightly, "A gourmet chef as well as all your other talents?"

"Not even close. I've just moved into my own place and most of my attempts have been disasters. Tonight I'm attempting spaghetti and I don't think that even I can mess that up too much. Spaghetti with a *bolognese* sauce and a tossed salad. Do you think that's all right?"

"Sounds wonderful," Glynis said. "She's a lucky lady."

Chapter 10

Later that evening Evan was standing in his kitchen, surrounded by saucers and bowls of chopped onion and garlic, minced beef, and tomatoes. *Survival Cooking for One* was propped on the shelf beside him. A large pot of water was bubbling on the stove and he was just heating some oil in a frying pan when the front doorbell rang.

"Damn," he muttered. It couldn't be Bronwen, surely? He'd begged her not to be early and made it very clear that he didn't want her to help him. He wiped his oniony hands on a tea towel and went to the door.

"Hello, Evan." Betsy was standing there, looking young and fresh and rather lovely. Usually she went in for ultrahip, sexy clothes that left little to the imagination. Today she was wearing jeans and a hand-knitted sweater a couple of sizes too big for her.

"Oh, Betsy. Is something the matter?"

"No. Nothing. I just thought I'd stop by and see how you're doing. I've just been over at Mrs. Williams's and had a bite to eat with Emmy. Mrs. Williams is a lovely cook, isn't she? She makes the lightest pastry, even better than my old *nain* used to. So we got to talking about you and Mrs. W hoped you were doing all right, so I said I'd pop in and see on my way home."

"I'm doing just fine, thank you," Evan said. "To tell you the truth, I'm in the middle of cooking — in fact, I have oil heating on the stove." He ran back into the kitchen and rescued the smoking pan in time.

"Oh, look at you!" Betsy said in admiration. "What are you cooking? Looks very fancy."

"I've got Bronwen coming to dinner in half an hour," he said. "I'm making a sauce for the spaghetti."

"You can buy that out of a jar," Betsy said.

"Yes, but it's not the same. I have to show Bronwen that I can do this."

"Do you want some help?" Betsy was already pushing up her sleeves. "I'm quite handy in the kitchen myself, having cooked for that ungrateful Harry Lloyd at the Dragon all this time. Want that lettuce washing, do you?" Before Evan could answer, she had it pulled apart and was running it under the tap. "He's regretting it already, I'm sure," she went on. "I peeked in there tonight and you know there's only a couple of blokes in there. Charlie Hopkins and Evans-the-Meat. Dead as a doornail in there. I knew it."

She shook out the lettuce so that spray went everywhere.

"Hey, watch it," Evan said, laughing. Betsy gave him a mischievous smile and flipped the

121

lettuce spray into his face. It was a deliberately flirtatious move and Evan stopped himself as he was about to grab her wrist. Any physical contact with Betsy and who knew where it might lead!

"Stop distracting me, will you? I've got to get this sauce simmering. Now let's see. First the onions and the garlic." They fell into the pan with a sizzle.

"So did you find out any more about that missing girl?" Betsy asked. "Bethan said you'd been back to the Sacred Grove today."

"Only that the girl was there for less than a week then left again. It's not much to go on."

"So she could be back in America by now."

"It's very probable."

"Too bad I'm not further along with my psychic training. I could just close my eyes for you and pick up her vibrations."

"Your guru, Randy, tried to do that and didn't come up with anything. How did your session go with him today?"

"It didn't. He wasn't there. I went to his office but he didn't show up. I expect he got called away for something more important than me. I know they had new guests arriving today. He'll fit in my sessions when he can." She leaned against the edge of the draining board, watching him. "Emmy says that my powers may be remarkable. She says that I may be able to see other people's lives and even make things happen. She says the most powerful psychics can just picture something in their head and it happens, just like that. Isn't it exciting?"

"I'd take it all with a grain of salt if I were you," Evan said as he dropped the spaghetti into a huge pot of boiling water. "These people believe in all that stuff, but I'd want some proof, myself. I've never yet met anyone who was truly psychic."

"My old *nain* used to see the Derin Corff, didn't she?" Betsy demanded.

Evan smiled. "I shall be only too delighted if you turn out to be a famous psychic. You've always wanted to be famous, haven't you?"

Betsy beamed. "Imagine me on a TV show someday with Randy."

"Sorry to remind you, love, but he's already married."

"Oh, he's too old for me. He's way over thirty. I like younger blokes myself." She hoisted herself up onto one end of the counter and sat there, swinging her legs. "Tell me, Evan," she said carefully, "if Bronwen wasn't around any longer . . . if there was no Bronwen Price in the world, do you think you might be interested in me then?"

"Betsy!" He laughed uneasily. "I really like you. Honestly I do. But I don't think I'm the right bloke for you. You need someone who's

123

more lively and fun. You know I don't like dancing and the type of thing you like."

"I'd also like to settle down with a steady bloke of my own someday," Betsy said. "Oh, well, I'm not going to give up without a fight. Do you think I could use my psychic powers to make Bronwen disappear?"

"Hey — that smells wonderful," came Bronwen's voice as she opened the front door. "You see, I told you that you could . . ." She stopped short as she came into the kitchen and saw Betsy sitting on the kitchen counter beside Evan. "Oh," she said. "I hope you haven't been cheating."

"I'm here on an errand from Mrs. Williams," Betsy said, sliding gracefully from the counter. "You don't have to worry."

Bronwen laughed. "I meant cheating by having someone who knows how to cook help you. You haven't been helping him, have you, Betsy?"

"Only washed some lettuce or you'd have eaten it full of caterpillars," Betsy said. "Well, I'll be on my way then. Enjoy your dinner. I think you're doing just fine, Evan."

Evan was conscious of Bronwen looking at him as Betsy closed the front door behind her. "You didn't ask her to come and help you, did you?" she said accusingly.

"Of course not. Mrs. Williams wanted to make sure I was all right. Betsy had been having dinner with the famous Emmy, so she stopped by on her way home."

"If you ask me, Betsy's all too influenced by the famous Emmy. She's been following her around like a sheep."

"And by the famous Randy," Evan said.

"Oh, who's he?"

"The star psychic at the Sacred Grove. You should see him, Bron. Hair over his shoulders like Samson. Very tanned and muscled and Hollywood."

She gave him a wicked smile. "Ooh, sounds interesting. Maybe I'll go and check him out for myself."

Evan grabbed her round the waist and pulled her close to him. "None of that, or I won't share my secret spaghetti sauce with you."

Bronwen laughed and kissed him.

"And none of that when I'm trying to concentrate," he added. "Make yourself useful and open the bottle of red wine I've put on the table."

"First sensible suggestion you've made all evening." She waltzed out of the kitchen. Evan came through to join her. "I haven't got as far as candles and tablecloths and things."

"This will do just fine. You've done a lot in a week."

"Especially since I've been up and down to that bloody Sacred Grove all weekend. Missing college student from America," he added. "Turns out she was there briefly then left a couple of months ago, so we're none the wiser."

Bronwen poured out two glasses of red wine.

"You sit down and I'll serve," Evan said. He went through into the kitchen, stopped in horror, and yelled, "Bloody hell!"

Bronwen came running through. "What? What is it?"

Evan pointed silently at the huge glutinous mound that was currently creeping out of the pot and down the side of the stove. "Spaghetti isn't supposed to behave like that, is it?"

Bronwen started laughing. "It's like something out of a horror movie — *The Blob That Swallowed Wales*. Evan — how much spaghetti did you put in?"

"Well, I started with one packet but that didn't look like very much, so I added another one."

Bronwen wrapped her arms around his neck. "My dear sweet twit, each packet is enough for eight people. You've just cooked enough to feed half of Llanfair."

"Well, I'm not inviting them to share," Evan said, annoyed and embarrassed at her laughter. "I planned a special dinner with my girlfriend and that's what we're going to have. Now go and sit down and don't watch while I serve up."

Still smiling, Bronwen went back into the living room.

It was very early the next morning when Evan's phone roused him from sleep. He staggered downstairs and picked up the receiver.

"Evan — are you all right?" He was surprised to hear Bronwen's voice.

"Me? Yes, I'm fine, as far as I know. I've only just woken up. What time is it?"

"I don't know. Early. I'm sorry I woke you, only I'm not fine, and I just thought maybe there was something in the food. . . ."

"You mean you're sick?"

"As a dog," she said. "I've hardly left the loo all night."

"I'll be right over," he said. He scrambled into his clothes and ran up the high street. It was a misty morning and the milk float loomed like a ghostly specter as it crept up the street, making the morning milk round. The schoolhouse was barely visible through the fog. Evan ran across the school playground and let himself in with the key Bronwen had given him.

"You shouldn't have come," Bronwen said as he came into her bedroom. "It might be catching."

"You look terrible. I'm phoning for the doctor."

She nodded. "I feel terrible. But you're

fine and we both ate the same things last night, so it can't be food poisoning."

"I like that," Evan said, smoothing her hair back from her forehead. "I cook her one meal and immediately she accuses me of poisoning her."

"I'm sorry. I didn't mean . . ."

"It's okay, love. You've probably just got a touch of flu. Would you like to try a cup of tea and some toast?"

She nodded. "I'm not sure if it will stay down, but I'll give it a try. And could you make a phone call for me? I have to let the Office of Education know that they'll need to send up a substitute for me today."

"You're lucky this is my day off," Evan said. "See, I knew there had to be some advantages to working every other weekend."

"Lucky me." Bronwen managed a smile. "If the first meal didn't finish me off, he's got a chance to try again."

Betsy sensed as soon as she entered the Sacred Grove that morning that something was wrong. Emmy had dropped her off at the entrance. "I've got some new prospects to interview," she said. "Fascinated as I am by your particular case, I'm supposed to be compiling a body of evidence about extrasensory perception among Celts. Just one Celt isn't likely to satisfy my professor at home. Let me know how your session with Randy goes today, won't you? I'll try to stop by later."

Betsy passed nobody apart from Blaine at the security post until she had almost reached the spa, where her first duty was to check towel supplies. She stopped when she heard someone yelling.

"You! Girl! What's your name — Betty?"

Lady Annabel, her hair for once not looking as if she had just left her hairdresser, came running down the steps. Betsy noticed that she hadn't made up her face either.

"I want a word with you, Betty. Can you come up to my office, please?" Her voice was shrill.

"My name's Betsy. I haven't done anything wrong, have I?" Betsy asked. "I loaded the dishwasher before I left last night and . . ."

"You've done nothing wrong. It's not that." Lady Annabel climbed the last of the steps at a great pace. "I wanted to ask you about your session with my husband yesterday afternoon."

Betsy shot her a glance. Was she jealous? Did she suspect her husband of flirting with an attractive young girl?

"I didn't have the session with him yesterday," Betsy said.

"But it was down on his schedule. Bethan said you went down to Meditation to meet with him around four."

"I did." Betsy nodded. "But he wasn't

129

there. I waited around but he didn't show up. After a while I thought that maybe something more important had come up, and I was supposed to be helping with dinner shortly. So I went up to the kitchen and decided he'd find me there if he wanted to."

Lady Annabel pushed open the door of the admin building and swept in ahead of Betsy, not seeming to care that the door swung back into Betsy's face.

"Why? What did he say about me?" Betsy asked with a tremulous voice.

"He didn't say anything!" Lady Annabel's voice rose almost to a shriek as she turned to face Betsy. "He didn't say anything because he's nowhere to be found!"

"You mean he's gone?"

"Of course I mean he's gone!" Lady Annabel snapped. "When he didn't appear for dinner, I sent Michael to look for him. He found Randy's desk with some notes about you scribbled on a pad, a half-drunk cup of coffee, and no sign of him. Nobody has seen him since midafternoon."

Betsy couldn't think what to say. What kept crossing her mind was that Randy was a rather gorgeous man and Lady Annabel was a chubby older woman. Maybe Randy had a good reason for slipping out for the night.

"I'm sure he'll be fine," she said, trying to be helpful.

Annabel gave her a poisonous stare. "If

you're as bloody psychic as they claim you are, then why can't you bloody well see him and tell me where he is?"

"There's no point in screaming at Betsy." Michael came out of Mrs. Roberts's office. "She obviously knows no more than the rest of us."

"You're all bloody useless," Annabel snapped. "And you more so than the rest of them."

"What do you want me to d-do?" Michael demanded patiently, blinking worriedly behind his glasses. "I've done everything I can. I've searched the grounds for you. . . ."

"Well, it's not enough. Call the police. Get that policeman back here. He's just spent the last two days annoying us. Now let's see if he can do something useful for a change."

"I don't think you can call the police to report someone missing when it's only been a few hours," Michael said patiently.

"He went swimming and was swept away by the tide, I know it!" Annabel wailed hysterically.

"Just think for a moment," Michael said in his low, reasonable voice. "It was low tide around five yesterday. There would have been no water in the estuary until almost dark. And he wouldn't have walked out half a mile through the mud, would he?"

"Then where the devil is he?" Annabel demanded.

"It's not going to help to upset yourself like this," Michael said. "You've still got guests, haven't you? You don't want to scare them off."

"Oh, bugger off, Michael, and don't try to tell me what to do. You, of all people!" She changed direction and headed for the main staircase. "I've got a terrible headache. Bring me up some tea and don't let anyone disturb me unless it's good news!"

Betsy stood there, feeling embarrassed and awkward until Annabel disappeared. Michael gave Betsy a sheepish grin. "Sorry about that," he said. "She flies off the handle rather easily."

He began to walk toward the kitchens. Betsy walked with him, feeling great sympathy.

"Why do you let her talk to you like that?" Betsy whispered when they were alone in the passageway. "And why do you stay here if she's so difficult? You've got an education, haven't you? You speak posh and all that. I bet you could get a better job easily. With more money too."

"That wouldn't be hard," Michael said, "as she pays me nothing except room and board."

"Room and board? Why do you stay here then?"

Michael looked amused. "Didn't anyone tell you? She's my mother."

"Your mother?"

"The resemblance isn't exactly striking, is it? I'm the product of her first marriage, to Colonel James Hollister. She married him at eighteen — big society wedding. Had me then dumped us both and ran off with a race car driver."

"Oh, it's like something out of a film, isn't it? Rather romantic."

"Except if you happen to be me, left alone in that drafty old castle, brought up by a succession of nannies and a father who hardly said two words to me in his life. He died when I was fourteen. As soon as I finished school, I sought out my mother again. The race car driver had killed himself by that time and she was working her way through a string of young and gorgeous men, of whom Randy is the latest. Unfortunately she was stupid enough to marry him."

"I wonder why —" Betsy began, then stopped.

"Why he married her?"

"Yes, I mean she's not —"

"No spring chicken? Not the greatest catch? She has a title and this property, but not much else. If he thought she was rich, he's been sadly disillusioned by now."

"It's strange that he should just hop it, though," Betsy said.

"He wouldn't be the first one who's done a bunk on her," Michael said. "As you've seen, she's not the easiest person to live with. Very possessive. And naïve too. Easily taken in. All this psychic stuff. It's her latest craze. She's already been through acupuncture and Buddhism and God knows what else. She thinks that Randy can see her future for her and help her straighten out her present as well."

"Don't you think he can?"

"If you want me honest opinion —" Michael put his head close to Betsy's "— I think he's a big phony. Why else do you think I'm here? I interrupted my university course so that I could keep an eye on her. What with Randy and that accountant of hers, I wanted to make sure that the property was here for me to inherit someday." He smiled at Betsy. "But don't let it worry you. It's not your problem. I'll see you later. I've got to take her a cup of tea, and a couple of tranquilizers, I expect — even though she claims to be a devotee of only natural healing these days." He shrugged his shoulders in a gesture of resignation, then went into the kitchen, leaving Betsy standing alone in the dark hallway.

Chapter 11

There was a rumbling in the darkness. Evan came to consciousness and lay there, listening. Thunder? Outside his window the sky was still lit with stars. Not thunder then. When it came again, he recognized it for what it was — someone was pounding on his front door.

He grabbed his dressing gown and fumbled for the hall light, his heart racing. *Bronwen,* he thought. *Bad news about Bronwen.* She hadn't seemed any better when he left her last night and he was worried, even though the doctor had dismissed it as probably nothing more than a twenty-four-hour bug — lots of it going around.

He opened the door. A small, waiflike figure, wearing an anorak over what looked like a white flannel nightgown and fluffy pink slippers, was standing there.

"Betsy? What on earth's the matter?" he asked.

Her eyes were as big as saucers. "I saw him, Evan. I saw him," she gasped.

"Saw who?"

"Randy. I saw Randy."

"The man from the healing place? Where?" He leaned out of the front door, expecting to see a figure running from Betsy's cottage, but the street was deserted.

"In my dream."

"Betsy, what are you talking about?" He wondered for a moment if this was Betsy's latest excuse to get into his house, but the terror on her face was genuine and she was shivering violently.

"Hold on a moment. Come on inside. I'll make you a cup of tea."

She put out her hand and grabbed at his sleeve. "No, you don't understand. I've got to get down there and tell them."

"Betsy, calm down," Evan said. "You had a bad dream, did you? Well, it was only a dream and your dad's in the house, isn't he? What do you want me to do?"

"Come with me, down to the Sacred Grove."

"At this hour? Can't it wait till morning?"

"No. I have to get down there now, because he's missing and I've just found him." Betsy's teeth were chattering so violently that she could hardly speak. "And Emmy said we should take you with us, just in case."

"Randy is missing?"

"Yes. Lady Annabel wanted to call you — she wanted to report him missing but Michael said you can't just go calling the police when someone has only been gone for a few hours. And then I fell asleep and suddenly there he was and I saw the whole thing —

him lying there and everything and I ran to tell Emmy and she believed me. She said things are often communicated to psychics through dreams and I should get you."

Evan looked out of his front door and noticed a car parked by the curb with a figure inside it. He strode out to it. Emmy had the window wound down and was sitting there, bundled in a dark jacket and hood.

"What nonsense have you been putting into her head?" Evan demanded. "You've scared this poor kid half to death."

"I think you should face the fact that this girl has strong powers. You should have seen the test results. She matched eight out of ten shapes. There is no way to fake tests like that. And if she has seen Mr. Wunderlich in her dream, then I think we had better take it seriously. I do anyway. I'm driving her down there now. I thought you should come with us, just in case."

"Very well. I'll get dressed," Evan said. "And Betsy should too. She'll catch cold the way she's shivering right now."

"The psychic experience often does produce intense physical side effects," Emmy said, "but I agree. She should get dressed. We may be doing some climbing."

A few minutes later they were driving in Emmy's rental car down the pass to the coast.

"So what's this about Randy going

missing?" Evan asked. "You'd better fill me in on the facts."

"I'm sure Lady Annabel can give you all the details," Emmy said. "I showed up to pick up Betsy yesterday evening and found the place in turmoil. Nobody had seen him since the afternoon before. They'd searched the grounds. Annabel was in hysterics."

"Wasn't it just possible that he'd gone off somewhere on a whim, without telling anyone?"

"His car was in the car park. The security guard didn't see him leave."

Beddgelert was in darkness and sleeping as they passed through it. A lone cat slunk through the deserted streets of Porthmadog.

"It would have been more sensible to call first." Evan was just realizing all the things he should have done, including making a cup of tea, as well as checking in with HQ, and he was annoyed at having been hustled into action by this forceful American woman. Emmy sat, tense and excited, staring at the road as she drove. "This will be a first for me," she said. "I've done plenty of research, I've read all the books, but actually seeing a psychic experience taking shape. I mean, wow — is that mind-blowing or what?"

Betsy sat in the front seat beside her, huddled in her coat, still shivering. Evan was jammed into the inadequate backseat. The light of the dying moon gleamed from water on either side of them as they crossed the estuary.

At last their headlamps illuminated the wire mesh of the security gate outside the Sacred Grove. Evan pressed the buzzer and hardly expected a reply at this time of the night, but a voice answered almost immediately and at the barked "North Wales Police," the gate swung silently open.

Lady Annabel appeared in a purple satin robe, looking pasty-faced and dazed. Mrs. Roberts, in a sensible gray wool dressing gown, hovered behind her, like a faithful dog. "Now tell me again," Annabel said as she came down the stairs. "This girl thinks she's found Randy?"

"She had a dream," Emmy said at the same moment that Betsy said, "I saw him in my dream."

"The preliminary tests show she has strong psychic powers," Emmy said. "I think we should take her seriously."

"At this stage I'm willing to take everything seriously," Annabel said. "I'm willing to grasp at any straw if she can only find my husband." She grabbed Betsy's arm. "Tell me what you dreamed." She glanced up at Emmy. "Should we wake Rhiannon? Does the dream need to be interpreted?"

"About as straightforward as you can get," Emmy said. "Tell her, Betsy."

139

"I went into a cave," Betsy said, "and I saw someone lying on the floor. It was dark in there and it smelled of seaweed. As I got closer, I saw that it was Randy — Mr. Wunderlich. He was just lying there. I went to touch him and I woke up."

"A cave! Why didn't we think of that? Of course. How stupid. Get Michael now. We need torches. Where's my mobile phone? How did Randy look in this dream? Had he had an accident, do you think? We might need a doctor for him — should we call a doctor now? Do you think he was taken ill? Or fell? Or you can be trapped by the tide in some of those caves . . ."

She was rushing around, her arms waving like fluttering wings.

Mrs. Roberts stepped forward to restrain her. "Just a moment, Miss Annabel. You're not going anywhere in your nightclothes. You go up and get some warm garments on and I'll make us all a nice cup of tea."

Annabel looked around in a dazed manner. "All right," she said. "You're right. I should get dressed first. And tea would be nice. Thank you, Mrs. Roberts. You're so good to me."

"Somebody has to be," Mrs. Roberts muttered as she moved away.

"And please wake Ben and Michael for me," Annabel called after her. "I need them to be here." She ran up the stairs, her slippers flapping and her silk gown flying out be-hind her.

Evan looked at Emmy and Betsy. "Are there caves on the property?"

Emmy shrugged. "Don't ask me. I've only seen two buildings so far. This one and the meditation center, but I understand the property is huge."

"I'll know it when I see it," Betsy said. "It was ever so clear in my dream."

"It has to be on the coast. You saw sea-weed. That's significant," Emmy said.

"I could do with that cup of tea," Evan said, "and so could you, Betsy *fach*. You're still shivering."

"I know," she said. "I can't stop my teeth from chattering."

"I'll go and see if I can help Mrs. Rob-erts." Evan struck out in the direction of the kitchen. He needed something to keep him busy. It was too unnerving being with the two women. This whole scenario felt so un-real, almost as if he had been cast as an actor in a play and nobody had given him his lines. He met Mrs. Roberts, on her way with a tray of teacups. She refused his offer to carry it for her with a polite, "I can manage very well, thank you, sir."

By the time they reached the foyer, Annabel had come downstairs again, this time in her purple velour tracksuit, and both Michael and a portly man Evan hadn't seen

141

before were there, the latter looking decidedly grumpy.

"I know you believe in this psychic stuff, Annabel dear," the man was saying, "but couldn't it wait at least until dawn. Couldn't we send someone out on a preliminary recky? Michael could go with the young woman for you."

"I want to be there myself," Annabel said. "He's my husband. I want to rescue him."

"But why the caves? What on earth would he have been doing there?"

"I suppose he might have been meditating in a cave. He chose the most unlikely places to meditate," Annabel said, as if the idea had just struck her. "He told me once he picked up incredible vibes in caves. I had completely forgotten we had those caves on the property. I've no idea how Randy found out about them." She took the offered cup of tea. "You are a gem, Mrs. Roberts."

"I do my best, Miss Annabel," Mrs. Roberts said gruffly.

Evan drained his own cup gratefully.

"If you want to get to the caves, we should be going then," Michael said. "We might not be able to reach them if the tide's in."

"It's not," Mrs. Roberts said. "Low tide at six, isn't it? You'll be able to get around all right."

It was a silent procession that made its way down the many steps, past the meditation

142

center. The copper pyramid seemed to shiver with an energy of its own and the sandy estuary below glowed ghostly gray in the dying moon. The tide was still far out and water channels made streaks of silver across the sand. Michael led with a large torch. Annabel and Betsy were right behind him, then Emmy and Ben, whoever he was, with Evan bringing up the rear. Down the last steps onto the sand. It was fine and soft and squeaked under their feet, making walking difficult. As they passed the last of the buildings, looming like a great black shadow perched above them, Evan saw that the land rose into a headland at the end of the bay. There was a line of dark cliffs on their right, and the sand on the beach was dotted with large rocks and rock pools, around which they had to skirt.

"There." Michael shone the torch on the cliff face. Just before the rocky headland were two black slits in the cliff face. One of them was almost down at beach level, one a little higher.

"My father always maintained that smugglers used to use them," Lady Annabel said. "I thought there ought to be a secret passage to one of the buildings. But I never found it."

"Are these the caves you saw in your dream, Betsy?" Emmy asked.

"I don't know," Betsy said. "I only remember being at the mouth of the cave."

"Watch your step," Michael said. "We have to sort of scramble here. Are you all right, Mother?"

"I'll manage," Annabel said. "You go ahead with the torch. I think I'll wait down here until you find . . ." She shuddered. "Oh, I hope he's there. I hope he's all right. He might have fallen and injured himself and not have been able to walk. That's probably what happened, don't you think? And he had to seek shelter in the cave. . . ."

Michael had begun to scramble up the boulders that formed a ramp to the caves. Evan went to join him. "Here, let me." He took the torch so that the boy could use two hands to find his way up. "There must be a huge tide here," Evan said. "These rocks are quite slippery even up here."

"There is a big tide," Michael said. "The lower of these caves is almost flooded at high tide."

"So someone could be trapped in there."

"And the upper one too," Michael said. "You can't climb up the cliff right here and your way back along the beach would be cut off at high tide. You'd just have to find a spot to sit it out. Of course, the upper cave stays pretty dry."

Evan didn't add that there had been at least a couple of low tides since Randy went missing when anyone could have reached safety again.

Betsy and Emmy scrambled up to join Evan and Michael.

"Come on, Betsy." Emmy held out her hand. "I'll go in with you, so that you're not too spooked." She went to drag Betsy to the upper cave.

Betsy froze. "No, not that one. The other."

"Surely not." Emmy gave a nervous laugh. "Why would anyone want to go into that cave? If he was hiding out with a broken ankle, he'd go up to the dry one, wouldn't he? Come up to the entrance and see what vibes you're feeling."

"It's this one." Betsy stood before the entrance to the sea cave. It was a narrow, diagonal slit in the rock, not quite as high as a person, and the opening was piled with seaweed-covered rocks. Betsy started clambering over them, slithering and sliding as she tried to make her way inside.

"I'm sure you've got it wrong, Betsy," Emmy called after her. "Do wait a minute. Wait for the light."

"He's in here, I know it," Betsy said. "Look. There." Evan had climbed down to her and shone the torch into the cave. Inside, the cave widened out, but the debris-strewn floor rose upward to meet the roof at the rear of the cave. The light cast grotesque shadows from rocky outcrops. The back of the cave was strewn with boulders and behind one of these they could make out a pale

145

hand and blond hair.

Betsy was shivering again. "It's him, isn't it? Is he trapped? Is he okay?"

Evan had pushed past her to where Randy lay. He didn't need to feel for a pulse to know that the man was dead. He looked up at the horrified faces, all of them like white death masks in the torchlight.

"I'm afraid we're too late. . . ."

Annabel let out a wail and Emmy hurled herself forward. "No, that can't be right. He's not dead. He can't be dead!"

Chapter 12

The first streaks of cold dawn were silhouetting the mountains across the estuary when reinforcements arrived in the persons of a paramedic team, Sergeant Watkins, and D.C. Glynis Davies. Evan had sent the others back to the center, Ben and Michael supporting the hysterical Annabel, Betsy and Emmy clutching each other sobbing. Evan had decided to stay with the body until help arrived.

"Just when I thought I could sleep in for once," Watkins muttered as Evan scrambled over the rocks to meet him. "Do you know I had to be at those training sessions in Colwyn Bay at eight in the morning? Today I thought I wouldn't have to show up until nine and what happens? I get called out at bloody four-thirty."

"You got an hour's more sleep than I did," Evan said, returning Glynis's friendly smile.

"I bet you didn't expect we'd be back here again so soon, and on a completely different matter too, did you?" Glynis accepted his hand to help her up onto a large, seaweed-draped boulder. "How very bizarre. Did you say you found him?"

"I was in the party that found him," Evan said. "We came to this cave because young

147

Betsy from our village dreamed he was here."

"Wow, and it turned out to be true." Glynis looked impressed.

"Looks that way," Evan said. He switched on the torch he had kept with him. "The body's in this cave, Sarge."

Sergeant Watkins ducked as he followed Evan into the cave. "Been dead long, do you think?"

"I can't say. I'd imagine the body has been covered with water more than once."

"So it might have been washed in from the outside?"

"I wouldn't think so. The opening's too narrow for one thing and I don't see how the waves would have been strong enough."

"Then what the devil was he doing in a place like this? Not exactly where you'd come for comfort, is it?" Watkins shivered.

"His wife says he liked to meditate in these caves, but there's a perfectly good large dry cave a little higher up. I can't imagine anyone choosing to meditate in here."

The torch shone down on Randy Wunderlich's body. The golden hair was plastered around his face and encrusted with sand. Evan shivered. He still wasn't able to handle death casually. Neither, it appeared, was Sergeant Watkins.

"Poor bugger," he said. "What a stupid thing to happen. Here — hold on a mo—" This to the paramedics who were now also trying to get to the body. "I don't want him touched until we've got the police doctor and photographer here. There's nothing you boys can do anyway. He's long gone." He took out his mobile phone. "I'll just go outside and report to HQ. You boys can come with me and put your own call in."

"It's very odd, isn't it?" Glynis asked when she and Evan were alone in the cave. Of the three she seemed the least affected, climbing over the body to view it from behind. "An odd way to die, I mean."

"Just a minute, Constable." Sergeant Watkins reappeared. "Don't go trampling on any potential evidence."

"You don't suspect foul play, do you?" Glynis looked surprised.

"Always suspect foul play until it's ruled out, and then you don't get into trouble with your chief," Watkins said, giving Evan a knowing grin. "Not that it matters much here. The tide's been over all this at least once."

"He must have drowned, obviously," Glynis said, peering down at the body. "But the question is why?"

"Trapped by the tide while he was meditating?" Watkins suggested.

"You'd have to be in a pretty deep trance not to notice cold water coming all over you, wouldn't you?" Glynis said. "And even then, he'd have tried to force his way out through the waves. It hasn't been stormy recently, so I can't think the waves would have been too strong for him."

Evan had been examining the body. "Hey, look here, Sarge. There's a makeshift bandage around his ankle." One foot was bare and someone had tried to bind up the ankle using a sock and a handkerchief. "That might be it. He might have slipped and sprained an ankle. Perhaps he couldn't get past the waves if he couldn't stand properly."

Watkins nodded. "I suppose it's possible that he passed out with the pain at the wrong moment — just as the water was coming in."

"And drowned, you mean?" Evan shook his head. "I don't think so. I passed out with pain once when I separated my shoulder playing rugby. Someone threw cold water over me and it woke me up pretty damned quick."

Glynis was down on her hands and knees. "There are plenty of loose rocks in here. Do you think his foot got trapped under one of them?"

"How could he have bound up his ankle if it was under a bloody great rock?" Watkins asked, grinning at Evan.

"I don't know. Maybe a rock rolled onto his foot, and then the waves rolled it off again."

"While he was lying there unconscious?

Then he woke up long enough to bind his ankle only to pass out again and drown?" Watkins finished for her.

"You're right. It doesn't make sense," Glynis said, laughing with them. "What does the brilliant Constable Evans have to say about it?" She turned to Evan. "You're the one who solves the really tricky cases."

"Only by luck," Evan said. "I'm as stumped as you are. Even if I'd got a broken ankle, I'm pretty sure I'd manage to fight my way out of a cave rather than stay there and be drowned."

"Perhaps he couldn't swim," Glynis suggested. "Perhaps he had a water phobia."

"There's one possibility we haven't considered," Watkins said. "Maybe he didn't want to get out."

"Suicide you mean?" Evan asked. Then he shook his head. "I don't think so. If ever there was a man who was full of himself, it was Randy Wunderlich. He thought he was God's gift."

"Anyway, Dr. Owens will be here soon. Young Dawson can take his photographs and then we can have the body removed and go and have a decent breakfast." Watkins frowned at Evan as he spoke. "You look frozen to the marrow."

"I am. Funny, because I don't often feel the cold. There's something about this place that's giving me the creeps."

Glynis nodded. "It is creepy in here. Do you think he was dabbling in something like witchcraft or black magic?"

"No more speculation, Constable Davies," Watkins said firmly, helping her out of the cave. "Wait until we've got the pathologist's report, then we'll know what we're talking about. Ten to one it will be very simple. We'll probably find he had a heart attack and dropped down dead."

"Ah, then the lungs wouldn't have any water in them. I know that much," Glynis said, grinning at Evan. "Look, the sun's up. It's going to be a nice day again."

It was a solemn tableau that greeted Evan and the two detectives as they came into the well-appointed lounge with its comfortable armchairs and sofas in muted pastels. Mrs. Roberts, still in her sensible dressing gown, was sitting straight-backed and grim beside another tea tray. Annabel, red-eyed and disheveled, was sitting on the sofa beside the large paunchy man she had called Ben, while Michael perched protectively on the sofa arm beside her. Betsy was on the floor, hugging her knees to her chest, while Emmy was sitting up straight, staring at the ceiling. They all looked up at the sound of approaching feet.

"Dr. Owens, the home office pathologist, and an incident team from police headquarters are down at the cave right now, Mrs. Wunderlich," Watkins said.

Evan started at the use of this name. Watkins was correct, of course. She had been married to Randy Wunderlich, but nobody had ever called her anything other than Lady Annabel.

"Your husband's body will be taken for autopsy," Watkins stated.

"I don't want him cut open." Annabel started to wail again. "I don't want that beautiful body spoiled in any way."

"I'm afraid there's no choice when the cause of death isn't obvious." He looked around at the group. "Now, if I could just ask you a few questions. We need to establish when he was last seen."

Glynis had taken out a notebook and pen and was standing looking efficient. Evan stood in the doorway, feeling superfluous.

"Right. Mrs. Wunderlich." There was a definite intake of breath from Mrs. Roberts this time. "When was it you first noticed that your husband was missing?"

"The day before yesterday. Two guests had arrived. We normally welcome guests at a private cocktail party before dinner. My husband didn't show up. I sent Michael to look for him and to remind him. He could be a little absentminded, especially when he — when his psychic receptors were open, as he put it."

"But I-I couldn't find him anywhere," Michael said.

"So I sent Michael to see if his car was gone from its parking space," Annabel continued.

"But it was still there," Michael finished.

"Which meant that he couldn't have left the premises?" Watkins asked.

"He could have gone for a walk," Annabel said. "He often went for walks."

"And what happened then?"

"When he didn't turn up all evening, I became very angry and frightened. I thought of calling the police that night, but I was told it was too early. And I was sure he'd call. I was sure he must have had a good reason —" She broke off and put her handkerchief to her mouth. Then she controlled herself again. "In the morning I had Michael and some of the young people who work here search the grounds, in case something had happened to him, but they found nothing."

"But you didn't think of looking in those caves?" Watkins turned to Michael.

"No. It never crossed my mind. Actually, I'd forgotten all about them. N-nobody ever goes near them. We advise people to use only the beach directly in front of the swimming pool, because it's so easy to be cut off by the tides and those caves are under water half the time. I'm surprised Randy even knew they existed. You can't see them from the beachfront."

"Lady Annabel mentioned that he used to meditate in the caves, I believe," Evan said.

Annabel nodded. "He said he picked up amazing vibrations."

"Let's back up," Watkins said. "Let's go back to the day he didn't show up for cocktails. When was the last time he was seen?"

"We had lunch together," Annabel said. "After lunch I usually take a little rest. I don't know where Randy went after that. You'd have to ask the staff."

"How many staff work here?" Watkins asked.

Lady Annabel fluttered her hands again. "We have a full-time masseur, and a team of experts in the healing arts on call, so the number would vary from day to day. Sometimes it's the Reiki therapist, sometimes the acupuncturist or the bio energy balancer. . . ."

A lot of people to pay when guests are almost nonexistent, Evan thought.

"And then there's the domestic staff. I'm not exactly sure how many of those we have at the moment. You'd have to ask Mrs. Roberts. She's the housekeeper."

"Let's see," Mrs. Roberts said. "At the moment there's the chef and the two kitchen helpers. Bethan helps me with the housekeeping. Then we have the maintenance man and the two groundskeepers and security.

That would be it. Oh, and the new girl, Betsy here."

Watkins looked at Betsy with interest. "You were the one who dreamed where Mr. Wunderlich was?"

Betsy nodded.

"Have you worked here long?"

"No, I just started a couple of days ago. The day before Randy — Mr. Wunderlich — was missing."

"Did you now?"

Evan noticed the glance that passed between Watkins and Glynis. He was just beginning to realize that the sequence of events must look suspicious.

"Well, yes," Betsy said, blushing bright red. "Miss Court, the American lady here, she brought me down to the Sacred Grove center so that Mr. Wunderlich could test my psychic abilities and Harry, my old boss at the pub, wouldn't give me time off, miserable old sod that he is, so Miss Court said she'd ask if they could give me a job at the center so I could be right on the spot when Mr. Wunderlich wanted to work with me."

"I see." Watkins looked at her for a long moment, then turned back to Lady Annabel.

"Could we have the staff assembled so that we could question them about Mr. Wunderlich's whereabouts after lunch that day?"

"The staff don't sleep on the property," Mrs. Roberts said. "The first of them will be

156

coming on duty at eight. I'll send word to the gatekeeper that they're to report in here first."

"So do we have any idea at what time Mr. Wunderlich was last seen?" Watkins asked. "Did he have appointments that afternoon?"

"He was supposed to be meeting with me at four," Betsy said. "But he didn't turn up. I waited in his office but he never came."

"Did any of you have contact with him after lunch?" Watkins asked, looking around the room. His gaze fell on Emmy, who had been sitting silent and withdrawn.

"Me? I wasn't here," Emmy said. "I'm not attached to this place. I'm a grad student, doing research work, and I brought Betsy here because I'd heard about Randy Wunderlich and the advanced methods he had developed for testing psychic ability."

"And I wasn't here," Michael said. "I went into town after lunch to run some errands for my mother."

"I saw Mr. Wunderlich after lunch," Betsy said. "I was asked to take him down a cup of coffee — around two-thirty, that would have been. I took it down and he was on the phone and he said, 'Thank you. Leave it there.' "

"You took his coffee?"

Betsy nodded. "And the empty coffee cup was still there on his desk when I went into his office at four. I was planning to take it away and wash it up, but I forgot."

"Rhiannon might know something," Lady Annabel said. "We should have her here."

"Rhiannon?" Watkins asked.

"Our resident Druid priestess," Lady Annabel said. "She runs our meditation center and directs our Celtic spirituality classes. She might well have seen Randy that afternoon — his office is in the same building."

"And where can we find her now?"

"She lives in one of the cottages, right behind the meditation center," Annabel said. "I can send Michael to find her for you."

"No, I think we'll go down that way ourselves and take a look," Watkins said. "If one of you would be kind enough to direct us."

"Michael will take you down, won't you, dear?"

"If you say so." Michael got to his feet. "This way, please."

Watkins followed him out through the etched-glass front doors. Glynis looked back at Evan and nodded that he should come too.

"A resident Druid priestess," Glynis muttered to Evan. "This place is too much, isn't it? Do you think they really believe in all this stuff?"

"Wait until you meet the priestess," Evan said. "She takes herself very seriously."

"So I might not have been so far off with

158

my suggestion of black magic down in the cave?" Glynis said as they descended the flight of steps.

Evan remembered the bone-chilling dread of that cave. Now, with the early morning sun sending steam rising from the grass, it seemed laughable that it was caused by anything more than inadequate clothes and an empty stomach.

They were halfway down the steps when they saw a figure walking up to meet them. It was wearing a white, hooded, floor-length cloak.

"Ah, Rhiannon," Michael called. "I was sent to find you."

"And I was coming to you." Rhiannon threw back her hood to reveal the striking gray hair. "They've found Randy, haven't they? I was awakened while it was still dark. I felt a tremendous disturbance in the cosmic forces."

Michael nodded. "Yes. They've found him. Dead, I'm afraid. Drowned."

"I knew it." Rhiannon said. "I sensed it all along. Not that one would have ever picked up vibrations from him, but the universe told me."

"Why wouldn't you feel vibrations from him?" Glynis asked, moving up beside Watkins. "Were you not on the same wavelength?"

Rhiannon's penetrating stare held Glynis

until the young woman blushed and laughed awkwardly.

"What we do here is not to be taken lightly," Rhiannon said. "Randy Wunderlich took it lightly and see what fate awaited him. The universe will not be mocked."

"So — uh — do you remember when you last saw Mr. Wunderlich?" Watkins asked. "So far, the last time any person had contact with him was around two-thirty in the afternoon that day."

"I'm afraid I can't help you there, Inspector. I was out and about all afternoon."

"It's not inspector, it's sergeant," Watkins said.

"Ah. Not inspector yet. I'm sorry. A little premature." Rhiannon's fixed her intense gaze on Watkins. "I try to shut Randy Wunderlich from my mind. I find his presence very disturbing, so I wouldn't have noticed him even if he were in the next room." She gave a curt little nod. "Good day to you. I expect I'm required at the great house."

She continued on up the steps.

"What a strange woman," Glynis muttered.

Watkins glanced back over his shoulder. "How did she know I was going to be promoted?"

"Rhiannon is a law unto herself," Michael said, watching her go up the steps, the white cape flying out behind her. "She'd like people to think she is in constant contact with the forces of the universe — whatever that means. You should go to her ceremonies some time. P-pretty impressive stuff. She knows how to put on a good show — I'll say that for her."

"I gather you don't go along with all the things they do here?" Evan asked the young man.

Michael laughed. "If you want my honest opinion, it's a load of cod's wallop. But if enough misguided people are willing to pay to have their auras put back into shape and find out that they were Cleopatra once, who am I to rock the boat?"

"Yet you choose to work here. The money must be good," Evan said.

Michael looked surprised. "Didn't anyone tell you that I'm Annabel's son? Rightful heir to the Bland-Tyghes, come home to claim my inheritance?"

"No, I'd no idea," Evan stammered. "You don't exactly look like . . ."

"The lord of the manor? No, I'm not exactly treated like it either, am I? And believe me, being here is not my idea. I should be back at university, finishing my degree, but someone had to keep an eye on my mother."

"Why was that?" Evan asked.

"I didn't trust Randy Wunderlich, if you really want to know. He had to have had some motive for marrying her, other than her charm and good looks. I rather suspect it was to get his hands on her property."

"In which case, his death should come as a relief to you, I'd imagine."

Michael gave an uneasy grin. "Put that way, I suppose you're right, Constable."

Chapter 13

Excerpt from *The Way of the Druid,* by Rhiannon

Druid Holy Places

The Druids did not create the great stone circles, the monoliths, the henges, but it is very possible that they incorporated native religious practices into their rituals and used these holy places for worship and divination. It is possible that they used them as calendars, which is what their builders had designed them to be. The accurate telling of the solstices was of paramount importance to the old Druids as their major festivals were held on solstice dates. Solstices were dates of very special significance when the passage between this world and the other was more accessible. We know, for example, that Druid-era window-tombs allowed shafts of light to fall onto the body only on the morning of the winter solstice.

Over centuries of worship holy places become imbued with power and awe. We sense the power in these holy places today and incorporate them into our ceremonies.

But our true holy places today are not amid standing stones or on mountain crags.

163

We worship wherever we are at one with nature. Druids have always venerated the oak tree. Therefore, we choose to hold our most sacred ceremonies in an oak grove.

Druids have always believed that mistletoe is a plant of mystical powers, maybe because it can live without roots, merely perching on other plants, green all winter in spite of frost and snow. We always incorporate "mistletoe" into our ceremonies.

We hold the hazel important for divination.

The yew has special powers for us.

We are at one with all nature — stone and water, wood and flower.

We are at one with the animals of the forest and the birds of the air and the fish of the ocean.

By midmorning Evan was riding with Betsy and the American woman back to Llanfair. Betsy had tried to protest that she should be staying to do her job, but even Annabel saw that Betsy was in no condition to work.

"We really don't need you, my dear," she had said, patting Betsy's hand. "Please go home and have a good rest. We've all had a terrible, terrible shock — you much more so, because of the psychic forces at work in you. Randy was always so tired after a session with —" She broke off, put her hand to her mouth, and fled into her office.

Betsy allowed Emmy and Evan to lead her

to the car. Emmy asked Evan to drive. "I'm in no fit state," she said. So Evan drove. Emmy sat silent beside him. Betsy huddled in the backseat. As usual on such occasions Evan was amazed to find life going on as if nothing had happened. Women were doing their shopping in Porthmadog high street, pushing prams or dodging in and out of traffic with shopping baskets. Tourists were taking pictures of the bridge in Beddgelert. Children were screaming as they ran around the playground of the Beddgelert village school, causing Evan's thoughts to turn to Bronwen. He hoped she was feeling better this morning. If it was a twenty-four-hour bug, as the doctor had predicted, she should be up and around again.

"I'll be sorry to leave Mrs. Williams," Emmy said as they drove into Llanfair. "Such a nice lady. We had already established a real bond between us."

"You're not going, are you?" Betsy asked.

Emmy pushed back her hair in a distraught gesture. "I can't stay here now. Not after what's happened. Too many bad vibes. I just wouldn't feel right working here. And with — Randy gone, there's no point, is there?"

"So will you go back to America?" Betsy asked.

"I don't know where I'll go or what I'll do at the moment. I'm too upset to think straight. I suppose I might go up to Scotland or over to Ireland. Anywhere to get away from here."

"So now we'll never finish testing my psychic abilities, will we?" Betsy said.

Emmy turned around to her and placed her hand over Betsy's. "Listen, kiddo, you have already proved that you have awesome powers. That dream — you were right on. Don't give up now, okay? See if they can still work with you at the center. At least they'll be in touch with others in the psychic community. You'll need to learn how to make those powers work for you."

"But I don't want you to go," Betsy said. "Couldn't you stay and help me?"

"Don't ask me to stay here. I just can't." Emmy shook her head violently, then she added, "Besides, I'm an academic. I can test people and measure ability, that's all. You need to work with another psychic."

"Don't go yet," Betsy begged. "I'm scared."

"Of what?"

"That something else bad is going to happen."

"Do you feel that, Betsy?" Emmy asked.

"Yes."

"Then stop working at that place, Betsy," Evan said. "Go back to your old job, for heaven's sake."

"Of course she shouldn't go back to her old job," Emmy said angrily. "Would you have advised Michaelangelo to stick to painting houses?" She spun around to Betsy again. "But I'll be here a few more days. I'll need to talk to my professor and decide what to do next. He'll understand that I can't go on working here. I really think the best thing for me right now is to go home, to the States — to regroup."

Evan parked the car outside Mrs. Williams's cottage. Mrs. Williams already had the front door open by the time they were getting out of the car.

"What on earth has been happening?" she demanded. "Running off in the middle of the night like that! I've been worried sick. Come inside, all of you. You look dreadful, Betsy *fach*. White as a sheet, and so do you, Miss Court. I've got the kettle on the boil and the bacon cooked in the over. . . ."

She ushered them into the house, like a sheepdog rounding up sheep. Evan turned down the offer of breakfast somewhat reluctantly, claiming that he had to check his messages at the police station and look in on Bronwen. He found that he was glad to have made his escape. This was all too much emotion for him. He went into the police station, found no messages, then set off for the schoolhouse. He could hear the voices of children chanting their twelve times table as he crossed the playground. Was that a good sign? Did it mean she was back in class with them? Then the door of Bronwen's living quarters — a gray stone cottage attached to one end of the school building — opened and Evan was amazed to see Mrs. Powell-Jones, the minister's wife, come out.

"Ah, Constable Evans. I don't think you should go in there now." She put up her hand to stop him.

"Why? What's wrong?"

"She's not looking at all well. I heard that she was sick and I thought it was my duty to minister to her, but she was so weak, she couldn't even lift her head to try some of my nourishing homemade calves foot jelly. And she wouldn't hear of my making her any soup either. She said all she wants to do is sleep, so I think we should respect her wishes, don't you?" She put a forceful hand on his arm and attempted to turn him around.

For once, Evan wasn't about to be turned. "Look, I promised I'd stop in on her this morning, and I was called out really early on a case, so she'll be wondering what has happened to me. Don't worry. I'll only stay a minute." He gave what he hoped was a winning smile and moved past the minister's wife.

"Try to get her to take a spoonful of the calves foot jelly," she called after him. "She needs to build up her strength."

Evan tapped lightly on the door, then let himself in. The schoolhouse felt cold and empty. He walked softly to Bronwen's bedroom and pushed open the door. Bronwen was lying quite still with her eyes closed. Her face looked gray and hollow.

"Bron?" He couldn't resist touching her, just in case.

Her eyes opened and a smile spread across her face. "Oh, it's you, Evan. I thought it was that dreadful woman coming back. Not only do I feel rotten, but having Mrs. Powell-Jones ministering to me was one affliction too many. Sleep seemed like the only way out of eating her awful calves foot jelly. You should have seen her, Evan. She sat on my bed and kept waving this spoon in my face. And then I wanted to go to the loo again and she told me it was only a question of mind over matter and I shouldn't let it get the better of me."

Evan perched on the edge of her bed and took her hand. "I'm sorry I wasn't here to protect you from her," he said. "How are you really feeling?"

"A little better, I think," she said, "but awfully weak."

"Do you think we should call the doctor again? It's been more than twenty-four hours now."

"Give it another day. If I'm no better by this evening, I'll ask him to drop in on his rounds."

"Is there anything you'd really like — not

calves foot jelly, I mean?"

Bronwen shook her head. "I can't say that the thought of any food appeals to me. Another sip of Lucozade, that's all."

He filled the glass for her. She sat up then lay back with a sigh. "I feel as if I'm made of putty. I'm going to have to take Mrs. PJ's advice and start using mind over matter. I can't just lie here, being sick!"

Evan bent to kiss her. "You just get a good sleep, all right? I'll pop round again later."

As he let himself out, he noticed that Mrs. Powell-Jones was pretending to work on the garden outside Capel Beulah while keeping an eye on the schoolhouse. As he let himself out of the playground, she came running down the street to him.

"It's all right. She's sleeping now," he said. "She'll probably sleep for hours. We shouldn't disturb her."

"That wasn't what I wanted to talk to you about," Mrs. Powell-Jones said. "I wish to lodge a complaint. You haven't been here doing your job for the past few days."

"I was called away on a case," he said. "I'm a mobile unit now, you know. Not confined to Llanfair."

"I should have thought your first duty was to protect the citizens here, mobile or not," Mrs. Powell-Jones said.

"Has something happened?"

"Only that there is a homicidal maniac at large."

"A what?"

"That lunatic postman," Mrs. Powell-Jones exclaimed in her booming voice. "Some stupid fool has given him a motorbike. He almost rode me down yesterday. I was crossing the road when he came careening down the hill, completely exceeding the speed limit. I had to leap for my life, Constable Evans. And he didn't even stop to apologize."

Evan was trying not to smile at the thought of Mrs. Powell-Jones leaping for her life. "I'm sorry. He hasn't quite got the hang of it yet," he said.

"Then he shouldn't be allowed to ride it, should he? I want you to arrest him for reckless driving. Confiscate the damned thing before he kills somebody or himself."

"I'll talk to him," Evan said. "I'll try and make him see sense."

"Talking is not enough. You have to learn to be more forceful, Constable. If you don't act now, someone is going to get hurt."

She strode off back to the chapel. Evan sighed and walked down the hill to the police station. Life was back to normal after the excitement at the Sacred Grove, he thought. Then he corrected himself: It wasn't back to normal. Bronwen was ill.

He wished he could stop feeling so damned guilty. Logically his cooking couldn't have caused Bronwen's illness, because he had eaten the same things, but doubt still nagged at the back of his mind. Maybe there was just one piece of tainted meat, one piece that was not fully cooked, and Bronwen ate it. If only the timing hadn't be so coincidental: Bronwen had fallen ill right after — Evan broke off in midthought and stood there, in the middle of the street — right after Betsy had stopped by to visit.

Disturbing snatches of remembered conversation flashed through his mind. He heard Betsy's voice — "If Bronwen Price wasn't around any longer . . . do you think you might be interested in me then?" And what else had she said? Something about harnessing her powers and how real psychics could just think something and it would happen. He knew that witch doctors in Africa could will somebody to die and that person died. He found that his heart was racing and his mouth was dry. Had Betsy, either knowingly or not, put a similar curse on Bronwen?

He was halfway down the hill, ready to challenge Betsy, when reason took over. What an absurd thing to think — that Bronwen had fallen ill because somehow Betsy had willed it! Everybody got stomach flu at some point in their lives. And Bronwen, exposed to all those children every day, was more at risk than most. She had even said that she was feeling slightly better, hadn't she? Evan shook his head and strode out in the direction of the police station. All the strange goings-on at the Sacred Grove had started affecting him. He was glad they'd found Randy Wunderlich's body and he wouldn't have to go near the place again.

Chapter 14

Life in Llanfair went on smoothly — that is, apart from the occasional motorbike ridden by a screaming postman careening into a row of dustbins. Evan had delivered his stern warning to Evans-the-Post but it didn't seem to be doing much good. Mrs. Powell-Jones rang the police station at regular intervals to complain. She threatened also to ring the postmaster in Llanberis and probably the postmaster general in London, but Evans-the-Post was not to be halted on his morning rides of terror.

There were no phone calls from Sergeant Watkins or Glynis Davies for the rest of that Tuesday or all day Wednesday. If the investigation was proceeding, then Evan wasn't part of it. Evan gleaned from a phone call to headquarters that the autopsy had revealed no sign of a heart attack; also that the bandaged foot had minimal if any damage. Randy Wunderlich would definitely have been able to walk out of the cave. The death was ruled accidental, if puzzling.

Betsy had gone back to work at the Sacred Grove on Wednesday morning. When Evan tried to dissuade her, she claimed that she liked it there better than at the Red Dragon, where she wasn't appreciated and had no chance to use her talents.

On Wednesday afternoon a board went up outside the Red Dragon, announcing Friday to be trivia night — Llanfair versus Beddgelert.

"He's getting desperate, wouldn't you say, Evan?" Charlie Hopkins muttered as he passed Evan on his way to the pub.

"Hurting for business, is he?" Evan asked.

"Indeed he is. Nobody in there but me and Evans-the-Meat last night. Quiet as a grave."

"And he really thinks a trivia contest will help, does he?"

"Trying everything, isn't he?" Charlie sucked through his remaining teeth. "It will be beauty contests next week, sheepdog trials, striptease acts. . . ." He shuffled on, his old body shaking with laughter as he walked.

It was just like old times when Evan entered the bar on Friday evening. Full of smoke and chatter and familiar faces. Evan was glad. He had had a hard week, spending every spare moment ministering to Bronwen while trying to drive two ministers' wives away. The moment that Mrs. Parry Davies learned that Mrs. Powell-Jones had been tending to the sick, she had shown up on Bronwen's doorstep with a bowl of home-made leek soup and some suitable reading material — mostly religious tracts on why everyone was going straight to hell.

Evan had had little enthusiasm for cooking since the Bronwen disaster. He had thrown the mound of spaghetti away, in case it was somehow poisoned, and he had lived on tinned soup and grilled cheese all week. As he made his way across to the pub on Friday, he decided that a couple of bangers and perhaps a meat pie would go down a treat.

"Here he is, the man himself," Evans-the-Meat greeted him. "We're going to need you on our team, boyo."

"Team?"

"The trivia contest. We have to show those blokes from Beddgelert that we're smarter than they are."

"I don't know if I'm much good at trivia," Evan said, but Evans-the-Meat waved down his protests. "Went to that posh grammar school in Swansea, didn't you? Of course you'll know all the answers."

Evan made his way to the counter. He remembered how nice it had been to see Betsy smiling at him and drawing his usual pint of Guinness. To the right of the counter, the blackboard had some words scrawled on it: "Not serving any food on account of the fact that the landlord only has one bloody pair of hands."

Evan ordered his Guinness.

"Over here, boyo." Evans-the-Meat beckoned Evan to join him. "We need to talk strategy."

As Evan joined the group, Roberts-the-Pump leaned close to him. "We don't hang around the bar these days. Harry gets that bad tempered. He wants Betsy back but he's too proud to ask."

"I don't think he'll get her back," Evan said. "She's having a good time at the Sacred Grove."

"What, down among the loonies?"

"They're loony enough to pay her for doing very little work, as far as I can see," Evan said.

"Talk of the devil." Evans-the-Meat nudged Evan in the side. The door had opened and Betsy came in, looking strangely elegant in a long dark coat and heels.

"What are you doing here, Betsy?" Evans-the-Meat asked. "Come to give Harry a hand?"

"Not likely," Betsy said. "I just popped in to see how things are. I'm meeting Emmy and we're going to dinner in Conwy. It's her last night — she's leaving tomorrow so she's taking me and Mrs. Williams out for a treat."

"I hope the restaurant can measure up to Mrs. Williams's standards," Evan said.

"She won't even notice. She's so upset, she's been crying all day. She says she lost a son and now she's losing a daughter. Terrible, it is."

"Make up your minds. I haven't got all day, you know," came Harry's gruff voice from behind the bar. "Dimple Haig? You bloody would — just because I have to stand on the stool to reach it!"

"He's not exactly making it fun to be here, is he?" Betsy said. "Still, he brought it on himself, didn't he?"

"So you like it down there, do you?" Owens-the-Sheep asked.

"It's a lovely place. Of course, it's very sad at the moment because Randy died, but they're all being so nice to me. Lady Annabel says she's coming to rely on me and even Rhiannon is being nice to me."

"Rhiannon? Who the hell's Rhiannon?" Evans-the-Meat demanded.

"She's the Druid priestess," Betsy said, ignoring the chuckles around her. "You can laugh, but you'd be surprised. Rhiannon says I'm a true Celt and all true Celts have the old religion, in their blood. She says we're bound to the forces of the universe, whether we like it or not."

"Never heard such a daft . . ." Evans-the-Meat began.

"You just wait, Mr. Evans, until I've got my powers developed. Then you'll be laughing on the other side of your face. Rhiannon has been telling me about the Goddess."

"Goddess? Betsy, don't let the ministers hear you talking like that!" Charlie Hopkins looked around to see if Mr. Parry Davies was in his usual corner.

"It's a free country, isn't it? And I think a Goddess might be rather nice after having to pray to an old man in a white nightie all my life." She gave Evan a challenging look. "She wants me to come to one of her ceremonies. I think it might be fun."

"Just watch yourself, Betsy," Evan said. "I don't like that place. Never did."

"That's because you don't have powers, Evan," Betsy said.

"Powers!" Barry-the-Bucket came up to join them. "Are you still on about those powers?"

"I've already had one psychic dream this week, for your information," Betsy said. "There's no knowing where my powers will take me next. Go on, test me."

"See if you can make that pint of Robinson's float off the counter and into my hands, will you?" Barry-the-Bucket said.

"Not stuff like that. I'm not a magician. Things like seeing into the future."

"All right. Predict something that's going to happen tomorrow," Barry said, still grinning.

"I won't be going on a date with you, that's for sure," Betsy answered. "Tomorrow, let's see." Her face became suddenly serious. "I think it's going to be a nice day. I can see myself feeling hot."

"Hot and bothered when I'm near you,

Betsy *cariad*," Barry said, but she pushed him away, laughing. "Never give up, do you?"

"Can you come up with someone better? And don't say Constable Evans here, because you'll have to get rid of Bronwen Price first."

Betsy tossed back her blond curls. "As a matter of fact I might well have someone in mind," she said. "A gentleman I work with at the Sacred Grove. He's a bit shy, but he's really nice when you get to know him." A car horn sounded outside. "That's Emmy. I've got to run." She pushed her way through the crowd, just as a group of strangers entered the pub.

"Here they are now, look you — the team from Beddgelert, come for the trivia contest," Harry said loudly.

"Come to be soundly beaten," a Llanfair voice chimed in. Harry ignored the comment and went on, "Welcome, gentlemen. Let's have the Llanfair team over here, at this end of the bar, and you gentlemen down at that table in the corner."

"How come we're put down near the fire?" a Beddgelert man demanded. "It's too bloody hot down here. We can't think straight."

"You lot couldn't think straight if you were standing on top of a bloody mountain," Evans-the-Meat said.

"Now, now, boys. Friendly contest, isn't it, not a bloody war," Harry interjected.

Evan decided to beat a hasty and well-timed retreat. He was in no mood for trivia contests, nor for keeping the peace between two sparring villages. He stepped out into the crisp night air. From one of the cottages came the smell of onions frying, reminding him that he'd had nothing to eat and wasn't likely to get anything now. He looked wistfully down the road, wishing he could have gone with Betsy, who was now on her way to a good restaurant with Mrs. Williams and Emmy.

He started to walk up the street. At least Emmy would be gone in the morning, which was a good thing. Evan wished she had never come in the first place and never picked Betsy for her stupid tests. All this nonsense about powers and goddesses — and yet was it all nonsense? Betsy had, after all, dreamed where to find Randy Wunderlich's body. He recalled her wide-eyed terror of that night, when she had knocked on his door.

A cold wind rushed up the pass, rattling branches and making Evan shiver. He didn't believe in rubbish like psychic powers, and yet he had been a witness at the extraordinary events that night. Was it also possible that she had used those newly awoken powers subconsciously to bring about Bronwen's illness? If not, why wasn't Bronwen getting better?

Chapter 15

Saturday dawned fine, if blustery, with white puffball clouds racing in from the Western ocean and the sigh of the wind moaning up the pass. Evan thought of going for a hike, but somehow the idea lost its appeal without Bronwen. He thought of driving down to the coast and searching for other domestic necessities at the flea market in Caernarfon, but that also lacked appeal alone. In the end he agreed to go and change Bronwen's library books for her.

"Nothing too heavy, please," she said as she handed him the books she had finished. "I don't seem to have the strength for more than the lightest books — I can't concentrate or hold them up either." She gave a sweet smile that twisted Evan's insides. She looked like a pale shadow of herself lying there. Why wasn't she getting better?

"I'll be back as quick as I can," he said. "Maybe we could play Scrabble later and I'll let you beat me as usual."

Bronwen nodded. "That would be nice, although you might even win for once."

He was just putting the books in the front seat of his old bone-shaker when his pager sounded. With a muttered damn he went back inside and dialed HQ.

"Constable Evans?" It was Megan, the witty dispatcher. "D.C.I. Hughes would like a word with you. One moment, please." He heard her say, "I've got Evans on the line for you, sir."

Then Hughes's clipped, high voice. "Ah, Evans. Good man. I want you to meet me at that place — the Sacred Grove — in half an hour."

Evan could hardly remind a newly appointed D.C.I. that it was his day off. Besides, if something was going on, it was a miracle that he was being included.

"Has something happened, sir?" He tried to keep the excitement out of his voice.

"Interesting development. Look, I understand there is a young woman who claimed to have had a dream that led people to the body. And I'm told she's working at the Sacred Grove as well. So I'll find her down there, shall I?"

"I think she has the weekend off, sir," Evan said, tempted to add, "like me."

"Then I'd like you to find her and bring her down to me, so that I can ask her some questions. Let's say — ten o'clock."

The phone went dead. Evan stared at it for a second, then replaced the receiver and went in search of Betsy.

"What's it all about then?" Betsy asked. "He wants to hear about my dream, does he? How exciting. Do you think he might want to use me as the police psychic someday? The police do use psychics, don't they?"

She grabbed her coat and ran out of the house. "Can we go on your new bike?" she asked. "I've always wanted to ride a motorbike."

"I don't think I'm supposed to give rides," Evan said.

"Oh, come on, don't be a spoilsport," Betsy pleaded. "It's official police business, isn't it? And you're taking me along as a witness. And that's your official police transportation."

"I suppose it is," Evan said. "All right. Jump on."

Betsy let out little yells of delight as they went around each of the hairpin bends down the Nantgwynant Pass. Evan had picked up some of Betsy's excitement. He had suspected that Randy Wunderlich's death hadn't made sense. Now maybe he was going to find out the truth.

The security gate swung open for them. As Evan pulled up in the car park, D.C.I. Hughes appeared from the security post. As usual he was immaculately dressed in a well-cut suit, a royal blue bow tie, and a white handkerchief showing in his top pocket. Not an iron-gray hair out of place. Neat little moustache trimmed to a slim line on his upper lip. He always looked as if he should be working in a high-class gentlemen's clothier's, not a police station.

"Evans!" He strode across to the motor-bike. "What do you think you're doing, man? Giving joyrides on a police motorbike?"

"Sorry, sir, but you did ask me to bring the young lady down here, and this is my only official police vehicle." Evan stared the D.C.I. in the eye.

"Oh, yes, well, I suppose it is." Hughes gave an embarrassed cough at the back of his throat. "Well, I'm glad you got here so quickly. I've spread the word that I want to question people up at the main house. Come along then, this way." He set off with quick, mincing strides, like a large windup toy. Again, as Evan watched him, he found himself wondering how such a person could rise so easily to the rank of detective chief inspector, while he, Evan, was still firmly planted on the very bottom rung.

"Rum sort of place, isn't it?" Hughes slowed to let Evan catch up with him. "Not quite real, if you know what I mean." Evan did know. He nodded.

"Still, I suppose there are enough people interested in New Age kind of things these days for them to make a go of it," Hughes commented.

Evan kept his views to himself.

"I'll need you to take notes, Evans," Hughes continued. "I thought Watkins and his team would be here to assist me, but there was a nasty hit-and-run outside Caernarfon this morning so I've sent them over there instead."

"Very good, sir." Evan tried to hide a smile. For once he wasn't being dismissed as soon as things got interesting. That was hopeful.

"And you, young lady." Hughes addressed Betsy for the first time. "I think we'll start by talking to you. A most interesting case, by the way. Fascinating."

"Excuse me, sir, but have they found out anything more about Randy Wunderlich's death?" Evan asked. "Is that why we're here?"

"What have you heard so far?" Hughes asked.

"Only that it wasn't a heart attack, there was no sign of external injury, and cause of death was drowning," Evan said. "But I always suspected there had to be more to it."

"Why was that?"

"A young, fit man doesn't wait in a cave to be drowned."

"Ah." Hughes gave a satisfied little nod. "Quite perceptive of you, Constable. As it turns out —" he moved closer to Evan so that Betsy couldn't overhear "— the lab has done a splendid job of hurrying through the toxicology, and we got the report this morning. It indicates that Mr. Wunderlich stayed in the cave, waiting to be drowned, because he was fast asleep at the time."

"Fast asleep. You mean in a trance?"

"No, I mean a damned great dose of flurazepam."

"What's that?"

"Sleeping pills. Sold under the name of Dalanine. Either he took them intentionally, to kill himself, or someone made damned sure he didn't wake up when the tide came in."

"I'd be inclined to go along with the latter," Evan said.

"Oh, and why is that?"

"I met Mr. Wunderlich. He thought a lot of himself. He acted the part of the famous psychic. He wasn't the sort of man to die in a cave where his body might never have been found. If he was going to commit suicide, he'd make damned sure he staged a good one."

Hughes nodded. "Interesting. I'll bear that in mind. So if he didn't kill himself, then someone else fed him enough drugs to knock him out."

"And then put him in the cave?" Evan asked. "It would take a strong person to carry him the length of the beach and up the rocks, besides its being damned risky that they would be seen."

"That's something we'll have to find out, won't we?" Hughes gave his birdlike nod again. "Interesting case, Evans. Come on

187

then. Let's get started." They had reached the former stately home that now housed administration and reception. Hughes went up the front steps, pushed open the swing door, and walked through as if he owned the place. Evan and Betsy followed. "I've taken over Lady Annabel's office," Hughes said, as if this were a perfectly natural thing to do. "Let her know that I'll be ready for her in about half an hour. We'll start with you, my dear. I'm sure you've got some fascinating things to tell us."

"I'll do my best, sir." Betsy blushed with pleasure.

"Right. Then let's get to it, shall we?" Hughes sat himself at Lady Annabel's desk and indicated an upright wooden chair for Betsy. He didn't motion for Evan to sit. "Your name is?"

"Betsy Edwards, sir. Well, Elizabeth Edwards really, but I've always been called Betsy."

"And you come from the village of Llanfair?"

"That's right, sir. Llanfair born and bred, as they say."

"And what sort of work do you do, Betsy?"

"Until last week I was working at the Red Dragon — that's the pub in Llanfair. Maybe you know it." Hughes nodded. "But then I started working here at the Sacred Grove."

"What made you change jobs? I'd imagine

it's a long complicated journey each day for someone who doesn't have a car. You don't have a car, do you?"

"Well, you see, sir, until now Emmy has been driving me to work each day."

"Emmy?"

"The American lady. She's the one who discovered my powers, sir."

"Emmy?" The D.C.I. consulted his list. "How does she come into this? She's not on my list as working here."

"No, sir. She doesn't work here. She's a university lady, studying about people who have psychic powers. And she was living up in Llanfair until — well until this morning."

Hughes looked across to Evan. "I don't think we should let this woman go without having a word with her first. Do you know where she is living, Constable? Get her on the phone and tell her that she's not to leave the area until I've spoken with her. Tell her I want her down here right away."

"Very good, sir." Evan picked up the phone and dialed Mrs. Williams's number, noticing that the D.C.I. looked impressed that he had the number down pat. He didn't mention it was his former landlady's house.

"You've just caught her," Mrs. Williams said. "You're lucky she's still here. She was planning to leave right after breakfast but her clothes were still wet on the line. She didn't realize there wasn't a clothes dryer in the village. 'Nobody has a dryer around here,' I told her. 'We don't go in for such things,' I said. 'Nothing wrong with a good old clothesline out in the wind, is there? You'd have to go down to Bangor to the laundromat if you want fancy things like clothes dryers,' I told her. So she said . . .''

"Mrs. Williams," Evan interrupted. "Would you run outside and bring her to the phone before she drives away?"

"Oh — *or gore,* right you are, Mr. Evans. Important, is it?" Mrs. Williams was startled by the abruptness of his interruption.

"Very," Evan said. "The chief inspector wants to speak to her."

"I was just heading out of the door," Emmy said as she picked up the phone. "What's up? I've got an afternoon flight to catch, so I don't have much time."

"The chief inspector wants a word," Evan said and handed the phone to Hughes. Let him be the one to tell her that she wasn't going to catch her flight. He didn't think Emmy was the kind of woman who would have her plans disrupted without protest. Sure enough, he heard the raised voice escaping from the phone and saw Hughes's pained expression as he held the phone well away from his ear.

"Just a minute, my dear young lady. I'm sorry if it's disrupting your plans," he said when he could get a word in edgewise, "but there has been a development concerning the death of Randy Wunderlich and you will be required to make a statement."

"That set her straight," he said as he put down the phone. "Damned American women always have to have the last word." He turned back to Betsy. "Now tell us how you came to be involved with this woman, Betsy."

"Well, sir, it was like this," Betsy said. "She came into the pub and started asking questions. When she heard about my old *nain* having the second sight and seeing the Cannwyll Corff — ohh, I just remembered!" Betsy put her hand to her mouth. "When I went into Mr. Wunderlich's office for the first time, what do you think I saw? There was a candle burning on his table. I should have known, shouldn't I?"

"I'd imagine that candles are a fairly normal occurrence for a New Age center," Chief Inspector Hughes said dryly. "Go on with what you were telling us about this — Emmy person."

"Well, when Emmy heard that I was an only daughter of an only daughter, she said it was very possible that I had the second sight too and she'd like to take me to get tested. That's when she brought me to the Sacred Grove, sir. And she did some tests with cards. She picked out cards with shapes on them and I had to guess what shape she was looking at and I got them nearly all right. So she said she wanted me to meet Mr. Wunderlich because he was a very famous psychic. So she took me down to see him and he tried a couple of tests, too, and then he said he wanted to work with me — to help me with my powers. Only . . ."

"Only what, Betsy?"

"Only he wasn't there when I went for my first session alone with him. He'd said four o'clock right enough, but he wasn't there. Well, sir, I was a little upset because I'd been looking forward to it. I just went home and I didn't think no more about it. But when I got to work in the morning, I found the whole place in a tizzy. It seems nobody had seen Mr. Wunderlich since I'd taken him his coffee after lunch the day before."

"So you took him his coffee, did you?" Hughes scribbled in his notebook. "And what did you think of Mr. Wunderlich, Betsy?"

"If you'll pardon the expression, sir, I thought he was ever so sexy. Like a film star, just."

"Did any flirting go on between you and Mr. Wunderlich? Did he come on to you at all?"

"Oh, no, sir. He's a married man, sir. And anyway, Emmy was in the room with us, helping with the testing."

"So you liked him, did you?"

"I didn't know him well enough to like him, sir. He was nice enough to me when we met — and he did give me a job at the center so that I could be there when I was needed. That was kind of him."

"So let's move on to the dream," Hughes said. "Tell us about this dream you had, Betsy."

"The dream, sir? Well, it was like this — I went to bed that night and suddenly I dreamed I was standing outside this cave. I went in and it was all dark and it smelled wet and seaweedy, if you know what I mean. I could see something white lying there at the back of the cave. As I got closer, I saw it was Randy. I thought he was asleep and I went to touch him, but then I woke up. I ran to find Emmy and she said, 'You've had a pyschic dream, Betsy. We'll have to go and wake Constable Evans and get straight down to the Sacred Grove.'" Betsy glanced up at Evan for confirmation. "It was about four in the morning, wasn't it, Evan?"

Evan nodded.

"When we got to the center, Lady Annabel said she knew where there were caves on the property, so Michael led us down to the beach and we found Randy's body in the cave, just like I'd dreamed it. It was horrible, sir."

"I'm sure it was, Betsy," the chief inspector said. "Tell me, do you often have dreams like this?"

"Oh, no, sir. This was the first one. Least-ways, it was the first one I knew about.

Maybe I'd been dreaming about things that had really happened before, but I never realized it until Emmy told me about my powers. I've always had vivid dreams, sir. But I thought they were just dreams. . . ."

"Look, why don't you go and get yourself a cup of tea and wait for us in the foyer," Chief Inspector Hughes said. "I have to talk to a lot of people and then Constable Evans can take you home again."

"Thank you, sir," Betsy said. "Glad to have been of help."

"Well, what do you think?" Hughes looked up at Evan.

"About what?" Evan asked.

"Did she do it?"

Chapter 16

Evan stared at Chief Inspector Hughes. "Kill Randy Wunderlich, you mean?"

"It wouldn't be the first time that a murderer has claimed to have dreamed where the body could be found — and she admits bringing him the cup of coffee, which could easily have contained the sleeping draught." The chief inspector was looking rather pleased with himself, Evan thought.

"With all respect, sir. That's bloody stupid," Evan said. "I've known Betsy for a couple of years now. Not the brightest girl in the world, a bit naïve, easily impressed, but . . ."

"She could have been working with someone else then. 'Easily impressed,' you say. Maybe someone else put her up to it."

"I can't think who," Evan said. "She only met these people a few days ago. And I said she wasn't the brightest girl in the world, but she's not stupid either. She's got enough common sense not to go poisoning someone or claiming she'd had a dream. I saw her that night — she was shaking with fright. It wasn't put on."

"I don't believe in powers myself, Constable. If you say Randy Wunderlich didn't kill himself, then someone had a good reason for wanting him dead. Let's see which of them, shall we?" He glanced at his list. "I think we should start with Lady Annabel. Always look nearest to home when it comes to murder — that's my number-one rule. Ten to one the spouse or next of kin did it! Tell Lady Annabel I'm ready to see her now." He raised his hand in an imperious gesture that somehow looked right as it came from Lady Annabel's chair.

Evan was tempted to bow. "I'll tell her, sir," he said.

Lady Annabel had dressed for the occasion. No warm-up suits today. She was wearing an expensive navy dress with a Hermes scarf at her throat and a large diamond on her finger. Her hair was lacquered into a perfect twist and her face was a serene mask of makeup. Even Hughes was a little taken aback as she swept in. He got to his feet. "Of course, you must have this chair, Lady Annabel."

"Thank you." She took it without protest. Hughes perched himself on the wooden upright.

"Now just a few questions about your husband's death, if you don't mind."

"Must we? This has been very painful for me, as I'm sure you understand, Inspector. All I want is his body returned to me for burial, and to be left alone in my grief."

"We'll do all we can to return the remains to you, Lady Annabel, but I'm afraid your husband's death can no longer be ruled accidental."

A little gasp came from Lady Annabel and she put her hand to her throat in a dramatic gesture. "Are you saying that somebody killed him?"

"Or that he killed himself."

"Oh, no. Not Randy. Randy loved life. He had so much to live for. He'd never, ever kill himself."

"Then the sooner we get to the bottom of this, the better," Hughes said. "With your cooperation, Lady Annabel?"

"But of course. What would you like to know?"

"Your name is Lady Annabel Bland-Tyghe? Is that correct?"

"Actually my name is Mrs. Randal Wunderlich," she said. "People around here have known me as Lady Annabel all my life, so I decided to keep it. Randy thought it created the right image for the place."

"And how long had you been married?"

Her face creased in pain. "Not even a year. We were married last summer, in Las Vegas."

"If you don't mind my saying so —" Hughes cleared his throat "— you seem a very unlikely couple. How did you meet?"

"Randy saved my life," she said simply.

"He did? How?"

"I went through a stage of intense depression. My father had died and I didn't know how I was going to be able to pay the death taxes to keep the property that I loved so much. I was just drifting. I didn't know what I was going to do next. I was visiting friends on the East Coast and my friend Dodie had become a real disciple of the New Age. She told me about this marvelous psychic hot line. So I called and Randy was wonderful. He told me so many things about myself and when he heard all my troubles — about trying to hang onto the property — he was so positive and supportive. I called him again and again and one thing led to another. He flew across from California to meet me and it was incredible. He told me his vision for a center he wanted to build — a place that would encompass healing and spirituality and psychic gifts. And when he described it — you won't believe this — it was my property he was talking about!"

Her face had become alight with joy. "When I showed him pictures, he was as flabbergasted as I was. It seemed as if we were meant to be together, didn't it? So we flew to Las Vegas, got married, and came here to put Randy's vision into action."

"When did you say that was? Last summer?" Hughes asked.

Lady Annabel nodded. "Our timing was poor, unfortunately. We had wanted to have the place up and running for the summer holidays, but by the time everything was in place, it was already mid-September — too late to attract many guests. We've had a pretty grim winter, actually. It's not inexpensive to operate a place of this scale. But we were so hopeful for this summer season. Bookings were coming in. We were starting to get some publicity. Everything would have been wonderful." She pressed her lips together and composed herself. "Now I don't know anymore."

"I'm sorry," Hughes said. "Do you think you'll have to close the place?"

"Not if I can help it," Annabel said. "It was Randy's dream. I can't let his dream die, can I? I'm going to soldier on, I suppose. I come from a long line of fighters."

She gave him a brave smile.

"If I could just ask you a couple of questions about Mr. Wunderlich's death, Lady Annabel."

She nodded.

"You say that things weren't going well. You were experiencing financial difficulties. And yet you don't for a moment consider that your husband's death might have been suicide?"

Annabel shook her head violently. "I'm sure of it, Chief Inspector. Randy was the eternal optimist. He was actually very excited this past week. He told me that good things were just about to happen. He saw the Sacred Grove as the center of lots of publicity

199

and the bookings rolling in. He was a well-known psychic, you know."

Evan thought of the man he had seen coming up from the beach. He had certainly looked like someone who was relaxed and confident — rather full of himself, in fact.

The chief inspector cleared his throat. "Which brings us to the next question, Lady Annabel. Can you think of anyone who wanted your husband out of the way?"

"Nobody — everyone adored him. He was a likable man."

"So you've no idea of who might have slipped him a powerful drug and left him to drown?"

Annabel looked horrified. "Is that what they did? Monstrous, absolutely monstrous. You have to catch him, Inspector."

"You sound sure that your husband's killer was a man."

"Well, yes. It never occurred to me that it could be a woman, but . . ."

Evan was watching her closely. Something had crossed Lady Annabel's mind. "But surely a woman couldn't have got Randy into that cave? Over all those boulders?"

There was a tap on the door and the middle-aged man Evan only knew as Ben came in. "I don't think it's right that Annabel should be questioned alone, in her delicate mental state," he said. "She's not herself at the moment, Inspector."

"It's chief inspector, sir," Hughes said, "and who might you be?"

"I'm Benedict Cresswell, Annabel's good friend and financial adviser."

"Do you live here too, sir?"

"No, I was just down for a few days to discuss financial matters, then this happened, so I stayed on because Annabel needed me."

"So you were here when the — tragedy — happened?"

"Oh, indeed, yes. Poor dear Annabel. I've never seen anyone so stricken with grief before."

Hughes got to his feet. "That will be all for now, Lady Annabel. Thank you. If you could notify your entire staff that I'd like to speak to them all later this morning. Can you have them assembled, say, at eleven-thirty?"

"If you wish," Annabel said, "although I really can't think that any of my staff . . ." She left the sentence unfinished and went out. Ben Cresswell went to follow, but Hughes held up his hand.

"A few questions first, sir, if you don't mind. Seeing that you were here on the night of the tragedy." He motioned to the upright chair as he walked around to resume sitting at Lady Annabel's desk. "Now, sir. You say that you are Lady Annabel's friend."

"Old and dear friend, yes. We used to play together as children. Our mothers were friends from finishing school days."

Evan had a chance to study the man for the first time. His was a formerly handsome face that, like Lady Annabel's, had gone to seed. There were bags under his eyes and too many chins, while the red nose indicated either a life of fox hunting or too many whiskies. He was wearing an Aran sweater one size too small for him. The sort of man who would call people like Evan "my dear chap" — or even "chappie." Probably ex-army.

"And you are now her financial adviser?"

"That's right. Went into the City right after my army days. I took over the affairs of this estate when the old man started going — how shall I put it — rather peculiar. Of course, he was always eccentric, but what old family doesn't have an eccentric now and then? What a boring old world it would be if everyone was sane and sensible, what?"

Hughes, who had never been anything other than sane and sensible, coughed in reply.

"And then the old Lord Bland-Tyghe died?" he asked.

"Actually he was Sir Ambrose. Knight. Not lord. Slight difference."

Evan noticed Hughes bristle at the condescension.

"Sir Ambrose then. Lady Annabel inherited on his death?"

"Yes. She was the only surviving Bland-Tyghe. That was two years ago now. The

202

property is so huge that the death taxes were horrendous, as you can imagine. Annabel begged me to come up with a way to keep her property. But I had no idea she'd get this crazy notion of turning it into a New Age center."

He leaned forward in his seat. "Between you and me, Chief Inspector, Annabel has always been very gullible. One day she was going to be an actress, the next she was going to fly out to Calcutta and help Mother Teresa. They were all passing whims. This would have passed too if that dreadful man hadn't latched onto her."

"Mr. Wunderlich, you mean?"

"Of course. When Annabel poured out all her troubles on that wretched psychic hot line, he realized he was on to a good thing."

"You think he only married her for the property?"

"Of course. Why else? Young, fit men don't often go for chubby middle-aged women, do they? The other way around, I admit, but . . ."

"I take it you didn't approve."

"It was a disaster. The man had big ideas but no capital to back them up. I warned them to get the enterprise up and running first and then put in amenities with the profits, but he wouldn't wait. He wanted the spa and the meditation center and the gourmet kitchen all at once. It has drained the very last of Annabel's inheritance, I can tell you that, Chief Inspector."

"Didn't Lady Annabel try to stop him?"

"She wouldn't listen to me. She was still at the infatuation stage. Everything Randy did was wonderful. It would only have lasted another month or two and then she would have tired of him anyway."

"So all in all, you'd say that Randy Wunderlich's death is a blessing?"

"As her financial adviser, I'd say it has come too late. She may well have to auction off the property. But as a friend I say better late then never."

"Do you take sleeping pills, Mr. Cresswell?" Hughes asked.

"Sleeping pills? Good lord no. I was in the Guards, man. I don't mamby pamby myself."

Hughes got to his feet. "Thank you, Mr. Cresswell. You've been most helpful. Can I ask you to stay around a few more days until we've got this matter sorted out?"

"Sorted out? What is there to sort out? The fool went into a cave and got himself drowned."

"Not exactly, sir," Hughes said. "Someone made sure he was asleep when the tide came in."

Ben Cresswell took a moment to register this. "Someone made sure — Good God! So that's why you asked me about sleeping pills. . . . Well, that changes everything, doesn't it?" His red face flushed even redder. "Listen, old chap. All that I said about not liking him and Annabel being better off without him — I don't want you to think . . ."

Ben Cresswell blundered out of the room.

Chapter 17

"Interesting." Chief Inspector Hughes looked up at Evan. "We've already come up with one person who didn't adore Randy Wunderlich."

"I don't think he'll be the only one, sir, from what I've observed," Evan said.

"Really? Well, let's bring in the next contestant, shall we?" He chuckled at his little joke.

Mrs. Roberts sat stiff and erect on the straight-backed chair and eyed the chief inspector coldly.

"You've no right to be putting Miss Annabel through this after what she's gone through already," she said. "The poor man is dead. Let him be. What good can come of asking questions over and over?"

"The truth, I hope," Hughes said. "Now, if he killed himself deliberately, for example . . ."

Mrs. Roberts gave a brittle laugh. "Kill himself — that man? I've never seen a person who thought more of himself. Never passed a mirror without stopping to check how he looked. Vain as a peacock. No, if he was going to kill himself, he'd want to be found lying somewhere special, looking lovely."

Evan nodded to himself. Mrs. Roberts was nobody's fool.

"You've been here long, Mrs. Roberts?" Hughes asked.

"Since Lady Annabel was born. I was only a housemaid at the time, of course, but I rose to housekeeper and I've stayed with her ever since — even though I never imagined I'd be running this kind of establishment. Sir Ambrose would be turning in his grave if he could see them cavorting on his lawns. Heathens! Devil worshippers, that's what they are."

"So why didn't you leave?"

"Leave Miss Annabel to him? I should think not. She might look hard on the outside, but she's as soft as marshmallow. He had her wrapped around his little finger, you know."

"So you didn't like Mr. Wunderlich?"

"I did not, sir. I couldn't stand the man. Quite wrong for Miss Annabel, he was. Not that she had much success in picking men after her first husband. Colonel Hollister was a proper gentleman. The rest have been ragtag and bobtail, if you'll pardon the expression, sir."

"So his death is a relief to you?"

"I wouldn't wish anybody dead, sir. That's not Christian, is it? But if you want my real feelings, yes, I'm glad he's gone. Now maybe things can get back to normal again, and she can marry someone suitable."

"Like Mr. Cresswell?" Evan couldn't resist asking.

"At least he has her best interests at heart," Mrs. Roberts said. "He wouldn't be turning the place into a fun fair."

"That will be all for now, Mrs. Roberts," Hughes said. "Would you please ask Michael Hollister to come in?"

"Very good, sir. And may I bring you in a tray of tea or coffee?"

"Thank you. Most appreciated."

She gave a curt bow before she closed the door behind her.

Hughes turned to Evan. "What made you ask that question about Cresswell?" he demanded.

"I'm sorry, sir. I shouldn't have interrupted you. I just wanted to prove to myself that Cresswell was sweet on Lady Annabel."

"Good lord. What made you think that?"

"Just a feeling. Why else would he stay on here? And she asked for him when she found out the news about Randy's body."

"Ah. Did she? So that gives Cresswell a real motive for wanting Wunderlich out of the way. And Mrs. Roberts too — she was frank enough, wasn't she? Clearly loathed the man. I'm afraid Annabel was sadly deluding herself when she said that Wunderlich had no enemies. It's fairly obvious that —" He broke off as there was a tap at the door.

Michael Hollister poked his head around the door, then came in reluctantly, blinking owlishly behind his glasses.

"Ah, come in. You must be Michael." Hughes waved him to the chair. "Take a seat. Now, if you don't mind, we're trying to fill in the background on Randy Wunderlich."

"S-something's happened, hasn't it?" Michael asked. "You've d-discovered something or you wouldn't be back here. Did he kill himself or did somebody do it for him?"

Again that interesting mixture of shyness and arrogance. He was stuttering more than usual, Evan noted, but that could be a shy person's response to facing D.C.I. Hughes.

"We are only at the beginning of our investigation. Just asking a few questions. Now, I understand that you are Lady Annabel's son. Is that correct?"

"Although she has often denied it, that is correct, yes."

"Why would she want to deny it, Michael?"

"B-b-because I make her look old, of course. How can she be thirty when she has a twenty-year-old son?"

Hughes smiled. "I also understand that you grew up with your father, not your mother."

"That was because she ran out on us when I was very small."

"And yet you are with her now."

"We met up again when I left school. By

that time I could understand why she had run out on my father. She liked life — not being stuck in some grim old fortress and only shooting and fishing for entertainment."

"I also understand that you were at university until recently."

"Until last Michaelmas Term actually."

"So you haven't completed your degree?"

"No. I broke off my studies because I was worried about my mother. When I heard what was happening to the place — well, I thought someone ought to be keeping an eye on her — and on my inheritance."

"So you didn't like Mr. Wunderlich?"

"I can't say I disliked him as a person. He was always pleasant enough to me, although we didn't have much in common. I think he thought I was a poor specimen, because I play the cello and like poetry and don't like sport much. Randy was very into the body beautiful — healthy mind, healthy body, always pumping iron and jogging."

"But his death is very convenient for you. Now your mother is free of him and you get your beloved home back."

"I wouldn't call it a beloved home. I hardly know the place. I only came here a couple of times in school holidays to stay with my grandfather. But it is family property. It should stay in the family."

"Well, now you'll be able to go back to uni and finish your degree, won't you? I expect you'll be happy to be with your friends again. It must be rather dreary to be in a place with nobody your own age around."

"Oh, absolutely — although I'm not a particularly social kind of chap. Not exactly the life of the party, like Randy was."

Hughes consulted his notes. "I see from what Sergeant Watkins has written that you were out on the afternoon Randy Wunderlich went missing."

"Yes. My mother asked me to run some errands for her, so I took her car after lunch and drove into Porthmadog. Not exactly a shopping metropolis, is it? But I had to pick up a prescription for her and mail a couple of parcels — that kind of thing."

"And you got back when?"

"Not exactly sure. I stopped off at the harbor to see some chaps who sail with me. I like to sail, you know. I spent most of the afternoon there. They were laying the tables for dinner when I got back here, so it must have been around five. You can check with security; they log cars in and out."

"Michael — did your mother take sleeping pills?"

Michael grinned, making him look suddenly very young. "She wouldn't admit to it, because Randy went in for alternative healing, but she popped quite a few pills. Mogodans, tranquilizers, diet pills."

"And what was the prescription for that afternoon? Do you remember?"

Michael grinned again. "It was some sort of vitamin A cream for her wrinkles."

"I see. Thank you, Michael. You've been very helpful. Let me ask you one last thing. Do you think anybody at the Sacred Grove wanted to see Randy Wunderlich dead?"

"I should have thought the question would be who didn't," Michael said. "Mrs. Roberts couldn't stand him. Ben loathed him and Rhiannon —"

"Ah yes, the famous Druid priestess. I'm looking forward to meeting her. Would you ask her to come in next, please?"

Michael swallowed hard so that his large Adam's apple bounced up and down. "She sent a message to say that she wasn't to be disturbed during her meditation. You can come down to her when you've finished up here."

"Damned cheek," Hughes muttered. "Does she always behave like this, Michael?"

"Oh, she fully believes this is her center," Michael said. "Or it should be. But you have to speak to her yourself. Then you'll get the idea. So there's nothing more you want from me now?"

"Make sure you check with security that he really was gone all afternoon that day, Evans," Hughes said as Michael shut the door behind him. "I'd imagine he'd be happier than anyone to be rid of his stepfather and get back to university life."

"Yes, but you don't go around killing people just to get back to uni, do you, sir?" Evan chuckled. "Or just because you don't like somebody. You have to be pretty desperate to kill in my experience — back against the wall."

"Yes, quite," Hughes said crisply, reminding Evan that it was probably rather tactless to talk about his experience in solving murders. On the whole he had been rather more successful at it than Inspector Hughes.

"So what do you want to do about Rhiannon, sir?" he asked quickly. "Do you want me to go and fetch her?"

Hughes gave a little half smile. "I don't want to risk your being turned into a toad or a tree stump, Constable. If we've finished up here, then I suggest we pay her that visit. The mountain will go to Mohammed."

Chapter 18

The Druid Ceremony

We believe in the concept of circularity.
Life is a circle.
Death, life, regeneration, and rebirth.
The soul does not die, but is reincarnated.
Death is merely a point of change in a perpetual existence.
Therefore, we use the circle as our symbol. It symbolizes wholeness and eternity.
In the center of the circle is the still point of being and not being.
The place inside the circle is the sacred area in which humans can reach the spiritual plane. In the center of the circle is the cone of power, creating a link between natural and supernatural, reaching to the otherworld.
This is why we cast the circle at the beginning of our ceremonies.
This is why our sacrifices take place within the circle, where the Gods can reach down to accept our offerings.

Evan expected to find Rhiannon sitting lost in contemplation on the floor of her meditation room. Instead, she came out to meet them before they had reached the building. She was dressed again in jeans and a black sweatshirt with a silver Celtic knot design. She looked like any middle-aged woman about to go hiking or even shopping.

"You've found something, haven't you?" she asked, in her deep, rather masculine voice. "I knew you would. It was only a matter of time. Please, come inside. I've made coffee — good and strong, not like that revolting decaf nonsense they drink up there."

Hughes gave Evan a quizzical glance as they went inside.

"Why did you expect us to find something?" Hughes asked as she went ahead of them to a little kitchen. There were three hand-thrown pottery mugs waiting on the table. One of them had sugar and milk in the bottom. Rhiannon poured coffee without answering.

"Did you have a premonition or some sort of psychic message that something had happened to Randy Wunderlich?" Hughes insisted.

Rhiannon handed him a coffee cup. "I assume you take it black."

"Yes, I do."

"And the constable here no doubt likes coffee only when it is disguised with milk and sugar."

Evan laughed. "Yes. I do. Thank you."

Rhiannon ushered them out of the kitchen to a small sitting room with comfortable

215

chintz-covered armchairs.

"Now," she said. "To answer your question — it had nothing to do with intuition or second sight. It was merely observation. The man was incredibly fit. I used to watch him jogging along the beach, swimming in the sea. He was a powerful swimmer. There's no way he'd have let himself be drowned in a cave — without outside intervention."

"If you don't mind, I'd like to ask you a few questions," Hughes asked in a rather subdued manner for him.

Rhiannon nodded graciously.

"Your full name is?"

"Rhiannon."

"And last name?"

"Just Rhiannon. Having a last name implies owning or being owned or belonging to the tribe. I don't subscribe to that idea. I am my own free person, belonging only to the universe."

"So when you file your income tax forms, you just put 'Rhiannon' on them?"

"I don't file income tax forms. I don't believe in money. Useless commodity. Nothing good ever comes of owning it."

"So you're not paid to be here?"

"I made what I thought was a good agreement. My own cottage on the grounds, my meals, and running expenses in return for my presence here and my endorsement of the center."

"So that's what made you come here?" Hughes asked.

"When I first heard about it — a center for Celtic spirituality and myself a key part of it — I thought I'd died and gone to what you Christians call heaven. Later I found that the reality didn't exactly measure up to the promise."

"It wasn't what you'd hoped for?"

"It was all a sham. They were playing at these things. Not a serious New Age believer among them. It was just another way to attract tourism."

"But Randy Wunderlich was a world-renowned psychic."

"Randy Wunderlich was a charlatan, or a showman, if you like. He wanted me to hold weekly ceremonies on the lawn for the guests, and could I throw in some more visually dramatic elements — a chalice or two, flaming brands, swords, probably sacrifice a white cockerel, for all I know. I asked him if he'd suggest the same to the minister of the local chapel. He looked surprised — stupid man."

"So you didn't like him?"

"I *dis*liked him, if you must know."

"But you didn't leave."

"If true seekers came here, I wanted them to find at least one person who could guide them. And I do get a chance to hold my ceremonies in a real sacred grove. We have one of the most important ceremonies of the year approaching, you know. Galan Mai, we say in Welsh. In English it's called Beltane. The spring festival of the new fire. You should come to it. I hope I've already persuaded Constable Evans to come — since he's one of us."

Hughes glanced at Evan.

"A Celt, she means," Evan said quickly.

"To get back to Randy Wunderlich," Hughes said. "Can you think of anyone who wanted him dead? Apart from yourself, of course."

Rhiannon did not return Hughes's grin. "What makes you assume that I wanted him dead? Negative thoughts are never productive, you know. They surround the thinker with her own negativity until it stifles her. I have never wished anyone dead. I wished him enlightenment — and a few brains wouldn't have hurt either."

"And if others were less charitable than you?"

"I wouldn't presume to read the intentions of others."

Evan noticed that Hughes was getting agitated.

"On the afternoon that Randy Wunderlich vanished — can you account for your movements?"

"I can. I was out and about, wandering over the property, looking for the perfect site for our ceremony on the First of May. There must be oak trees, you know, and enough space for a bonfire and a large circle. I expect a good crowd."

"Did you see anyone?"

"If you mean did anyone see me, the answer is probably no. Although I did hear somebody or something."

Hughes looked up from his notes.

"Some large presence was moving through the woods, out of my range of vision. It could have been an animal, of course — a large dog — but it could have been a person in a hurry."

"About what time was this?"

"I have no idea. After lunch and before dark. I have little idea of time when I'm contemplating."

"Thank you." Hughes got to his feet. "You've been most helpful."

"I should say I've probably been most unhelpful, but I've told you all I know. Randy Wunderlich invited his own death, you know. The universe will not be mocked. The Goddess especially will not be mocked. Good day to you."

They had been dismissed.

"Well, that about rounds out the principal players, doesn't it, Evans?" Hughes asked as they climbed the stairs. "What a strange woman. It's amazing how odd some unmarried women get after fifty, isn't it?"

219

Evan decided that Hughes would never win a medal for tact. It was amazing that a similar comment hadn't managed to offend someone of importance on his way up the promotion ladder. Lucky that the chief constable wasn't a woman.

Hughes checked his watch. "They should have the staff assembled by now. I'll give them a little speech and then you can take their statements after I've gone. I have a luncheon appointment in an hour, so I'm in a bit of a rush. We just need to find out what they remember about the afternoon Wunderlich disappeared, whether they noticed anything unusual, and whether anybody saw him after two-thirty. See if you can pick up any gossip as they talk to you. I'd be interested to know whether Annabel adored her husband as much as she claims. Just let them chat, Evans. They'll probably feel comfortable with you. They might even want to speak Welsh and I know that's your forte. . . ."

"Very good, sir," Evan said. Again he wondered how Hughes could have risen so easily through the ranks when even his compliments managed to turn into insults. He attacked the flight of steps at a good pace. He noticed that Hughes was huffing and puffing by the time they reached the top.

"Where have they assembled the staff, do you suppose?" Hughes managed to gasp when the front doors were swung open and

Emmy Court came striding out to meet them.

"How much longer exactly am I to be kept waiting?" she demanded. "I've got a flight to catch, you know, on a nonrefundable ticket. Do you guys plan to buy me a new ticket if I miss the plane?"

"And we have a possible murder investigation to conduct," Hughes said. "We'll let you know when you are at liberty to leave the area."

"Murder?" The bluster left her and for once she looked as young as the image she tried to project.

Hughes nodded. "So we'll need to ask you a few questions."

"Hey, wait a second." Emmy's eyes darted nervously. "What has this got to do with me? I hardly knew the man. I only came to the place a couple of times, you know, and I had Betsy with me. Ask her. She can tell you."

"We have already questioned her, and everyone else," Hughes said. "There are just a couple of points I'd like to check on." He went to usher her back into the building.

"We can talk out here," Emmy said. "I hate being cooped up inside."

"As you wish." Hughes nodded. "Your name is Emmy Court, is that correct?"

"Uh-huh."

"Do I take it that is an affirmative?" Hughes asked dryly.

"Yes." She looked away.

"And you are a student?"

"I'm a Ph.D. candidate — paranormal psychology. University of Pennsylvania. My thesis is on second sight among the Celtic populations. Which is why I came here to do my research."

"And what is your connection to the Sacred Grove?"

"I read about it when it opened last year. Randy Wunderlich had a great reputation, so I thought I'd use him to verify my findings if I came up with a truly psychic person. Betsy seemed to have strong psychic potential, so I called Mr. Wunderlich and asked if he'd test her independently. He agreed to do so. I took her down to the center. We met with him once for testing. He was impressed and wanted to work with her . . . and then he vanished. End of story."

Evan detected a veiled bitterness in her voice. Was she annoyed that her potential thesis material had been ruined?

It was past one o'clock when Evan finished interviewing the staff. His stomach reminded him that it was a long time since breakfast. He found himself longing for the meals at Mrs. Williams's house. He had complained that she was overfeeding him, but right now he would have given anything for a generous helping of steak-and-kidney pie.

He came out into bright sunshine and stood on the terrace with the wind from the ocean blowing on his face. The pseudo-Italian village below him glowed in the sunlight. It was hard to believe he was still in his own corner of Wales. It was hard to believe much about this peculiar case. If you wanted to kill someone, wouldn't there be easier ways than drugging him and then leaving him to drown in a cave? Why the cave? Annabel was the only one who mentioned that Randy had gone there before for its fantastic vibes. Had somebody known he was planning to go there that afternoon, or had the murderer somehow dragged him, unconscious, to the cave and left him to die? What sort of person would have done that?

Evan glanced at his list of notes from the staff. One or two interesting things had emerged: Several of the staff reported that Randy and Rhiannon had had disagreements. The day before Randy disappeared, the groundsman had heard his raised voice yelling, "And if you don't like it, you can always leave, you know."

That same groundsman had been mowing the lawns on the fateful afternoon. He remembered seeing Annabel coming down the steps toward the meditation building, then returning shortly after. He also remembered seeing Ben Cresswell striding out across the property.

Not one of the staff remembered making the cup of coffee that Betsy took to Randy Wunderlich, or telling Betsy that Randy wanted a cup of coffee. Evan frowned. This wouldn't look good for Betsy. She had admitted taking him the coffee, which might have contained the sleeping pills, but she had nobody to corroborate that she had been instructed to do so. No one even remembered seeing her in the kitchen after lunch.

Not one of them had seen Randy Wunderlich after he went into his office in the meditation building around two.

Most interesting of all — Bethan reported that Lady Annabel and Randy had had several arguments recently. She had overheard things when she was making beds in the big house.

So there had been plenty of friction at the Sacred Grove. But arguments didn't always lead to murder, did they? Well, it wasn't any of his business. D.C.I. Hughes and his team would be handling the investigation from now on and Evan would be lucky if he heard how it was progressing. He should take Betsy home, make his report to D.C.I. Hughes, and get on with the task of changing Bronwen's library books. But he found he was looking down toward the meditation center and the path beyond, leading down steps to the swimming pool and then the beach. He had to go and take another look at that cave for himself.

Evan hurried down the long flight of steps. As he passed the pyramid, a pale-faced woman in a turban and robe came out and stood blinking in the sunlight.

"Amazing," she said to Evan. "I'm a new person. Even my skin feels younger. Amethyst, you know."

Evan nodded politely and went on his way. Down the last steps and onto the beach. The tide was still quite high at this time of day and Evan had to pick his way along a thin strip of beach. Where the tide had receded, the sand was still waterlogged and each footstep sank in with a deep sucking sound. How could anyone have possibly dragged an unconscious man this way — unless there was more than one person. He paused to consider this thought. Was it possible that several of them had conspired to get rid of Randy Wunderlich — Rhiannon and Mrs. Roberts, Mrs. Roberts and Ben Cresswell, even Annabel and Michael? All of the above? Such alliances seemed highly unlikely when he considered them, but desperation has driven people to even stranger alliances.

After five minutes of slithering along the water's edge, he came to the rocks before the cave. He scrambled up nimbly and stood at the entrance. He knew that forensics had given the cave a thorough going-over, and the sea had been in and out a number of times since the body was discovered. Even so, he ducked his head and went inside, wrinkling his nose at the dank, rotting smell. He found himself shivering as he looked around. As he had expected, he found nothing and was thankful to step out into the sunlight again. He couldn't imagine that Randy Wunderlich would have chosen to meditate there.

Now the higher, dryer cave definitely looked more inviting — a wide hole above the waterline, the sort of cave that would have attracted a boy wanting to play at smugglers. He scrambled up to it, using all fours over the precariously loose rocks, and stood peering into the darkness. He could see where the sea level reached the entrance. There was a line of seaweed and jetsam about three feet into the cave. Beyond that, however, the floor was sandy and dry. He noticed footprints in the sand, but they were indistinct and there was no way of knowing how long they had been there. As he turned back to face the entrance, he was met with a stunning view. The whole estuary of sparkling blue water spread before him, with the green hills rising on the other side to Cader Idris, second in height only to Snowdon.

He could see that somebody would want to come to this cave to get away from it all and think. In fact, Emmy Court had assumed the same thing. He remembered how she had tried to convince Betsy that she was heading

226

for the wrong cave. Well, anyone would have assumed the same thing, wouldn't he? He then realized something else about Emmy Court. When she had woken him that night, she had been bubbling with excitement as if the whole excursion was a grand adventure. But that had changed when they discovered Randy's body. He remembered her wail of horror, "He can't be dead!"

And yet today, in her interview with Hughes, she had acted as if Randy's death was merely a nuisance, a hitch in her plans. Evan turned and carefully skirted around the edge of the cave, examining every inch of the floor. There was really nothing to see. There was no jetsam above the high tide line, just sand and rocks. Toward the back of the cave his eyes strained in the darkness and he wished he had brought the flashlight he kept in the glove compartment of his car. He could see something on a small rock ledge. Evan reached for it. It was a wrapped granola bar. Half-buried in the sand beneath it was a full bottle of water and beside that a miniature torch. Using his handkerchief, Evan retrieved the torch and wrapped it carefully before tucking it into his pocket. It might be nothing more than kids playing at camping out, but it could also mean that someone recently intended to spend some time in this cave.

Chapter 19

By the time Evan returned to look for Betsy, he found her with Emmy Court. Emmy seemed calmer and resigned to missing her plane.

"If I've got to stay on a few days, I might as well give Betsy a ride home," she said. "I hope Mrs. Williams hasn't let my room yet."

Evan accepted her offer. He was glad he wasn't about to incur anyone's wrath by giving Betsy a ride home on the motorbike. Instead, he drove straight to drop off the torch he had found at the forensics lab. Then he remembered he had promised to change Bronwen's library books for her. That was the very least he could do. He felt that he should have been taking better care of her. Instead, he'd been running around all week — doing his job, to be sure, but still not there when she needed him.

When he finally reached Llanfair and pulled up outside the police station, the clouds had closed in and the formerly bright day was now heavy with the threat of rain. The first drops of rain spattered onto the tarmac as he climbed off the bike and wheeled it into the shed. No hiking today then! On the ride home he had decided to take a stiff hike up to Crib Gogh and back.

He had noticed his muscles complaining at all those steps at the Sacred Grove. That's what happened after several weeks without exercise — he was getting soft and needed some conditioning. Also, walking in the high country had a wonderful way of clearing his head. Up above the rest of the world, he was able to see connections that hadn't been obvious before, and Evan was a great believer in connections. Find the missing links and you were well on the way to solving the case — if he was going to be given the chance of future involvement. Evan kicked at a pebble and sent it skidding across the wet street. Then he tucked Bronwen's books under his jacket and plodded up the hill to the school-house.

He was about to open the gate to the school playground when he heard his name being called and sighed as Mrs. Powell-Jones came bearing down on him, her unbuttoned cardigan flying open like the wings of an avenging angel.

"Constable Evans! Stay right where you are. I wanted a word with you, urgently."

Evan was in no mood to be forbidden to see Bronwen again. "I'm taking Miss Price the library books she wanted," he said quickly.

"It's not Miss Price I'm concerned about. It's Betsy Edwards," Mrs. Powell-Jones said.

"Something's happened to Betsy?"

"To her immortal soul, if we're not careful. I was speaking to her not an hour ago, and what I heard has appalled me, Constable. Absolutely appalled me." She pushed a rain-sodden wisp of hair from her face. She wasn't wearing any kind of raincoat and her pea green hand-knitted cardigan was giving off a strong odor of wet sheep. "I had my doubts about this so-called healing center since I first heard about it," she went on, wagging a finger at Evan. "Pagan spirituality indeed! As if pagans can have any spirituality. But now I've had a chance to question Betsy thoroughly and what I've heard is worse than I feared. Did you know there is Druid worship going on at that place? Betsy says there is actually a Druid priestess who holds her ceremonies there. No wonder someone has been murdered. The Druids were a most bloodthirsty sect, you know. They went in for human sacrifices. It must be stopped, Constable Evans. Stopped now, before it's too late!" She thrust her face into his, peering at him with her sharp, pale eyes. "I take it that the police will be shutting it down, after what has happened?"

"I don't know, madam," Evan said. "I'm just the local constable. I don't make the decisions."

"Then I shall call your superiors immediately. And if the police don't close it, then steps will have to be taken. We Christians have a moral obligation. I've told young Betsy that I forbid her to go there again."

"She has a good job there, Mrs. Powell-Jones," Evan began, but the minister's wife peered into his face again.

"A good job, you say? No good can come of cavorting with the devil, you must know that. You must stop her, Constable Evans, before it's too late. Good day to you."

She stalked back to her house, her shoes making an unpleasant squelching sound as she walked. Evan watched her go, then pushed open the schoolyard gate.

"Goodness, you're soaked," Bronwen greeted him from where she was sitting, wrapped in her eiderdown in the armchair by the fire. "Were you caught in the downpour when you were on your bike?"

"No, I got caught by a belligerent Powell-Jones," Evan said. "I've been told to close the Sacred Grove immediately, or else steps will be taken. And she's forbidden Betsy to go there again."

"Oh, dear." Bronwen managed a weak smile. "I wouldn't like to be the people at the Sacred Grove if Mrs. Powell-Jones gets her teeth into them."

"So how are you feeling?" Evan crossed the room and gave her a little kiss on the forehead. "You're sitting up. That's a good sign."

"I hope it is. I still feel as weak as a new-born kitten."

"You need building up again."

"Not Mrs. Powell-Jones's calves foot jelly, please."

Evan smiled. "I'd offer to make you some soup, only my cooking doesn't seem to agree with you too well."

"Don't say that. This obviously wasn't anything to do with your cooking. Just an unluckily timed bug, as the doctor says."

"I hope so. But most bugs I've seen don't linger on as long as this. I've got you some new library books, by the way. I hope you approve of my taste."

"In women at least." She gave him a weak smile, reached for the books, and let them flop onto the eiderdown beside her.

Evan gave her a worried glance. The hands that took the books from him seemed frail and transparent as alabaster and belonged to an ethereal creature, not the Bronwen he knew.

"So what's the latest excitement from the Sacred Grove?" She patted the arm of her chair and he perched beside her. "Has Betsy had any more psychic dreams and found any more bodies?"

"Plenty of excitement," Evan said. "It turns out that Randy Wunderlich's death wasn't an accident. It looks as if someone drugged him so that he was asleep when the tide came in."

"What a horrible thing to do!" Bronwen

shuddered. "Any suspects?"

"Plenty, it seems," Evan said. "He wasn't very popular with several residents of the Sacred Grove, and one of the maids said he argued with his wife a lot too."

"So what do you do next?"

"Me, nothing, I expect. Hughes will no doubt bumble his way through, insulting everybody, unless he puts Watkins and his partner on the case."

Bronwen reached out and touched his hand. "You know you're cleverer than any of them, and they know it too. What are your thoughts so far?"

Evan shrugged. "It could be any of them. His wife took sleeping pills, but not the same kind as were used on him. Betsy took him a cup of coffee that could have contained the sleeping pills but she doesn't know who poured the coffee."

"It doesn't necessarily have to be any of them, does it?" Bronwen asked. "I mean, you said this man was a famous psychic in America. I'd imagine men like that make enemies."

"Someone came over here specifically to kill him, you mean?"

Bronwen laughed. "It does sound rather ridiculous when you put it like that, doesn't it?"

"No, but . . ." Evan paused, staring at the flames dancing in the fire.

"You've thought of something, haven't you?" she asked gently.

"Emmy Court is American," Evan said. "She just appeared over here, right before this happened. Why pick this place to start doing her research?"

"I'd have someone look into this man's background in America," Bronwen said, "and maybe check out Emmy Court too, while they're at it."

Evan kissed her forehead again. "Smart girl," he said. "I'll suggest it to Watkins if I can catch him between his training sessions."

"Training?"

"They're promoting him to inspector, didn't I tell you?"

"Oh." Bronwen looked up. "Does that leave a vacancy, do you think?"

He stared past her, into the fire. "Not that I've heard. They've just taken on Glynis Davies, haven't they?"

She reached out and squeezed his hand. "Your turn will come. And there's really no hurry, is there? You were quite content here to start with. You said you liked the quiet life — and your hiking and climbing."

"Yes, that was before . . ." He paused. *Before I thought of supporting a wife and family,* he didn't finish out loud.

That evening Evan was attempting to cook a leg of lamb. *Rather stupid really,* he thought, *to cook a whole leg for one person.* But he liked leg of lamb on weekends, and he was considering using the bone to make Bronwen a lamb stew. His mother always served him lamb stew with dumplings when she wanted to build him up. Maybe he'd have a go at dumplings tomorrow and take some over to Bronwen.

The lamb was beginning to smell appetizing and Evan was just putting frozen peas into a saucepan when there was a tap at his front door.

"Ooh, smells good. What are you cooking?" Betsy asked.

"Roast lamb." He saw her eyes light up. "Have you eaten yet?"

"No, and there's nothing in the house except baked beans. The old man's down at the pub already and I didn't fancy baked beans on my own."

"You're welcome to join me. I can't eat a whole leg on my own." Evan stood back to let her in.

"Lovely! Diolch yn fawr, Evan *bach*." She gave him a beaming smile as she came in. "Do you want me to lay the table?"

She had opened the kitchen drawer and was taking out knives and forks without being asked, laying them swiftly on the table in the living room. Then she went back into the kitchen and perched herself on the counter again as Evan took the roast from the oven. "I've never carved one of these things before," he said. "Where do you think I should start?"

"Absolutely clueless, aren't you?" Betsy slid from the counter. "Your mam must have spoiled you something rotten. Look you — this is how you carve a leg. You make a vee in the top like this and then you work backward. Got it?" Her hands covered his and he was conscious of how warm and real her hands felt after Bronwen's fragile icy ones.

"All right. I've got it now." He laughed her off awkwardly. "Let me try it. I've got to learn."

Several large and not very elegant chunks of lamb were put on each plate, followed by roast potatoes and a generous spoonful of peas.

"I've got a jar of mint sauce on the shelf, I think," he said, "but I'm not sure what to do about the gravy. Mrs. Williams used to make lovely thick gravy with lamb."

"I make mine with gravy mix," Betsy said, "but I'll do what I can with the drippings."

"You're quite handy in the kitchen," Evan commented.

"I've had to be, haven't I? With my *mam* gone all these years and my *tad* only good for staggering to the pub? And I'm learning a lot by watching the way they do things at the Sacred Grove. You should see how lovely they make the food look. Little swirls of color and bits of flowers and things on the plate. Ever so pretty it looks." She sat down opposite Evan, took a mouthful of meat, then looked up. "That crabby old cow wants me to stop working there," she said.

"Mrs. Powell-Jones?" Evan smiled. "Yes, she gave me a long lecture about it this afternoon."

"She doesn't know what she's talking about," Betsy said. "Going on about devil worship and all that nonsense. I think Rhiannon makes a lot of sense. Why shouldn't the spirit of the universe be all around us in nature? She's asked me to help her with the ceremony this week — you know, the Galan Mai? It's going to be so exciting — lots of people coming from all across Britain, all wearing white robes and then the fire and everything. I always did love Guy Fawkes Night when I was a little kid."

Evan watched her as she spoke, her face alight with excitement like a small child's.

"This is cozy, isn't it?" She beamed at him. "I've waited a long time to be asked to dinner alone with you, Evan *bach*."

Evan couldn't think of the right thing to say and went on eating.

"So Bronwen's no better yet, is she?" Betsy asked suddenly.

"A little better, but not much," Evan said. "I don't know why it's taking so long. Those bloody doctors just say it's an unknown bug and leave it at that. I hate to see her as weak as this. She still won't eat —" Suddenly a picture formed in his head of Betsy sitting on the counter as he carved the lamb. She had sat on his counter like that on the evening that Bronwen became ill. She had been in the kitchen as he prepared the meal. And she had asked him that question — if there was no Bronwen, would he notice her then? Was it too absurd to think that she might have put something in Bronwen's food? Was it also too absurd to think that she might have spiked Randy Wunderlich's coffee?

Chapter 20

Excerpt from *The Way of the Druid,* by Rhiannon

The Cycle of the Druid Year

We believe there is a deep and mysterious connection between our individual lives and the life force of our planet. Therefore, we recognize eight occasions during the yearly cycle that are significant to us and we mark them by special ceremonies.

Four of our special ceremonies are solar, four are lunar — a balance between the feminine and the masculine, the Goddess and the Sun God.

At the solstices the sun is revered — in the glory of its maximum power in midsummer and in the quiet of its near-death in midwinter. At the equinoxes day and night are balanced. These are the times of planting and of harvest. In spring we sow and in autumn we reap the fruits of our toil.

Then there are four more ceremonies, during the year. This is the cycle of the land of planting and harvest.

At Samhuinn, on October 31st, livestock used to be slaughtered before the winter when there was no fodder. At Imboic, on February 2nd, lambs were born. Beltane, on May 1st, was the time of mating and purifying. Lughnasadh, on August 1st, was the time of harvest.

We celebrate these festivals to remind us that our lives are interwoven with the cycle of the year. We see them as more than festivals of farming. On October 31 time stands still. The veil between this world and the other is lifted. The spirits of the dead walk among us. We make contact to share their wisdom and inspiration. The dead are honored and feasted as guardians of the tribe.

The winter solstice, called in the Druid tradition Alban Arthan — the Light of Arthur — is the time of death and rebirth. In the darkness we throw away those things that have been holding us back. One lamp is lit from flint and raised to the East. A year is reborn and a new cycle begins.

On February 2nd, called Imboic in the Druid tradition, is the celebration of the first snowdrop, the melting of the snows. Lambs are born. It is a gentle festival in which the Mother Goddess is honored with eight candles rising out of the water at the center of the ceremonial circle.

It is interesting to note that the Christians have adopted our ceremony as Candlemas. Our aspect of the Goddess is as inspiration of poets and healers. We celebrate in poetry and song. *It is a good time for the eisteddfod.*

At the spring equinox we celebrate the equality of night and day, the flowers of spring, and the time of snowing.

Beltane, which we Welsh call Calan Mai, is the feast of fertility, fire, and purification. We light the twin fires. In former times cattle were driven between them to assure fertility. Those who wish to conceive a child jump over the fire. Those who wish to be purified walk through it.

At the summer solstice we hold our longest ceremony. On the eve of the solstice we hold a vigil throughout the night. We mark the coming of dawn with a ceremony to celebrate the Sun God at his most powerful.

On August 1st is the ceremony of hay gathering. It is a ceremony of gathering together, of marriages. A wheel is passed around our circle to symbolize the turning of the year.

Last in our year is the autumn equinox, September 21st. In this ceremony we give thanks for the fruits of the earth and for the goodness of the Mother Goddess.

And what do these ceremonies truly mean for us? We no longer plant and sow, most of us. They represent the cycle of our lives. In the spring ceremonies we rejoice in youth. Spring makes us feel young again. The fires give us new life and vitality. In summer we celebrate the fullness of our blossoming into

241

maturity, of parenthood, and our place in so-
ciety. In autumn we rejoice in the harvest of
our lives — be it creative works, children, or
material success. As winter comes, we ap-
proach our declining years without fear and
rejoice in the wisdom of age.

On Monday morning Evan opened up the police station at nine o'clock sharp and started on his report for the previous week. He hadn't slept well last night. He knew he was being ridiculous to suspect Betsy, but the nagging doubt wouldn't go away. He remembered how devious she could be when she tried — how she had shown up in her bikini and even dressed herself as a grandmother to try and get a part in a film when a film crew had come to the area a few months ago. She was a person who would take strong measures to get what she wanted, that was for sure. But to go as far as hurting somebody, even trying to kill somebody? Evan had always thought that Betsy had a kind heart. Now he didn't know what to think, or how to follow up on his suspicions.

Wait and see, he decided. *Let the detectives do their work and see what they come up with.* He had only been working for a few minutes when his phone rang.

"Evan, this is Glynis. How are you?" As always she sounded bright and cheerful, full of energy and enthusiasm. Before he could answer, she went on. "Listen, I had to call you right away about that torch you found. That was brilliant of you to find it and to wrap it so carefully in your handkerchief like that. We got some super prints, not smudged at all."

"Do you know whose?"

"Oh, yes. They all belong to Randy Wunderlich. His are the only prints on the torch."

"Interesting," he said. "So I was right in my hunch. He did intend to do his meditating in the upper cave, not the lower one. I couldn't imagine why anyone would even go in that horrible place, especially not when the upper cave has such a fantastic view and is high and dry."

"So what do you think happened? Why did he change his mind?" Glynis asked.

"I really don't know. . . ."

"Oh come on, Evan. You're really good at this. Your hunches are always spot on. What made him go down to the lower cave?"

"My guess would be that he didn't go there. If we know that he fell asleep before he drowned, then it's logical that the person who drugged him could drag him down to the lower cave. It's a pity that the rocks and cave floor get so thoroughly washed over by the tides or we might have found scraps of fiber on some of the rocks."

"So somebody knew he was planning to

have a long meditation session in that upper cave and made sure he was drugged enough to put him to sleep. That's right. You don't have any hunches about which of them it could be?"

"That's the tricky part. Everyone we spoke to had a good reason for wishing Randy Wunderlich wasn't there — including his wife, I might add. But I wouldn't go jumping to any conclusions if I were you," Evan said. "My girlfriend had an interesting observation. She said he'd been a famous psychic in the States and people like that make lots of enemies."

"So you think it could have been someone from outside?"

"I think it wouldn't hurt to look into his background in the States."

"Brilliant. I'll run a computer search and see what comes up. I'll let you know what I find."

Evan smiled to himself when he hung up. At least Glynis was grateful for his help and happy to keep him updated on new developments, even if she did get the credit and he didn't. He tried to concentrate on adding up figures for the last week. Then, some half hour later, the phone rang again.

"Evan, you've got to get down here and see this," Glynis's excited voice echoed down the phone.

"Your search engine turned up good stuff?"

"I'll say. I've put in a call for Sergeant Watkins to come over and see it too. The D.C.I. is out at a regional meeting or I'm sure he'd want to see it."

Evan ran straight to his motorbike. He was in on the action at a meeting where there would be no D.C.I. Hughes to ask him what he was doing there and to remind him that it was none of his business. He took the bends faster than he ever had before, now more comfortable with leaning inward and feeling the pull of gravity. "Next year, Isle of Man TT races," he said to himself and laughed.

Glynis was sitting at the computer, printing out Web pages as he came in.

"This search engine has turned up over seven hundred mentions of his name." She looked up excitedly.

"Popular man."

"Or unpopular, as the case may be." She handed him some sheets of paper. "Look what I've printed out so far."

Evan took them from her and read the top headline: "Psychic Hot Line Guru Sued for Five Million." His eyes scanned down the page. "Randy Wunderlich, whose psychic hot line has made his face familiar to every TV viewer in the country, is being sued in a Florida district court by Mary Sue Harper of Dade County. The suit alleges that Randy Wunderlich duped her out of her life savings by encouraging her to keep in daily contact via the 900 number and that his advice made her make disastrous life changes."

"Five million," Evan said. "So he must have been wiped out financially."

"He won the case." Glynis handed him another sheet of paper. "The jury decided that nobody forced Ms. Harper to keep running up phone bills by consulting him every day. But the judge warned him that what he was doing was morally wrong and he was going to recommend that the hot line be investigated by a federal commission."

"And was it?"

"It's all here." Glynis waved papers excitedly. "He was investigated, the hot line was shut down, and he had to pay restitution to a whole lot of angry people who claimed he had tricked them out of money and wrecked their lives."

"Not that great a psychic then." Evan flicked through the pages she had given him.

"Not a legit psychic at all. No kind of credentials, anyway. Did some undergraduate work at a state college in California but that's about it. A con man, actually."

"Fascinating." Evan continued to read case after case of people, mainly women, telling stories of how Randy had kept them dependent on his advice, which often turned out to be bad.

"Do you think one of them could have tracked him down over here and then killed him?" Glynis asked.

Evan stared at the computer screen, thinking. "The person who killed him had some inside knowledge of his routine. That person knew he was planning to go and meditate in a cave. I can't imagine he'd have announced that fact to the whole world."

"So it still comes back to those closest to him — someone else who works closely with the center."

"Maybe the next step should be to find out who had a prescription for the right kind of sleeping pills," Evan said. "If it was someone from the center, they wouldn't have had the prescription filled too far away, would they? We know which chemist handled Lady Annabel's prescriptions. Her son went to pick one up for her that afternoon."

"Too late to drug Randy."

"Yes, and according to Michael, it wasn't a drug he picked up. It was some kind of medicated face cream to get rid of wrinkles."

Glynis grinned. "If she's so vain, you'd think she'd go on a diet, wouldn't you?"

"I get the impression that —" Evan broke off, staring at the computer screen. The Web page was a report of the federal commission's investigation into the psychic hot line. Names of a lot of women registering complaints filled the page. Evan had been scanning them idly. None rang a bell. But at the bottom of the page: "Also indicted for fraud is Mr.

Wunderlich's partner, Mary Elizabeth Harcourt of Philadelphia, Pa."

"That's it!" Evan stabbed excitedly at the screen. "I knew something about her didn't add up."

"Do we know her?" Glynis asked.

"Emmy Court. It has to be. Her name wasn't Emmy. It's M.E. Short for Mary Elizabeth."

"Oh my goodness. You're right."

"I've been wondering about her all along," Evan said. "It always struck me that something didn't add up about her. Let's look her up on your computer."

Evan watched in admiration as Glynis's skillful fingers tapped in information. The only time Emmy's name appeared was in conjunction with Randy Wunderlich's.

"She's a pretty good actress," Evan said. "Pretending not to know him. Why did she come here, I wonder?"

"Obvious," Glynis said. "He married someone else, didn't he? I can't imagine she'd be Randy Wunderlich's partner without being romantically involved with him. She expected him to marry her, but he was broke and he latched onto someone with money."

"He probably thought Lady Annabel had money, but she didn't," Evan said.

"Even so, she had the property. Once the center got going, I'd imagine it would have been very lucrative — and safely far away from his former enemies."

"So you think Emmy came here to kill him because he ran out on her?" Evan asked.

"It makes sense, doesn't it? And it's the most compelling motive we've had so far, especially if he left her behind in the States to face the music."

Evan nodded. "Do you want me to go and bring her in?"

Glynis looked up at him. "Just make sure she doesn't go anywhere in a hurry, while I alert the airlines, just in case she's already done a bunk on us."

Betsy found it strange going to work at the Sacred Grove that day just as if nothing had happened. She wasn't even sure she was still employed there now that Randy was gone and Emmy Court was planning to go too. When Lady Annabel passed her just as she was taking off her jacket in the staff cloakroom, she fully expected to be asked what she was doing there and to be sent packing. But Lady Annabel drifted by like a ghost and hardly seemed to notice her.

All in all, Betsy hoped she could stay. For one thing the work was so easy and, for another, it was like living in a fantasy world, with all those fountains and pools and the beautiful view across the estuary. It was sad that Randy was gone, but she hoped that Rhiannon might be able to help her with her newfound psychic powers. Rhiannon had already told her that the ancient Druids were also seers. They had all kinds of ways of looking into the future. She often saw the future herself. It was just a question of harnessing the power of the universe. In a way Rhiannon scared Betsy. She was so intense, as if there were a fire burning inside her. But she was also being very kind at the moment, taking time to answer Betsy's questions. "We'll make a Druid of you yet," she had said when they last spoke. "You're going to be a great help to me at the coming ceremony. I'm relying on you."

Betsy helped clear away breakfast then went down to the meditation center to bring up any dirty crockery waiting to be washed. As she went in, she heard a low humming sound coming from the main meditation room and wondered what it could be, until the door opened and she saw that it was Bethan, with a vacuum cleaner.

"Hello, Betsy," Bethan called cheerily. "How are you then? I've been thinking about you, having that dreadful dream and seeing poor Randy lying there and then actually finding him just like you'd dreamed. It must have been a terrible shock for you."

"It was," Betsy said. "I couldn't stop shaking all day."

"Did you really dream the whole thing?" Bethan asked. "They're saying he was murdered now. Did you see the murderer in your dream?"

"No, just Randy lying there."

"Perhaps you'll have another dream and see the murderer," Bethan said excitedly.

"I hope not. It was horrible." Betsy hugged her arms to herself. "It's funny, but it already seems as if it wasn't real. I know it happened, but it's like something I saw on TV, you know."

Bethan nodded. "It's funny how life has gone back to normal, isn't it? Lady Annabel is the only one who looks upset. She doesn't seem herself at all, poor thing. She wasn't even wearing makeup today and I've never seen her without her makeup on before. They say people can die of a broken heart, don't they?"

"She's a bit old for a broken heart, isn't she?" Betsy moved closer to Bethan as the latter maneuvered the heavy vacuum cleaner out of the room and into the passage. "I mean she's got a grown-up son. Middle-aged people don't die of broken hearts, surely?"

"Oh, I think she was gaga for him." Bethan moved closer to Betsy. "You should have heard her shouting and crying when she found out he'd been paying attention to another woman. 'I trusted you and you let me down,' she was yelling. I was up making the beds and I was embarrassed to be caught up there with them yelling outside the door. 'I thought I was the only woman in your life,' she said. 'And now I find out about *her*.' And now he's gone. Funny old life, isn't it?"

Betsy nodded.

Bethan coiled up the vacuum lead and started to wheel it down the hall. "You know, I never expected to find him dead, did you? When I heard he was missing, I thought to myself, well, here we go again."

"What do you mean?" Betsy asked.

"Well, he was the second person who's been missing here, isn't it? And both Americans too. They say there's been no sign of that American girl Rebecca since she left here. I often wonder what happened to her. I was just getting friendly with her, you know, when she went. And you know what was so strange? It was her coat. I often wondered about that coat, I mean —"

A door opened on their left and Rhiannon appeared. "Will you girls stop gossiping and get back to work?" she snapped. "Bethan, put that thing away and get about your duties. Betsy, would you come into my office? I'm going to need you to help me prepare for the ceremony."

Betsy spent the next hour helping Rhiannon assemble a collection of objects she needed for the ceremony. They included robes and tools — a cauldron, a dagger, a pentacle, a large stone that Rhiannon said was sacred. "And now," she said, "you are going to help me to build a very large basket."

It was noontime when Betsy was finally released, and she rushed up to do her job at the spa. She was supposed to have wiped down the walls of the sauna and steam room by now. The spa was scheduled to open again at twelve-thirty. She hoped she wouldn't get in trouble for being late. Luckily she didn't pass anybody as she went through the foyer with its lovely underwater murals. She gave the sauna a quick once-over, then she went into the steam room. That was a harder job. Mildew grew so easily in the hot damp conditions and Betsy had to stand on tiptoe on the tiled bench to reach the corners at the very top. She was on the bench with her back to the door when she thought she heard a noise outside. Immediately the steam came on in a great rush. *That's funny,* Betsy thought. She was supposed to trip the switch to turn the system on when she had finished. The room filled quickly with hot steam so that by the time she picked up her cleaning materials and climbed down from the bench, the door was hardly visible.

Betsy experienced a brief moment of panic and disorientation. *Don't be so daft,* she thought to herself. *People pay a lot of money to come in here and sit in this steam and you can't wait to get out of it!* She laughed at herself as she located the door and turned her shoulder to push it open.

It wouldn't move.

Betsy put more effort into it and tried again. The door was stuck fast. She put down the cleaning rags and spray and tried with both hands. Behind her the steam kept on hissing as it poured out, filling the tiny room and raising the temperature. Betsy coughed. It was getting hard to breathe.

Not to worry, she told herself. The steam was on a timer. It came on, then a thermostat shut it off after a few moments. She'd seen it working. Seconds ticked by but the steam didn't go off. The room was now so full of steam that the glass panel in the door was the only real thing in the world. Betsy could feel sweat and steam running down her face into her eyes. She hammered on the door with both fists, realizing that nobody was likely to hear her. The spa wasn't scheduled to open for another half hour and Bethan had obviously done her share of the work and gone by now.

Half an hour. Could she hold out that long? The heat was overpowering. Betsy could feel the blood singing in her head. She was starting to feel dizzy. *Help!* she tried to shout. *Help!* But every breath she took only resulted in a fit of coughing. With the last of her strength, she pounded on the door again.

Suddenly the door was wrenched open.

Bethan and Michael stood there, staring at her with frightened faces. "Betsy, what on earth were you doing in there?" Bethan demanded as a gasping, sobbing, red-faced Betsy staggered out.

"I — I couldn't get the door open," Betsy said.

"Oh, no." Michael took her arm and led her to a chair in the foyer. "That damned door must be sticking again. Remember it stuck once before, Bethan? I thought the janitor had fixed it. I'll get onto him again this afternoon."

"It was horrible," Betsy said. "The steam came on and it wouldn't go off. It just kept on coming. I would have passed out if you hadn't heard me."

"Lucky I'd just gone to get Michael to show him a crack in one of the tiles," Bethan said.

Michael gave Betsy an encouraging smile. "I think you probably had a bit of a panic attack, don't you? I know what it's like when the steam comes on — it is rather frightening. But it only lasts a minute or two, honestly."

"It was much longer than that," Betsy said. "The whole place was full of steam."

"It only seemed longer, I'm sure." He put a hand on Betsy's shoulder. "Come on. Let's go and get some lunch. I'll make sure the janitor fixes that door properly this afternoon.

We don't want any panic-stricken guests, do we?"

Betsy allowed herself to be escorted up the steps between Michael and Bethan. Had she just panicked? she wondered. Had it not been as long as it seemed in there and would the steam have gone off by itself? She felt a bit of a fool.

"Thanks for rescuing me, anyway," she said. "Sorry if I was making such a fuss."

"I'm sorry, Mr. Evans, but she's not here," Mrs. Williams greeted Evan at the front door.

"She's left, you mean?" Evan's heart lurched at the thought of arriving too late.

"Oh, no. She just drove young Betsy to work at the center. She said she didn't want to sit around doing nothing and she liked visiting the center."

"So she's down there now?"

"I expect so. She told me not to cook lunch for her, she'd be eating out, but she'd be back for dinner. I'm making her a steak-and-kidney pie tonight. You remember my pies, don't you, Mr. Evans? I'm a dab hand with pastry, although I shouldn't say it my-self."

Evan did remember her pastry. Vividly. He could almost taste the thick brown gravy with tender morsels of steak and kidney buried in it and the light, flaky crust on top. He sighed. "I'd better go and look for Miss Court then."

But as he turned away from the front door, a car drew up and Emmy Court got out. Evan noticed a momentary flicker of alarm on her face before it became an expressionless mask again. "What do you want now?" she demanded.

"I've been asked to bring you down to headquarters to ask you a few more questions, if you don't mind."

"I do mind. I've already told you everything I know. I've already missed my flight home. Do you know what kind of penalty they charge to rewrite a ticket these days? I'm a student, you know, trying to live on a grant. I sure hope you guys are going to write some kind of letter to the airline for me."

"I'm sorry, miss. I'm just doing my job. It shouldn't take long and the sooner we get things sorted out, the sooner you can go home, isn't it?"

Emmy glared at him, but she allowed herself to be shepherded to the squad car that Evan had borrowed from Sergeant Watkins.

"It's harassment, that's what it is. I'm going to complain to the U.S. embassy." Evan said nothing and Emmy remained silent all the way down the pass. When they reached the Caernarfon police station, Evan

257

ushered Emmy into one of the interview rooms.

"Would you like a cup of tea or coffee while I tell them you're here?" Evan asked as Emmy sat defiantly with her arms folded across her chest.

"Your British tea is disgusting and your coffee is even worse. I haven't had one decent cup of coffee since I got here. Mrs. Williams's idea is to put a spoonful of instant in a cup and then fill it up with hot milk. Don't you people have a clue about anything?"

At that moment D.C.I. Hughes came into the room, followed by Watkins, who had clearly just arrived. Watkins was still wearing his wet raincoat and there were droplets of rain on his sandy hair. He grinned at Evan.

"Thank you, Constable," Hughes said, waving him away. Evan retreated, but only as far as the door. Hughes took the only other chair in the room, leaving Watkins standing also.

"I take it you don't mind if our conversation is recorded?" Hughes leaned across the table to turn on the portable recorder. "For your protection as well as ours."

Emmy shrugged. "Do what you like. I've already told you what I know. You're just wasting your time as well as mine."

"Not quite all you know, I think," Hughes said. He spoke into the machine. "Detective Chief Inspector Hughes, interviewing Emmy

Court, Monday, April twenty-ninth. Now let's go back to square one, shall we, Miss Court? Would you mind repeating your full name for us?"

"I told you. It's Emmy Court."

"And you are a student?"

"I told you. A doctoral candidate at the University of Pennsylvania."

"Now that's odd, isn't it?" Hughes looked across to Sergeant Watkins. "I understand, Sergeant, that your search of the records at the University of Pennsylvania came up with no doctoral candidate by the name of Emmy Court."

"No student of any kind registered under that name."

"Well, I took a quarter off for this field-work, didn't I? If you'd checked back . . ."

"Ah, but Sergeant Watkins did check old records. He found only one similar name. Mary Elizabeth Harcourt, who took a bachelor's degree in psychology ten years ago. And a woman of the same name shows up in the records of the federal commission looking into Randal Wunderlich's psychic hot line scandal. This Mary Elizabeth Harcourt was mentioned as Randal Wunderlich's partner."

There was utter silence except for the hiss and whir of the tape recorder and the rhythmic tick of the clock on the wall.

"Do you still maintain that you are Emmy Court, a student at the University of Pennsylvania?" Hughes asked. "I can always send to America for fingerprints."

She turned to glare at him but said nothing.

"This might be a good point to have my sergeant read you your rights, Miss Harcourt, and to ask you whether you would like to have a lawyer present."

Until now Emmy had been aggressive but composed. Now suddenly her face flushed. "Hey, wait a second. You don't think I had anything to do with his death, do you? I loved him."

"Of course you did," Hughes went on smoothly. For once Evan was impressed. "But he married someone else, didn't he? He left you behind in the States to face the music while he came to live in luxury in Wales. What more perfect motive for murder?"

"Bullshit," Emmy said. "You British cops are really stupid, do you know that? If you really want to know the truth, we planned the whole thing, Randy and I."

"Planned his death?"

"He wasn't meant to die." For the first time her voice had a desperate edge to it. "It was meant to be a stunt — a publicity stunt."

"Go on," Hughes said.

"Okay, this is what was supposed to happen. Randy was in deep shit at home. The

260

feds were watching his every move. He decided to get out for a while. This Englishwoman had been calling his hot line and in talking to her he found out that she was a lady with a title and a stately home. He'd always dreamed of opening a New Age center someday and he thought this woman was loaded. She was also looking for a new guy in her life. Randy's great at that kind of thing. He can have any woman eating out of his hand in seconds. He told me what he was going to do and I agreed. He said it wouldn't be more than a year, two years, max. So he married her and then he found that she wasn't loaded at all. She had the house and all these debts. She hadn't been quite honest with him, it seemed."

That was poetic justice, Evan thought. Randy Wunderlich had been a little less than honest with her too.

"So now he's stuck with this bloody great house and he's just started work on the center but there's no money to get it going properly. You need publicity to launch a project like that. So he decided we needed a crazy stunt to make headlines. If you want to know the truth, I thought it was a little too crazy, but once Randy gets an idea, it's hard to stop him."

"And what was this idea?" Hughes asked.

"He decided that he'd go missing and he'd make psychic contact with some complete stranger and she'd find him. Great story, huh? World-renowned psychic vanishes and is found through psychic message. The plan was supposed to work like this — he'd go down to meditate in a cave he'd found. He'd fall into a trance and only wake when it was dark. It would be hard to get out of the cave because the rocks were slippery by this time. He'd try and twist his ankle so badly that he couldn't walk then he'd spend a miserable night in the cave, cut off by high water. In the morning his ankle would have swollen so that he couldn't put any weight on it. So he'd have to sit it out and wait to be found — but he would send out psychic messages because he was getting desperate. One of them would be picked up by a young girl who would lead the search party to find him."

"Wait a minute," Evan interrupted, before he remembered that he wasn't supposed to be in the room. "How was he so sure that Betsy would get the message and find him?"

Emmy gave him a withering stare. "We picked the right girl."

"You detected her strong psychic powers?" Evan asked.

"We detected gullible and suggestible. We've done enough psychic work to know how to plant an idea in someone's mind. You know — hypnosis. While I was working with Betsy, I suggested to her that she would have a dream and I told her exactly what she was going to dream about. The only thing was — she went to the wrong cave. And he was there. And he was dead."

She covered her face in her hands and lowered her head. A great heaving sob escaped from her. Hughes shut off the tape recorder.

Chapter 21

In the middle of that night, a storm broke over Llanfair. The thunder echoed, alarmingly loud, in the narrow confines of the pass. Lightning illuminated the mountaintops before more clouds rushed in to hide them again. Evan had woken in the still-unfamiliar room at the first rumble of thunder and had lain there, unable to sleep, counting the pauses between each flash and the following crash. Not more than a second or two. The storm was almost overhead and moving closer. Rain started drumming on the roof, almost drowning out the thunder. He was glad he wasn't out in this one. A real drencher.

He certainly wasn't going to be able to fall back to sleep until the storm was over, so he lay there, mulling over the events of the previous day. Emmy Court was being held in custody now, not having the funds to post bail. D.C.I. Hughes was satisfied that they'd got the right person, but Evan wasn't so sure. He wasn't sure what to make of her at all. Usually he was a pretty good judge of character but Emmy Court had got him stumped. Scheming. Manipulating. She showed no remorse about using Betsy so shamelessly. Apart from that one outbreak she had shown little emotion. Evan could easily imagine her dragging Randy Wunderlich to the sea cave and leaving him there to die if it suited her purposes. But then he thought back to the night when they had found Randy's body. All the way down to the Sacred Grove, Emmy had seemed keyed up, but excited, like a child setting out on an adventure. She had tried to persuade Betsy that she was going to the wrong cave and then there was the anguished outburst: "He can't be dead!" Surely there was true shock and despair in that wail. Randy's death had taken her by surprise. But it was no use expressing his doubts to D.C.I. Hughes at this stage. Hughes would want a better suspect before he'd let Emmy Court go.

The thunder crashed, louder than ever before. It went on and on, growing in intensity. It took a few moments for Evan to register that the noise wasn't thunder, but someone banging on his door. He grabbed his dressing gown and ran downstairs.

Betsy was standing outside the front door, wearing her anorak and nightdress, exactly as she had that previous night. She stared at him with terrified eyes and then flung herself toward him.

"Betsy, what on earth is it?" Evan asked.

"I'm so scared and my dad's passed out, as usual, and I'm so frightened that the murderer will come and get me."

Evan took her inside and shut the door. "It's all right. Calm down. You're safe now." He took the trembling girl into the kitchen and sat her down. "Look at you. You're soaking wet."

"I know. I didn't want to stay in the house any longer," she said. "I thought I could hear someone coming up the stairs so I just grabbed the first coat and ran."

"Take that wet coat off. My cardigan is hanging on the hook in the hall," he instructed. "I'll make you a cup of tea." He put the kettle on and Betsy came back, her hair still plastered to her forehead. She looked like a lost orphan in Evan's oversized cardigan.

She came to stand beside him, holding out her hands to the flame under the kettle. "I'm chilled right through," she said. "I don't know what's the matter with me."

"So tell me what happened," Evan said. "What frightened you?"

"I had another dream," Betsy said. "Only this one wasn't clear like the other one. It was just that I knew someone was after me. It was someone in a cloak and hood and I couldn't see the face but I knew it was the real murderer. Then I woke up and the storm was horrible and I thought I heard noises outside my door. I was so sure it was the murderer come to get me."

Evan patted her shoulder awkwardly. "You

just had a bad dream. Nobody's after you."

"But look what happened last time I had a bad dream. It all came true!"

Evan poured the boiling water into the pot. "Betsy, there's something you should know. It might stop you from worrying like this —" He paused, wondering how to phrase what he was going to say. "Betsy, all that rubbish about psychic ability, that's all it was — rubbish. The police are holding Emmy Court right now. It seems she planned a hoax with Randy Wunderlich. They worked together at this psychic hot line in America, you know. He was going to disappear and some unknown person was going to find him through a psychic connection. They picked you. They set you up. You didn't have a psychic dream. You were hypnotized. Emmy Court put those images into your head."

Betsy was staring at him, a bewildered look on her face. "You mean I'm not psychic at all? I don't have powers?"

"I'm afraid not," Evan said.

"You really mean I'm not psychic after all? They only pretended I had powers?"

Evan nodded. "It was a cruel trick to play." *But she did get the cave right,* he thought. *Was that just coincidence?*

"But why did they do it?"

"Publicity, that's all. They wanted to generate publicity for the Sacred Grove because it wasn't going very well. They thought this kind of thing would capture the media's attention."

"That is so unfair." Betsy's voice cracked. "How could she do that? I thought she liked me. And I was so excited about my powers. I really believed I was special at last."

"Look on the bright side of this," Evan said. "The murderer has nothing to fear from you. You won't be seeing his face in another psychic dream. You can't give him away — or her away," he added.

"Do they think that Emmy killed Randy?" Betsy asked. She picked up the mug of tea that Evan had poured for her and took a hesitant sip.

"They seem to. But that doesn't mean that I do, Betsy. I really think you ought not to go to that place again."

"But I want to. Even if I'm not psychic and they won't be helping me to develop my powers after all. The people are nice to me, honestly. I really don't feel I'm in danger there . . . except that . . ."

"What?"

"Something happened to me yesterday. I thought it was just a horrible accident —"

"What was it?"

"I got shut in the steam room by mistake. The steam came on and I couldn't get out. I nearly passed out before Bethan and Michael came to rescue me. They said the door had stuck before and they didn't seem at all worried. In fact, I get the feeling they thought I was being silly and hysterical."

Evan looked at her sharply. "So who knew you were going to be in the steam room?"

"I'd just left Rhiannon, so she knew. But then anyone only had to look at the staff schedule to see that I was supposed to be cleaning the spa at that time. I almost didn't make it to the spa. Rhiannon kept me doing other things. I had to rush."

"I really wish you wouldn't go back there, Betsy. Take that scare as a warning. If somebody does want to get rid of you, there are plenty of easy ways to do it at that place."

"I'll let them know about Emmy Court tomorrow and how she tricked me. It won't be easy to admit that I'm just ordinary after all, but I'll do it. When they hear that I'm not psychic, I'll be safe, won't I?"

"You'll be safer if you don't go back at all."

"No. I'm being silly again. I'm sure that steam room thing was just an unlucky accident. Michael said the door had stuck before, didn't he? And he was going to get it fixed right away. 'Can you imagine how one of the guests would freak out if it happened to them?' he said. He can be funny if he wants to, can't he? A bit shy, of course, but sweet. And Bethan's nice too. Those two will take care of me."

She took another sip of tea. "And you say

you don't think that Emmy killed Randy. Then that's all the more reason for me to keep on working at the center. I can be your eyes and ears for you, can't I? I've always wanted to help you with your work. Maybe I can track down the killer for you and you'll get all the credit for once."

"Betsy, you're something else." He ruffled her wet hair. "I'm going to get a towel to dry you off. You're dripping like a wet dog."

When he came back, Betsy was sitting on the chair, hugging her knees to her. She looked about twelve years old.

"Come here." He flung the towel over her head.

"Ow," she yelled playfully. "Lct mc out. You're suffocating me!" She pushed the towel back from her face and looked up at him. One minute they were both laughing, the next she was somehow in his arms and he was kissing her. Her lips were icy but her mouth was warm and inviting.

"I'm sorry —" He broke away and stepped back from her. "I don't know how that happened."

"Don't apologize," she said, still looking up at him adoringly. "I liked it. I've been waiting a long time for you to kiss me, Evan Evans." She slipped her arms around him, pulling herself close to him again. "Hold me. I'm still so cold."

He could feel her slender body shivering.

He wrapped his arms around her. "You should never have come out in this storm, you dafty."

"I know. I didn't stop to think. I was in a real panic again. Don't make me go home again tonight. I'm scared of going back there alone."

As if on cue the room was lit with blue light and a great crash of thunder shook the house. Hail bounced off the pavement outside.

"No, I can't send you home in this." Evan hesitated. Part of his brain was whispering that this whole thing might have been one of Betsy's famous schemes. But he could feel her body shivering against him. He glanced up the stairs. "All right. You can sleep in my bed. Come on."

She allowed herself to be led up the stairs and scrambled into the bed, pulling the covers over her. "I'm still freezing," she muttered.

"You'll soon get warm. That Welsh quilt is terrific. Half a dozen sheep have been stuffed into that." He grinned at her.

"Where are you going?" she asked.

"I'm not rightly sure. I don't have an armchair or a sofa yet."

"Don't go, Evan. Stay here with me. Come on, there's room."

Evan gave an embarrassed laugh. "Look, Betsy, I'm only human."

271

"No, it will be all right, honestly." She patted the bed beside her. "I just want to feel warm and safe." She sat up, hugging the quilt to her. "I promise I'll behave myself," she said. "Honestly, Evan. I mean that." She looked up at him, her big, blue eyes holding his. "Look, I know I've tried everything under the sun to get you to notice me, but now that I'm here and I could have what I wanted — I know you love someone else. It's okay. I'm quite trustworthy. And if you really want to know and promise not to tell another soul in the whole world — I'm still a virgin. I'm not going to lead you astray." She gave him a little smile.

Cautiously Evan climbed in beside her. He hoped that he was quite trustworthy too. He wasn't at all sure of it. He was sure Betsy didn't realize how many times he had thought about being with her and what it would be like. Now she was here and all he could think of was Bronwen.

"Goodnight, Betsy." He leaned over and gave her a little kiss on her forehead.

He woke early to find himself alone in bed and wondered if he had dreamed the whole thing. Then the smell of frying came to his nostrils. He went downstairs to find Betsy in the kitchen, the tea already in the pot and eggs and bacon sizzling in the pan.

"Toast just popped up," she called. "If you

272

hurry up and butter it, the eggs are ready."

He sat down to his best breakfast in weeks.

"I thought I'd better get going early, before too many people are about," she said. "I don't want to ruin your reputation."

"What about yours?" Evan laughed.

"Me? Oh, they all think I'm a loose woman anyway. And what do I care? Let them think what they like."

"Too late," Evan said. There was a tap on his front door. He went to answer it.

"Oh, good, you're up." Bronwen breezed past him into the hallway. "I felt so much better this morning that I thought I'd come over and surprise you. Look, I'm walking again. Isn't that wonderful?"

"Oh, yes," he managed to say. "That's wonderful."

"Do I smell bacon frying, on a workday?" she demanded. "Evan Evans, what about that healthy diet you were promising. When I'm not around to keep an eye on you, you go —"

She broke off. Through the half-open kitchen door she had just caught a glimpse of Betsy in her nightdress, standing with a frying pan in her hand, looking trapped and guilty.

"My God, you didn't wait long, did you?" Bronwen demanded. "Did you think I wasn't going to recover and you were going to hedge your bets?"

"Bronwen, wait. It's not —"

"Did she spend the night here?"

"Yes, but —" He tried to grab her but she pushed him off and ran out of the house again.

"Bronwen, please — stop. Just let me explain. It wasn't like that at all . . ."

"Go away," she shouted. "Go away and leave me alone. I never want to see you again."

Without warning she teetered and collapsed to the ground.

The next moments passed as if in a nightmare. The ambulance seemed to arrive in no time at all. Evan watched the medics scoop Bronwen up and cart her off on a stretcher as if she were a piece of meat. He tried to go with them and was pushed back.

"Are you next of kin? Well, then ring the hospital later and they'll let you know when you can see her."

He stood there in his bare feet, in the street, watching it go, hearing the siren as it disappeared down the pass. He had only felt this bad once before in his life, and that was when he sat beside his father in the Swansea hospital and watched the life ebb out of him. The words of guilt screamed through his head: "You did that to her. It's your fault."

Chapter 22

It was still raining when Betsy arrived at the Sacred Grove. For the first time she had had to take public transportation and was out of breath after the long walk from the nearest bus stop. She had run all the way from the gate, not wanting to be late. Her heart was thumping as the electric security gate swung open — and it wasn't just from running. She had tried to seem brave to Evan, but truly she was scared about coming here now. Yesterday's incident in the steam room had unnerved her more than she cared to admit. The morning's incident with Bronwen had unsettled her even more. She knew that she had done nothing wrong, but she couldn't help blaming herself. She got the feeling that Evan blamed her too. What if something awful happened to Bronwen because of her? The stupid thing was that she had fantasized over and over about something happening to Bronwen and Evan turning to her for love and support instead. But now that something had happened to Bronwen she just felt sick and scared.

She reached the main house and went to hang up her coat in the cloakroom. Evan had made her promise that she'd not be caught anywhere alone again. "Stay in public areas and if you're sent anywhere, get another girl to come with you," he had instructed. If Evan was worried for her, then she should definitely be on her guard. She decided she'd go around with Bethan all day, just for safety.

"Where's Bethan?" she asked as she went into the kitchen. Bethan usually cleared up after breakfast with her and the dining room looked like a disaster area.

"I don't know," Michael said. "She was looking for you a little while ago. I think she must have gone on down to the meditation center. Rhiannon wants you down there too, as soon as you can." He leaned closer to her. "I'll warn you that she's in a bad mood. It's raining on her bonfire and she had absolute confirmation from the universe that it would be fine tonight. But you'd better get on with clearing up in the dining room first. Chef's in a bad mood this morning, too. Must be the weather. Come on, I'll give you a hand."

Bethan put down her bucket as she pushed open the main door of the health center. Rhiannon had them all in a tizzy today, because the big ceremony was tonight. She'd almost snapped Bethan's head off when she had tried to be helpful.

"Get your other tasks done and come back here as quickly as possible. I want you and

Betsy together. We need to carry all this stuff across to the ceremony site and attempt to keep it dry. And tell the groundsman that I want him to find me dry wood too. The fire can't be allowed to smolder. It must flame up instantly."

Bethan thought it was a lot of fuss about nothing. She'd been to a ceremony before and thought they all looked pretty silly, dancing around the grove in their long robes, calling on the East and West and the spirits of animals. But she was afraid of Rhiannon. There was something about her, the way she looked at you, that made you not want to get on her bad side.

She decided to get her share of the spa cleaning done right away, then she wouldn't get in trouble with Annabel. She paused and looked up at the main house. It wasn't like Betsy to be late. And why did it have to be today, when Bethan really wanted to talk to her? She'd had a bad night last night, wondering who to tell — because Rebecca's disappearance had been playing on her mind. At the time she hadn't thought much about it. They'd told her Rebecca had gone and she'd accepted it. And when she had found Rebecca's raincoat still hanging in the staff cloakroom, she hadn't thought twice about that either. Rebecca was American, after all. They were all supposed to be rich. She probably didn't care that she'd forgotten her raincoat. She'd just buy another one.

But now that Randy had died, things were different somehow. She remembered that it had been cold and rainy the night Rebecca had left. She began to wonder what had made Rebecca run off, leaving her raincoat behind. She had inquired, innocently, of Mrs. Roberts whether Rebecca ever wrote and asked them to forward her raincoat. Mrs. Roberts said she hadn't heard a peep out of Rebecca since she left. So Bethan decided to do some snooping of her own.

Betsy finished up in the dining room and went down to Meditation to see if Bethan was down there. The sooner she teamed up with Bethan, the easier she'd feel.

"Ah, good, you're here," Rhiannon said in greeting. "Now where's that lazy child Bethan? Go and find her, will you? It will take two of you to carry the Wicker Man and I don't want him damaged."

Betsy went back up the steps. Bethan was nowhere in the main building. She wasn't in any of the cottages. Then Betsy opened the health center door and saw a bucket sitting in the hallway.

"Bethan?" she called. "Are you in here?"

That's when she was aware of the hiss of steam. She rushed to the steam room and struggled with the door. Finally she was able to wrench it open. Steam rushed out to meet her. She forced her way through it to the shape that lay huddled on the floor.

"Bethan!" she screamed, and dragged the lifeless figure out into the fresh air.

By midday Evan had completed his morning patrol of the area and was back at the station reporting in to HQ. It had been horrible feeling so powerless and cut off from Bronwen. He had followed the ambulance down to Bangor, only to be denied admission to the casualty ward where they had taken her. He'd called the hospital twice since but the news was the same both times. Miss Price was resting comfortably and they were conducting tests. He'd be able to see her during visiting hours that afternoon if she was done with her tests and back in the ward. *What could it be?* he asked himself over and over. *It must be something terrible to make her collapse like that — cancer, heart attack, stroke.* A terrible fear overtook him that she might die before he'd had a chance to explain and say he was sorry.

He looked up as the door opened and Glynis came in. "Hello there, Evan. How are you?" she asked, bright as ever. "I hope you don't mind my popping in, but I've got Rebecca's parents with me and you said you'd help me out with them. They are so devastated, poor people. Worried out of their minds. Terribly earnest types. God-fearing and all that."

Evan got to his feet. "What do you want me to do?"

"Take them around the places you went before, maybe, and then I thought we'd run them down to the Sacred Grove so that they can see for themselves."

"All right." He sighed as he reached for his coat.

"What's the matter?" Glynis asked. "You look terrible."

"Bronwen's in the hospital. She collapsed this morning and they don't know what's wrong with her." It just came out, even though he hadn't meant it to.

"Oh, I am sorry. How rotten for you. Look, it shouldn't take more than an hour or so to do this and then you can sneak away to the hospital if you like. I'll cover for you."

"Thanks, Glynis." He managed a smile. "All right then. Let's go and meet Rebecca's parents."

"By the way," she said as they walked out to the waiting car, "the hostile American woman posted bail this morning. We've had to let her go."

"Emmy Court, you mean?"

Glynis nodded. "She had the money wired to her. It's all right, though. She can't go anywhere. We've got her passport. Not that we had enough to keep holding her anyway." She opened her car door. "Mr. and Mrs. Riesen. This is Constable Evans I told you

280

about. He was the one who went around with Rebecca's picture."

The couple sitting in the backseat of the squad car looked like a typical American couple to Evan. The husband was wearing a San Diego Padres baseball cap. The wife was dressed in colors brighter than the average Welshwoman would wear. They both looked gray and haggard, but they shook Evan's hand warmly and thanked him for his trouble.

"I just wish there was more we could do," Evan said as he climbed into the passenger seat beside Glynis. "So you've still heard nothing from her. There's no possibility she went home to the States but hasn't contacted you yet?"

"Oh, no, Rebecca would never do that," Mrs. Riesen said. "She was a real homebody, if you know what I mean. We had the hardest time persuading her to go away to college, and my, was she homesick that first year! She really didn't want to come over to Britain for the semester, but she was awarded the scholarship and my husband told her, 'Honey, it's a wonderful opportunity. It might never come around again,' so she went."

"I encouraged her," Mr. Riesen said in a voice that cracked with emotion. "I made her go."

"Honey, you thought you were doing the right thing." She put her hand on his. "We all thought we were doing the right thing. We didn't worry about her once. She was never any trouble, all the time she was growing up. Other kids went through the rebellious stage, but not Rebecca. Didn't have to set her curfews or anything. She was never out late. All she cared about were her studies and her music. Only ever had one or two close friends — never the partying kind, you understand."

Evan nodded. "Do you have any idea at all what would have made her come to the Sacred Grove?"

"None at all. A place like that just wasn't Rebecca. She was always very involved in our church — she'd never have been lcd astray."

"Do you think that maybe she wanted to convert the people at the Sacred Grove?" Evan asked. "Someone mentioned she did some of that kind of thing."

"I can't see Rebecca doing that either." Mrs. Riesen looked to her silent husband for confirmation. "She was too shy. And she was tolerant too — live and let live. No, that doesn't sound like our Rebecca."

They had reached the top of the pass and Glynis pulled up outside the youth hostel. "Constable Evans asked about her here, but nobody recognized the photo," she said.

"I don't know why she'd come to a place like this," Mrs. Riesen said. "I can't see her wanting to hike with a backpack. How would she have carried her violin? She never went anywhere without it."

"Then maybe we should go straight down to the Sacred Grove," Evan said. "I don't know what good it will do, but there was one of the maids who had become friendly with Rebecca. You could talk to her and see if there was any clue she could give you."

Mrs. Riesen looked at her husband and nodded.

"Another thing I've been wondering, Mrs. Riesen," Evan said as the car swung around to the right and started to zigzag down to Beddgelert. "What made Rebecca stay on after the end of her course? Had she made friends she didn't want to leave? If she was the homebody you describe, wouldn't she have wanted to spend Christmas with you?"

"You know, we were rather surprised about that," Mrs. Riesen said. "I was quite upset at the time, wasn't I, hon? 'She doesn't want to spend Christmas with her family anymore,' I said to Frank. She had a couple of fellow American students who were taking an apartment in London and she spent the holidays with them. But they're both back home again now and neither of them has been in contact with Rebecca since the first of the year. She stayed on alone in London for a couple of weeks, apparently, then she went touring. She said she wanted to see something of the countryside — which is understandable. But we were surprised she was doing it alone. She was always a little cautious, our Rebecca."

"And I take it you've been to Oxford and seen where she lived?"

"Oh, yes. That was one of the first things we did. She lived in a dormitory for American students who were attending the institute. It wasn't actually part of Oxford University, you know. It was a separate program just for Americans. They got the chance to audit lectures with the Oxford undergraduates, but they did their assignments for the AIAO. That stands for the American Institute at Oxford, I believe."

"Everyone who knew Rebecca was gone, except for the faculty and staff," Mr. Riesen said, leaning forward in his seat. "It's only a one-quarter course, you see. All new students each quarter. Nobody had anything to tell us at all. The faculty hardly remembered her. 'She was quiet and shy and hardly ever spoke up' — that's what that one professor said, didn't he, Margaret?"

"And she didn't make any friends among the Oxford undergrads then?" Evan asked.

"She lived with other Americans, of course. And from what she told us, the British students were not particularly welcoming. Not that she was the social kind but she went to concerts and lectures with girls from back home. She loved her concerts, didn't she, honey? Crazy about her music."

Evan noticed they were using the past tense, as if they had mentally already accepted that she was gone from them.

Mrs. Riesen rummaged in her purse and produced a photograph. "That's her, playing with the orchestra at home. Second from the left. She was assistant concert mistress. Very talented. You should have heard her play — it brought tears to your eyes sometimes, didn't it, Frank?"

Mr. Riesen merely nodded.

As they reached the gate of the Sacred Grove, they saw that their way was blocked by an ambulance. Evan jumped out and ran ahead.

"What's going on?" he yelled.

The security guard went to yell something back, then noticed his uniform and recognized him. "Nasty accident, Constable. One of the girls got trapped in the steam room. She was dead by the time they found her. Poor little thing."

"Betsy?" Evan pushed past the guard, ready to run down the path.

"No, not Betsy. That wasn't the name. It began with a B though — Bethan. That was it!"

Evan was back in Llanfair by early afternoon. He was sure that it hadn't been an accident and had hinted as much to Glynis.

Fortunately, she was ready enough to believe him. She had the spa area cordoned off and the body sent for immediate autopsy. Again Evan was impressed with her coolness under stress. He had to admit that she had been promoted ahead of him not because she was female or dating the chief constable's nephew, but because she was bloody good.

Glynis had asked him to drive the Riesens, visibly shaken, back to their hotel in Bangor, while she stayed on and waited for D.C.I. Hughes to join her. Evan paced around his tiny police station, unable to settle. The hospital was still maddeningly uncommunicative about Bronwen and he was also worried sick about Betsy. In the light of today's tragedy, Betsy's incident in the steam room the day before had most probably not been an accident either. He wished she would have let him drive her home, but Rhiannon had interrupted when he was talking to her. "She is needed for a very important ceremony tonight. There is no question of her leaving early," she had said. "But don't worry. I'll see she is taken good care of. We don't want anything to happen to her."

Rhiannon's assurances had done little to still Evan's fears. He had no reason to trust her any more than the rest of them. But he had to admit that Betsy was probably safe for the rest of that day. There would be a forensic team arriving from police headquarters at some stage, and lots of people due for a big ceremony that evening.

At least he would have a chance to go to the hospital, as soon as he finished his day's work at the police station. He tidied the papers on his desk before leaving. Rhiannon's book, *The Way of the Druid*, was lying on his desk, as yet unread. Evan fingered it uneasily. It had a picture of a robed figure standing in an oak grove on the front cover. He couldn't make out what the figure was holding but it could have been a knife. He picked up the book and stuffed it into his pocket. Something had made Rebecca interested enough in Druids to seek out the Sacred Grove. Maybe the book would give him the insight that had been lacking. It would also help him pass the time down at the hospital if they wouldn't let him see Bronwen straightaway. Knowing hospitals, he'd have some waiting to do.

"She's resting at the moment." The starchy ward sister blocked his access to Nightingale Ward, where he had been told he'd find Bronwen. "We'll let you know when she wakes. She was severely dehydrated, you know. It took us ages to get a vein up enough to put the IV in."

"Do they know what's wrong yet?" Evan asked.

She looked at him as if he were a visiting worm. "Patient records are entirely confidential," she said. "Now please take a seat. We'll let you know."

Evan sat. The chair was orange vinyl and not big enough for him. Did they actually design hospital chairs to be uncomfortable, just so that people wouldn't hang around too long? he wondered. Part of National Health cost-cutting measures, maybe. He looked around for a magazine. There was a choice of *Golf Digest* and *Woman's Weekly*. Then he remembered the book in his pocket. He took it out and started to read. An hour later he still hadn't been called and he had reached chapter 10.

Chapter x. Sacrifices.

Sacrifice was a usual part of Druid ritual, although most sacrifices involved animals, not humans. Human sacrifice, greatly exaggerated and distorted by ancient Roman observers, did take place, but only in exceptional circumstances. Prisoners were ritually sacrificed so that their death twitches could be observed and the way they fell could provide divination answers to the oracles. Oracle Druids also disemboweled living victims so that their entrails could be read for answers from the gods.

Small numbers of ritually sacrificed bodies have been found throughout Britain, showing that ritual sacrifice was only performed in very special circumstances. Several bodies have been discovered, perfectly preserved, in bogs. The way they were decorated and the fact that their arms were bound with leather thongs show that they were put into the bog to die, although whether this was meant as punishment or as an appeasement to the gods is not certain.

In times of extreme emergency, or when the high priests felt that the gods were displeased or unapproachable, a perfect specimen from the tribe would be selected as an appeasement sacrifice — usually a young warrior or a virgin. In some locations they would be killed on a stone table with a ritual knife, but this does not seem to have been the preferred method in Wales or Ireland.

The more curious phenomenon of the Wicker Man has been reported by many ancient observers and was surely a part of the fire rituals, although whether on a regular basis or only in times of war is not known. The Wicker Man described in ancient literature was a figure made of willow branches and stuffed with straw. It was burned rather like our Guy Fawkes, on a bonfire to insure prosperity, fertility, or the success of the crops or as an offering to the gods in war. It is suggested that live victims were at times placed within the Wicker Man, although whether these were captives or victims selected from the tribe for a specific tribute is not clear.

As he read, Evan had been experiencing a growing uneasiness. Why was Rhiannon suddenly showing such an interest in Betsy? "She needs me to help her with the big ceremony." Evan flipped back to the chapter on Beltane. "Beltane, the ceremony of new fire. Sometimes sacrifices were performed to ensure success of the crops and fertility of the herds." He heard Betsy's soft whisper from the previous night: "Promise not to tell another soul in the whole world. I'm still a virgin."

The big ceremony tonight! Evan jumped to his feet. "Oh my God!" he gasped as he ran down the echoing tiled hallway. Beltane was tonight. The Wicker Man. He had to get to the Sacred Grove before it was too late.

He hadn't ridden down on his motorbike this time, because there was still a chance of rain, and his own old bone-shaker didn't do more than fifty miles an hour without protesting groans. He pushed it as hard as he dared along the expressway to Caernarfon, then on the coastal road to Porthmadog. Across the estuary, where the setting sun streaked the outgoing tide with pink, then into the twilight of the oak woods, and finally to the gate of the Sacred Grove.

As he approached the security gate, figures loomed out of the gloom and surrounded his car. They were waving placards and Evan soon recognized the song they were singing.

It was "Cwm Rhondda." "Strong redeemer, strong redeemer, I will ever cling to thee!"

"Go back, Satan. Back to the place God has ordained for you!" shouted a voice and Evan saw Mrs. Powell-Jones brandishing a sign as if it was a weapon. The sign read, DRUID WORSHIP IS DEVIL WORSHIP. Other signs proclaimed, PAGANS GO HOME. KEEP WALES CHRISTIAN. NO HEATHEN CERE-MONIES.

Evan wound down his window. "Let me get past, Mrs. Powell-Jones. It's me. Constable Evans."

"Constable Evans! Well, I never . . . I hope you don't intend to participate in the heathen orgy?"

"No, I want to try and stop it! Let me get past."

"Good man. Good luck to you! I hope they'll let you in. They closed the gate as soon as we got here."

Evan pushed the intercom button. "Let me in. It's Constable Evans. It's very urgent."

"I'm sorry, Constable," came the scratchy voice through the intercom. "I've had orders not to open this gate. There's a lot of raving loonies out there. If you can radio for police backup to keep the loonies out, then I'll let you in, but until then it's more than my job's worth to open this gate."

"The ceremony?" Evan shouted over the hymn-singing and chanting going on around

291

him. "Are they going ahead with the ceremony?"

"Oh, yes, that will have started by now. They were heading down to the oak grove about an hour ago."

"Where is it? Where is this oak grove, man?"

"Not exactly sure. Over toward the point, it must be. That's where they were heading."

"Send someone over there and stop it before it's too late!" Evan shouted.

"I can't do that. There's only me on duty and I can't leave my post."

"Call someone. Get someone over there, man, do you hear?"

"All right. All right. Keep your hair on, Constable. I'll call them at the big house. What's all this about then? What will I tell them?"

"To stop the bloody ceremony before somebody gets hurt, that's what!" Evan shoved the car into reverse and backed through the milling crowd, making them scatter before him as he sounded his horn. Then he drove a mile or so back along the road, parked the car on the muddy verge, and ran through the woodland. He had to be able to reach the point from here. The property was on a narrow strip of land between two estuaries. It couldn't be very wide at this point. It was just a question of cutting across at the right place. Darkness was falling rapidly now and trees loomed like ghostly figures, reaching out spiky arms to grab at him as he ran past. His breath started coming in gulps as he reached the crest of a hill and got his first view of the estuary beyond. At least he couldn't see the glow of a bonfire yet. Maybe he was in time and they hadn't started the ceremony.

He plunged down the other side of the slope, his feet swishing through unseen bracken, stumbling over tree roots, and tearing through gorse bushes. Then he heard the voice. It was colder and deadlier than ever before, but he recognized it and made for it through the darkness.

"I have cast the circle. The seen and the unseen are now one. Now I call the four quarters. I call the East, quarter of the air. I call all winged things, inhabitants of the air, to our circle. Come birds, come angels, be one with us. And I offer up the blade, tool of the East."

The voice echoed through the woodlands. Still there was no fire and Evan could only push on, guided by the voice.

"I call the North, quarter of the Earth, quarter of winter, midnight, darkness, and death. I invite anything that walks on the earth, two-legged, four-legged, to join us. I invite rocks, stones, leaves, branches to be one with our circle, one with us, and I offer up the sacred stone to be part of our ceremony.

"I call the West, quarter of water. Come tides, come dolphins and whales and fishes. Be one with us. And I place in the center of the circle the cauldron, tool of the West."

The cold, clear voice rose in pitch. "And last I call the South, quarter of fire, quarter of today's feast. Come lions, come dragons, salamanders and be with us. Be one with us. Be one with us as we make the new fire. Fire that purifies and cleanses and strengthens.

"I take the flint and I light the new fire."

Suddenly a glow appeared in front of Evan and he could hear the crackling as the bonfire came to life.

"Twin fires for Beltane — for Calan Mai. Whoever passes between the two fires will be purified and made fruitful for the coming year.

"I stand at the middle of the cone of power. We are all one in the cone of power and our power rises to be one with the power of the universe. A bridge has been made between natural and supernatural, between human and divine.

"This is Calan Mai — time of new plantings, new fruitfulness, and young womanhood. Tonight is the festival of fire — the union of the Goddess with the Horned God. I call on them to come down among us and accept our sacrifice, just as our ancestors sacrificed to them back until the dawn of time."

Evan was close enough to see them now — a group of shadowy figures in white robes stood around twin bonfires. Between them there was something on a pole. It looked like a large basket, but as he came closer he saw that it was fashioned in the shape of a crude human. The central figure, who had to be Rhiannon although she was hooded and robed, plunged a torch into the fire, then held it up above her head. She threw back her hood. She was wearing a torque around her neck, which shone in the firelight.

"Accept our sacrifice!" she intoned. "Cleanse your people. Make us fruitful. Let our religion be fruitful and grow and prosper. We give you what is living and perfect. Take it. Make it yours!"

Evan, watching in horror as he ran, didn't see the tree root until too late. He went sprawling, feeling the scratches on his hands and face as he went into the gorse. He staggered to his feet again just in time to see the Wicker Man go up in flames. An unearthly scream came from it.

With a great cry "No!" Evan pushed aside robed figures, threw himself into the circle, and knocked the burning wicker structure to the ground. It crashed down from its pole, scattering sparks. As he tried to put out the fire with his bare hands, he heard a horrified voice shouting, "Evan! What are you doing? Now you've ruined everything!"

Betsy, robed like the other figures, stood behind him, holding a chalice in her hands.

Chapter 23

The next morning Betsy went to work as usual at the Sacred Grove. It had taken a lot of courage to go there again after Bethan's death, but if Evan was being so clueless, she decided, then somebody ought to be on the spot, solving things. His disruption of the ceremony last night had been the one funny incident in a series of terrible, tense days. Of course, it hadn't been funny at the time. She had been really embarrassed and Rhiannon had been furious.

"You have spoiled the whole atmosphere of our ceremony," she had yelled at him. "You have driven away the gods! What on earth put it into your head that I would consider using a human sacrifice? If you had read my book, you would have known that Druids only resorted to human sacrifices in the most extreme circumstances. And since we are not in the middle of war, plague, or famine, I hardly think that now would be an appropriate time."

Evan had apologized, of course. He was obviously embarrassed about the whole thing. In fact, it was lucky that he'd discovered that Rhiannon had put a live rabbit into the wicker cage. That gave him grounds to cite her for cruelty to animals, which made him feel a little better and at least gave him an excuse for his action.

Now that she looked back on it, Betsy was rather flattered that Evan had been willing to risk so much to rescue her. It proved that he did care, after all. Not every girl had a champion who was willing to dash into a fire for her. He'd got nasty burns on his hands and would be off work for a few days for his trouble. All the more reason for Betsy to do some snooping of her own at the Sacred Grove.

One of the conclusions she had reached was that Bethan's death was not an accident. If the door had merely stuck, then how could she, Betsy, have wrenched it open after a few tugs? Bethan was bigger and stronger than she was. Why couldn't she have pushed it open? She decided to go down to the spa building and take a look for herself. The actual spa area was cordoned off with yellow police tape. That was good. It meant that the police weren't treating this as an accident either.

Betsy started looking around outside the building. She wasn't sure what she was looking for, but there was no lock on the steam room door. Something had to have been used to prevent it from opening. After several minutes of looking she found something promising. In the flower bed across from the spa building, she found a wedge-shaped sliver of wood. It wasn't large, but it might have been enough to slip under the door. Carefully she picked it up and put it into her overall pocket.

"What are you doing there, Betsy?"

A voice behind her made her jump with fright. Lady Annabel and Mrs. Roberts were coming down the steps together. Lady Annabel was looking at her suspiciously.

"I — I saw a weed in the rose bed," Betsy stammered. "I thought I'd better pull it out."

"That's why we employ gardeners," Lady Annabel said coldly. "Your job is to help out in the buildings. Please leave the grounds-keeping to the professionals."

The two women sailed past Betsy. With her heart thumping she went on up the steps. She was so intent in getting to the safety of the kitchen that she almost ran past Michael without noticing him.

"Hey there!" he greeted her. "What's wrong? You look terrible. You look as if you've seen a ghost. Don't tell me there are ghosts here too. That's all we're lacking."

"No. It's just that my nerves are on edge," Betsy said. "I keep thinking about poor Bethan."

"You too, eh?"

Betsy nodded. "Do you really think it was an accident, Michael?" she asked cautiously. She had promised Evan to trust nobody but she had to talk to someone.

Michael looked surprised. "She got trapped by a door that sticks, Betsy." Then a wave of suspicion spread across his face. "Wait a second. You don't think that her death had anything to do with . . ." He glanced around uneasily.

"I don't know what to think," Betsy said. Her fingers closed around the piece of wood in her pocket. Better wait until she could show it to Evan before she made any claims. "This place is beginning to give me the willies," she added.

"Me too." Michael lowered his voice. "You can't help wondering who's next, can you?"

"Don't say that." Betsy shivered.

"Look here, Betsy." Michael swallowed hard. "I'm not going to be here this afternoon. Can you go home early today? I don't like to think of leaving you here when I can't keep an eye on you."

"Yes, maybe I will try to get off early today. Thanks." She gave him a shy smile.

"Great." He smiled back. "Promise me you'll be careful. I'm off sailing, you see. A group of friends from Porthmadog and I sail together every Wednesday, and we use my boat, so I can't let them down —" He paused. "I suppose you wouldn't like to come with us, would you? It's quite fun. We usually bring food and have a picnic."

"I'd love to," Betsy said. "I've never been sailing."

"Haven't you? It's one of the things I live for." He smiled at her shyly. "See you around four then. Down at the dock."

Evan lay on his bed, unable to sleep. For one thing his hands were hurting him. The hospital had dressed them for him and given him painkillers but they still throbbed. But the hurt was nothing compared to the turmoil that was going through his head. He had made such a fool of himself tonight. How could he have got things so wrong? Now he wouldn't have another chance to find the real killer at the Sacred Grove. The doctor had said he wasn't to return to work until his hands had healed. So he was stuck home alone, in a barely furnished, cold, and bleak cottage, with more than enough time to brood and worry. And to top everything else he hadn't had a chance to see Bronwen. By the time he had reached her hospital ward, visiting hours were over and the starchy sister wouldn't listen. "No exceptions," she said frostily. "The young lady needs her sleep. You'll just have to come back tomorrow."

So another night of worrying about Bronwen and whether or not she would forgive him. The sister wouldn't even give him a phone number so that he could talk to her.

"The nearest phone is out in the corridor and I'm not having her standing out there, getting cold. I've said you can see her in the morning."

Sleep was impossible, so Evan got up and went downstairs to make himself a cup of tea. A beer would have been better, but he hadn't got around to stocking beer in his pint-sized refrigerator yet. How could he have read all the signs so wrongly? It made such sense that Rhiannon had killed Randy Wunderlich. She had Chief Inspector Hughes's favorite *m* words — means and motive. It was just possible, he decided, that he hadn't got it wrong after all. Maybe Rhiannon's intention had been to get rid of Betsy as the sacrifice last night, but with all the attention and the protesters at the gate, she had changed her mind at the last minute. Which meant that Betsy could still be in danger. If he wasn't working, the least he could do would be to go down to the Grove and let them know that he was keeping an eye on her.

Let's start at square one again, he said to himself. *Let's get back to the facts.*

Fact one: Randy Wunderlich was killed. Emmy Court admitted to her part in the hoax, but she said she didn't kill him. The person who killed him must have overheard enough of the plot to know that Randy would be hiding out in the cave. That could have been any of them, of course. They all disliked him, except for his wife. Most of them had the means, too — except it would need to be someone strong enough to drag his body from one cave to another.

Fact two: Bethan was killed in the steam room. Why? Obviously because she knew something about Randy's killer. She had seen something and, not being the brightest girl, it had taken her a while to put two and two together.

Had the killer also meant to kill Betsy? he wondered. If she hadn't been rescued, would it have been too late for her too? He suspected that Betsy had been a trial run — to see if being locked in the steam room with the steam full on really could kill somebody. And also to set up the premise that the steam room door stuck.

Another fact struck him: Bethan was the only one who remembered anything about Rebecca. It was ironic that she was killed just before Rebecca's parents arrived. Could Rebecca's disappearance somehow be tied to Randy's death? How? Something had brought her to the Sacred Grove and that something was to do with Druids — which brought him back to Rhiannon again.

Surely somebody in Oxford must have known Rebecca. You didn't spend a whole term in a place without making any mark. He took a big gulp of tea and came to a conclusion. If he wasn't allowed to work, he would drive to Oxford and ask some questions for himself. He wasn't supposed to drive, but he couldn't see that holding a steering wheel would make him feel worse than he already did. It took him a while to get dressed — he found it hard to negotiate buttons and zippers with his sore and bandaged fingers — but he left the house as the first streaks of dawn appeared in the eastern sky.

Oxford was just coming into full morning bustle as Evan drove into the city center, past the grand yellow sandstone buildings and the ancient spires. The streets were clogged with students on bicycles, their black gowns flying out behind them, making them look like flocks of penguins. He had never been there before and marveled at how quaint it still was, like a scene from an old film, then felt a pang of regret that he had never had the chance to experience any of this. He parked and got out, savoring the scene. Two serious young women, piles of books in their arms, their gowns flapping out as they walked, passed him. "Are you going to the OUDs thing tonight?" one asked.

"I can't. I've got Stebbins for a Greats tutorial in the morning and I haven't prepared a thing."

It was like visiting a different world. He remembered then that Bronwen had once been one of those young women — not here in Oxford but in rival Cambridge. He imagined life would be pretty much the same in both places. The thought of Bronwen generated pangs of guilt and alarm. What would she think if he didn't show up this morning? He'd have to make sure he was back in time to see her this evening or she'd think he'd given up on her.

He had stopped at a garage just outside of the city to consult a telephone book and get directions to the AIAO. It turned out to be on a ring road at the edge of the city in a building not at all like the old sandstone colleges — all modern concrete and glass. The receptionist looked at him suspiciously and he had to produce his warrant card before she would take him to the institute director. The director was a typical American and very friendly. He went to shake Evan's hand and Evan only managed to draw it away just in time, explaining about the burns.

"I guess you've chosen a tough profession," the director said. He listened to Evan's story, checked the records, then shook his head. He didn't remember that particular student personally but Evan was welcome to talk to her course directors. Half an hour later he was back in the street, not having learned anything. The faculty members he had spoken to couldn't even put a face to her name. They handled so many students that they remembered very few of them. And there were no students remaining from the fall program.

Sorry they couldn't be of more help.

They did direct him to the hostel where Rebecca had lived. It was a large and rather ugly Victorian on the Banbury Road. It was called the Laurels, although any bushes in the front garden had been paved over to make a parking area. Evan spoke to the hostel administrator, a no-nonsense, middle-aged woman. She remembered the name. Quiet girl. Wasn't in any kind of trouble. But everyone would have gone now who remembered her, apart from the cleaning staff. He could talk to the maids if he liked, but they usually cleaned during the morning when the students weren't around.

"What about her violin?" Evan asked, with sudden inspiration. "Did you ever get complaints about her practicing her violin?"

The woman wrinkled her brow. "I don't remember any violin. She can't have played it here. We do occasionally get students who play the piano in the common room, but I don't recall any violin practice going on."

That was odd, Evan thought. Her parents had stressed that she loved her violin. Could she have gone a whole term without playing it? Which had to mean that she played it somewhere else. He got back in the car and drove back to the city center. At the student union building he stood studying the overflowing notice board. Chess club match against Moscow University, rowing eights, drama club auditions . . .

"Is there a music club or an orchestra?" Evan stopped a young man who was looking for an inch of space to pin another notice to the board.

"OUMS," the boy said. Then, as Evan looked puzzled: "Oxford University Music Society. They're the ones who put on concerts. Is that what you mean, or do you mean pop music?"

"No, they'd be the one I'm looking for," Evan said. "Any idea how I could contact them?"

"Ask at the office. They'd have the yearbook with a list of the society officers."

Evan did as suggested. A serious-looking young Indian girl peeked at him from beneath a veil of long dark hair. "If you're interested in joining, why don't you give them a buzz and find out when the next meeting is?" she suggested in a flat southern counties voice polished with overtones of a good education.

"I'm not interested in joining. I'm a police officer and I need to talk to them about a missing girl."

The mane of hair was shaken back so that Evan saw two kohl-edged dark eyes. "Katherine Sparks, you mean? But that was ages ago. I thought they'd found her remains at last, haven't they?"

"Katherine Sparks?" Evan was confused.

"Yes, you said the girl who was missing, so I thought you meant her. LMH student, disappeared last year, didn't she, and they never found her. I'm not sure, but I think I read recently that remains on the south coast had been identified as hers. She's not the girl you're asking about?"

"No. This one was an American exchange student — not officially part of the university."

"Oh. American." She paused for a moment. "Well, I don't know where you'd contact any of these people during the day. Some of them might go back to college to eat lunch in the refectory if they're not too far away, but most of us just grab fast food these days. If I were you, I'd leave a note with one of their college porters and have them call you."

"It's rather urgent," Evan said. "I'm just here for the day and I have to get back."

"Then I'd go round to the president of the society's college and see if they'll give you his class schedule. Or you could ask his college servant. They usually have a pretty good idea where students can be found."

Evan left with directions to Baliol and was asking at the porter's lodge when an arrogant voice behind him demanded, "Nicholas Hardy? Who wants him?"

"I'm a police officer, making inquiries about a girl who might have been a member of his music club," Evan said. "Any idea where he is?"

"I left him wolfing down a large plate of spaghetti *bolognese* about five minutes ago," the young man said. "Across the quad, through those double doors and turn right. You'll find it by the smell."

Evan did as instructed and soon located the pale, fair-haired young man, who eyed him nervously. "Rebecca Riesen? The American girl? Yes, I remember her. Bloody good violinist, isn't she? She asked if she could sit in on our rehearsals and I think she ended up playing with us in the Christmas concert."

"Could you tell me anything about her, any friends she had, anything at all?" Evan asked.

The young man wrinkled his nose. "When I'm trying to conduct, I really don't notice that much. I think she was chummy with some of the other violinists. There's a group of three or four of them from LMH."

"LMH?" Evan asked.

"Lady Margaret Hall. Sandra Vessey, Jane Hill, and what is the dark girl's name? Greene, that's it. Rachel Greene. I've no idea where you'd locate them at this time of day, but we're having a rehearsal tomorrow night if you'd care to come to that."

"Thanks, but I have to get back to North Wales. I'll try their college if you could direct me from here."

"Let's see." The boy wrinkled his nose

again. "It's not that simple. Nothing is around here. I'd better draw you a map."

Evan found Lady Margaret Hall without too much trouble. A helpful registrar's office found him a course schedule for each of the girls. Rachel Greene seemed the easiest to locate. She had a tutorial with her history professor starting at twelve-thirty. Evan found the appropriate room, and didn't have to wait long before the petite dark-haired girl came along the paneled wooden corridor toward him. She stopped abruptly when she saw him blocking the way.

"Nothing's happened to Professor Overton, has it?" The light from a leaded window threw sunlight onto her black hair and made dust motes dance around her.

"No, I just wondered if I could have a few words with you. I'm a police officer from North Wales and we're looking for a missing girl. Rebecca Riesen."

"Rebecca?" she looked at him in alarm. "She's missing, you say?"

"Her parents have come over, trying to find her."

"But that's terrible. Poor Rebecca."

"You knew her well, did you?"

"Not well, I wouldn't say. She was only here for a couple of months, you know, but she sat next to us in the orchestra and we went out for a coffee afterward sometimes. A nice girl — and a very good violinist."

"You didn't keep up with her after the end of her term here?"

Rachel made a face. "I meant to, but you know how it is. You promise to write but you don't."

"So you've no idea of her plans when she left here?"

"I think she was staying with friends in London for the holidays. She said she was having such a good time she wasn't ready to go home."

"She didn't mention wanting to go to North Wales?"

Rachel shook her head. "No, never. She wasn't really the outdoor type, was she? She used to complain about the rain and cold in Oxford. I don't know what she would have done on Mount Snowdon. Concerts in London I could understand, but not North Wales."

"And yet she did go there. To a New Age center."

She gave him an incredulous stare. "A New Age center — whatever for? Wasn't that against her religion? She wasn't trying to convert them, was she? She was one of those dreadfully earnest Christian types. You had to be careful not to swear around her, and she'd never come to the pub for a drink."

"Did she have any boyfriends, do you know?"

"Not that I know of. She was almost painfully shy and like I said, she'd never come to the pub and places where we go to hang out and meet blokes. Although —" She broke off, frowning in concentration.

"Yes?" Evan asked hopefully.

"She was keen on one bloke, I think. I'm not sure actually if she was keen on him or if she merely wanted to help him. I got the feeling she was the type of person who went around wanting to save people — lame ducks, you know. There was this bloke in the orchestra. Like I said, I don't know if she fancied him or if she just felt sorry for him because people were being unjust."

"Unjust?"

"Yes, there were rumors circulating, you know, because the police had had him in for questioning — about Kathy Sparks. They were from the same sort of social set, you see. Both titled families and all that, ridden to hounds from the cradle, friends of the royals. All that sort of bosh."

"Kathy was the girl who disappeared last year?"

"Yes. She was from this college too. It was horrible. I don't think they've ever found her. It must be awful for her family, mustn't it?"

"And who was this young man who was questioned by the police?"

"He was in the orchestra with us. Rather geeky — socially inept type."

"Do you remember his name?" Evan asked.

An elderly woman in academic gown over tweed suit came down the hallway toward them. "Ah, there you are Miss Greene. Are we ready to debate the causes of the Hundred Years War, do you think?"

Rachel gave Evan an apologetic smile. "Sorry, I don't think I ever knew his name. I have to go to my tutorial now," she said as the professor swept her in through the paneled door.

Chapter 24

Evan turned and ran down the hallway, nearly barreling into another group of female students. He drove straight to the Oxford CID headquarters and was shown to the desk of the D.I. who had been part of the Katherine Sparks investigation.

"No, we're still no nearer to solving it, I'm afraid," the inspector said. He was a young man, not much older than Evan by the look of him, but he was already losing his hair. "The girl vanished from the face of the earth. We thought she'd run away to start with, because some of her clothes were gone, but she's never been seen since, so we have to assume the worst."

"And you questioned a young man?" Evan could hardly get the words out.

"We questioned lots of young men. The girl was not short of male escorts."

"This was a shy sort of bloke, who knew her family."

"Oh, you mean Michael Hollister? Yes, we questioned him, and for a while that lead looked hopeful, but in the end nothing came of it. He had an alibi on the day she went missing."

"Michael? Oh, my God." Evan held out a hand, remembered the burns, and withdrew it again. "Thanks for your help. I've got to get home."

"Anything more I can tell you?"

"No, you've already told me what I needed to know," he said. "Sorry but I have to rush. I'll let you know how if this turns out the way I think it will. We may be some help to you in solving your case. Oh, but I tell you what — can I use your phone?"

Dispatch in Caernarfon told Evan that D.C. Davies and D.S. Watkins were not available at the moment. If he liked to leave a message, she'd see that it was passed to them.

"This is Constable Evans," Evan began.

"Oh, Constable Evans. I heard you got yourself badly burned last night. How are you feeling?"

"I'm fine. Listen, tell D.C. Davies to send someone down to the Sacred Grove to keep an eye on Betsy until I get back. I'll explain everything. All right?"

"I'll pass it on to her," the dispatcher said. "And we think you were very brave to try to rescue that rabbit last night. Some people are savages, aren't they?"

Evan hung up and rushed out to his car. He hadn't eaten all day but he dared not stop now. His old clunker groaned and protested up the M6 and then along the A55 into Wales. Surely Betsy would be smart enough to stay around people, as he had instructed her. He felt a horrible sense of urgency.

He reached the Sacred Grove about twenty past four and rushed down the cobbled alleyways to the main building.

"Betsy? I think she must have gone home," the girl at the reception desk said. "I saw her getting her coat, about half an hour ago."

Evan hesitated. Should he drive up to Llanfair and see if Betsy had indeed gone home, or should he double-check the premises first? There was no point in phoning her house. Old Sam, her father, would probably be at the pub by now and he never answered phone calls anyway. And Betsy would take a while to get home if she was taking a bus. He started back to his car, then, on impulse, changed his mind, and ran back into the center. Nobody stopped or questioned him as he searched the spa building, startling an elderly guest as she emerged, clad only in a towel, from the sauna. He reached the meditation building. Rhiannon looked up in annoyance as he burst in. She was sitting, cross-legged, with two other people, on the floor of the main room. The two people sitting with her looked as if they were finding the position uncomfortable.

"What is it now, Constable?" Rhiannon asked in clipped tones. "Any more dramatic rescues to be carried out today?"

"I hope not," he said. "You haven't seen

Betsy recently, have you? Or Michael Hollister?"

"I saw Michael a while ago. He was down at the dock, rigging his sailboat."

"Thanks. Look, if Betsy shows up, keep her with you. Don't let her go anywhere."

"What's this about?"

"I'll explain later. I've got to find Michael."

He ran past the swimming pool, down the steps to the dock. There was no sign of Michael or a sailboat. Betsy had been seen putting on her coat but he hadn't passed her on the road or at the bus stop. Of course, somebody could have given her a ride home, but it was also possible that she had gone out with Michael Hollister in the boat. She had admitted she was keen on him, after all. And Michael did come across as a harmless kind of chap. The panic was making it hard to breathe or think clearly. He had to get to her before it was too late. It might already be too late. . . .

He should call for help, call in reinforcements, get the police launch sent out from Porthmadog, but how long would that take? If Betsy had only been getting her coat half an hour ago, the sailboat couldn't have gone too far. There wasn't much wind this afternoon. It would take a while to sail clear of the estuary.

Then he noticed the dinghy bobbing at a mooring about a hundred yards offshore.

And it had an outboard motor too. He tore off his jacket and swam out to it, gasping for breath as he hauled himself on board. Lucky that he'd just learned to ride a motorbike, he thought. This couldn't be too different. He pulled the choke full out and then yanked hard on the cord. The engine popped, sputtered, and died. The saltwater was making his burned hands start to smart. He tried it again, then again with mounting frustration. On the fourth try it sprang to life with a satisfying roar. He put in the choke a little and untied the rope as the engine warmed up. He increased the speed to full throttle as he steered the dinghy out to sea. The sound echoed back from the banks of the estuary and wide ripples spread across the flat surface. He reached the point and met the first slap of waves from the open sea beyond. Still no sign of a sailboat. He hesitated, not sure whether to turn left or right. Which way would they have gone? Where would Michael be heading if he wanted to get rid of Betsy? Straight out to sea, obviously. Less risk of her body floating back in to shore. He shuddered as the thought crossed his mind.

"Dammit," he shouted. Which way?

To his right he could see the channel markers indicating the channel into Porthmadog Harbor. It had been an important port once, during the time of the slate industry. The further — red — marker caught his eye.

There was something on it. He turned the dinghy toward it. As he came closer, he saw that it was a person, clinging onto the buoy for dear life.

"This is lovely." Betsy leaned out across the bow of the sailboat and trailed her hand in the spray. "I'm so glad you asked me, Michael." She looked back at him and smiled. "To tell you the truth, I was getting jittery about staying at that place a minute longer. I keep wondering — do you think the person who killed Bethan meant to kill me as well?"

"I don't know why you think somebody killed Bethan," Michael said. "I told you we've had trouble with that door before. I suppose the wood swells when it gets hot and wet."

"But the funny thing is that I managed to get it open," Betsy said. "I had to pull hard, but then it came open for me. Bethan was a lot bigger and stronger than me. How come she didn't have the strength to push it open from inside?"

Michael shrugged. "Maybe she passed out quickly. Panic makes people hyperventilate, doesn't it?"

"Yes, but . . . I found this in the flower bed." She put her hand into her pocket and produced the piece of wood. "Look, it's a wedge, isn't it? Not very big but it would have kept the door closed. I'm going to show

319

it to Constable Evans tonight anyway. Maybe they can find fingerprints on it." She turned back to him suddenly. "Your mum was furious with me when I found it. 'Leave the groundskeeping to the gardeners,' she said." She put her hand to her mouth. "I say, Michael, you don't think, do you? It's not possible — she couldn't have done it, could she? Killed Randy, I mean."

"Anything's possible," Michael said. "Nobody every really knows anyone else in this life."

Betsy shuddered. She found that she was shivering and drew her hand in from the water. The wind in her face had become stronger. She looked up. The point was behind them.

"Shouldn't we be heading right now, if we're picking up your friends in Porthmadog?" she asked.

"Not right, Betsy. Starboard. You've got to learn nautical terms if you're going to sail."

"Starboard, then. Shouldn't we be going starboard?"

"All in good time. We'll get there eventually. We've just picked up a good breeze. Sit back and enjoy it."

Betsy turned back to look at him. He was sitting at the tiller with a smile on his face. For once he didn't have that hangdog, defensive look. He was in control, master of his boat, handling it perfectly. She just wished she could stop feeling nervous. She told herself to relax. It didn't matter if they were going out to sea. Michael was a good sailor. Nothing would happen.

She watched as the coastline receded to a dark line on the horizon, with Snowdon and its sister peaks just jagged bumps on that line. She wanted to go back in to shore, but she didn't want Michael to know she was nervous. So she concentrated on looking over the side. The water was dark blue and so clear, going down, down, down. As she looked, she became aware of something deep below them, moving up through the deep water. A fish? No, it wasn't sleek and silvery. It was whitish in parts but parts of it were dark too. As she stared, fascinated, it came closer to the surface and she saw that she was looking at a girl's face with dark hair floating out around it. The amazing thing was that the girl didn't seem to be in any distress. She was moving quite comfortably up from the deep water, her eyes open and focused on Betsy. She was only a few feet below the surface now and she reached out her hand to Betsy. Then she opened her mouth to speak and a bubble came up to the surface.

"Rebecca." The word wasn't spoken out loud. It just resounded through Betsy's head.

"What are you looking at?" Michael asked.

"Nothing. I just thought I saw a fish."

Betsy spun guiltily as Michael left the tiller and came up beside her. He looked over the side. "You're right. It was nothing."

Betsy looked again and saw only deep, clear water.

Michael looked at her oddly, then went to grab the tiller again. "Keep looking," he said. "Sometimes you see dolphins around here."

She did as instructed, watching him out of the corner of her eye. She knew with startling clarity what she had just seen. Rebecca really was here, down at the bottom of the ocean, probably with a weight tied to her — and Michael had brought Betsy here for only one purpose. She wanted to kick herself for being so blind, so stupid. Why had she never suspected him? Because he had seemed so nice and so vulnerable, of course. But he was the one who had let her out of the steam room and . . . now she remembered. He was the one who had given her the cup of coffee to take to Randy. "He always has a cup of coffee after lunch," she heard him saying. "Why don't you take it down to him?"

On the floor of the boat she noticed a length of rope. There was a heavy weight tied to one end. That was for her, she was sure. A rope like that had taken Rebecca down to the bottom. Well, she wasn't going to go without a fight. Now that she knew, she wasn't going to be caught unawares. She turned around and sat demurely on the seat, facing him.

"I think it's time we went back into shore, don't you?" she said.

"Not just yet. There's one thing I've got to do first."

"I want to go back to shore now, Michael."

He laughed then. "And I don't want to. What are you going to do about it?"

Betsy made a lunge for the tiller. "This!" she shouted, wrenching the tiller hard across. The boom came flying across and the boat keeled.

"Are you crazy? You'll have us both in the water!" he shouted.

"Which wasn't what you'd planned, was it?" She wrenched the tiller the other way. He was grabbing for it, but still off balance. She saw the boom beginning to swing in his direction and pushed it hard so that it caught the side of his head and he was knocked to the floor.

"You're not going to kill me, Michael," she yelled. "Not like you killed Rebecca. She warned me, you know. You didn't think I was really psychic, did you? But she came up from the bottom of the sea and warned me. Why did you kill her, Michael?"

"I had to. She realized the truth about Kathy. She wanted me to turn myself in — stupid cow!" Michael slithered to his feet and made a lunge for her. "It won't help you,

you know. I'm still stronger than you."

The boat was leaning heavily to starboard. Betsy took a calculated risk. She flung herself toward the boom and pulled it downward, so that it had her weight and Michael's on it.

"What are you doing, you idiot!" he shouted as the boat teetered and then capsized.

Chapter 25

Michael Hollister clung to the swaying channel marker, his arms wrapped around it for dear life. "Help me!" he shouted again.

Evan brought the dinghy nearer. "Where's Betsy?" he demanded. "What have you done with her?"

"Betsy? What are you talking about? I've no idea where Betsy is. I was sailing alone — just get me off here."

"What happened to your boat?"

"It capsized. Freak wind."

"I thought you were supposed to be a good sailor."

"I am. A bloody good sailor."

"Who lets his boat capsize? How far away?"

"Out there, somewhere. I grabbed onto the top of an ice chest and the current brought me this far."

"I'm asking you again — what happened to Betsy? You're not getting off that buoy until you tell me."

"She — she went down with the boat. I'm sorry. Freak accident. I'm not the greatest swimmer. There was nothing I could do."

"Like hell there was," Evan said. "Just like there was nothing you could do when you killed Kathy Sparks and Rebecca? Did you throw both of them over the side? Convenient way of getting rid of somebody, isn't it? It's no good denying it, Michael. The police know everything."

"It wasn't my fault." Michael started to cry. "How was I to know? She'd had sex with plenty of other blokes — I didn't think she'd mind. She said she'd report me for rape, so what else could I do?"

"And Rebecca? Did you have to kill her too?" Evan shouted.

"Rebecca started following me around. I think she was keen on me at first. But then she began to put two and two together. Now get me off this bloody thing. I can't hold on much longer."

"When I've found Betsy," Evan yelled. "Now where did the damned boat capsize?"

"I told you, it's too late. I saw no sign of her in the water when I swam away."

"If you don't tell me, I'll go home and forget I ever saw you," Evan roared. "If you ever want to get off that buoy, you'll tell me exactly where it is."

"Sort of due southwest from here. It can't be too far. I'm not a strong swimmer."

Evan gunned the motor, leaving Michael yelling after him. "Don't leave me. I can help you find it. I can't hold on much longer!"

There was more of a swell now. The little dinghy rose and fell as it cut through the waves. Spray splashed into Evan's face and his wet clothing clung to him. His hands were stinging like crazy. He was shivering, though more with fear than with cold. How would he find her out here? How would he ever spot the hull of a capsized boat, if it hadn't sunk completely by now? Betsy! He felt tears warm on his cheeks. He should have done more to protect her. He should have forbidden her to go to the Sacred Grove again. He stood up in the bobbing boat, scanning the sea for anything that could be a body. Then he saw it — the upturned hull of a small boat.

He made for it, his heart racing.

"Betsy!" he yelled. "Betsy? Can you hear me?"

Then a small white hand rose from behind the boat. She was clinging to the rudder, her arms wrapped around it, looking like a small, lost mermaid. Her face broke into a big smile when she saw him.

"I'm glad you got here, Evan," she managed to croak. "I couldn't have held on much longer."

It took him a while to haul her into the dinghy. She slithered to the floor and collapsed, coughing and gasping. "Michael," she managed to say. "It was Michael. He was going to kill me. I had to capsize the boat. It was the only thing I could think of doing."

"It was bloody brilliant," Evan said.

"I don't know what happened to him. I

ducked under the boat and stayed there. I thought he might give up looking for me and think I'd drowned. I suppose he must have drowned by now."

"He was alive when I last left him clinging to a channel marker," Evan said. "We'll go in to Porthmadog and get the police launch to pick him up."

"How could I have been so stupid?" Betsy sat hugging her knees to herself. "I thought he was the one person I could trust, but he killed Rebecca."

"How did you find out?" Evan asked.

"She told me."

"What? When?"

"I saw her, Evan. She came up through the water and she told me who she was. That's when I realized she was warning me." She looked up, her face alight with excitement. "Oh my gosh, you know what that means, don't you? I really am psychic after all. That's why I dreamed about the right cave. I really do have powers."

"Is this the way you take it easy when you're given the day off?" Sergeant Watkins stormed into police headquarters, followed by Glynis Davies.

"We went to the Sacred Grove — the whole place is in an uproar. Rhiannon called us," she said.

"And we've got Michael Hollister in custody," Watkins added. "He's blubbering like a baby, asking for his mother."

"His mother suspected him all along, can you believe that?" Glynis demanded. "She brought him home from Oxford because of another missing girl. She said she couldn't turn him in — her own flesh and blood."

"And then he went and killed her husband," Watkins added.

"Do we know why he killed Randy?" Evan asked. "Was it just to get him out of his mother's life?"

"No, he had a better reason than that. Randy saw him going out on the sailing boat with Rebecca. When you came showing pictures, he remembered and questioned Michael about it. So he had to go. Luckily, Michael has a good brain. He overheard Randy extolling the virtues of the cave he'd just discovered on his jogs. The rest was easy."

"And he established the perfect alibi for himself too," Evan added. "I only realized afterward how easy it was to cut across country to the point."

"Ah, so that's how he did it," Glynis said. "His mother was still swearing that he couldn't have killed Randy because he was in Porthmadog all afternoon."

"Some family," Evan commented.

"Yes, so much for the aristocracy," Watkins agreed. "Too much inbreeding, I suppose."

Evan sighed. "In a way I can't help feeling sorry for that boy. Abandoned by his mother when he was little more than a baby."

"Don't start on that," Watkins said. "The psychiatrists will have a field day trying to prove that he was a product of his unhappy childhood. I didn't have the best childhood but I don't go around killing people."

Evan smiled.

"She's a plucky kid, young Betsy, isn't she?" Watkins went on. "Kept her head out there in the boat."

"Yes, she's something else," Evan said.

"She told me she only kept going to work at the Sacred Grove because she wanted to help you," Glynis commented, watching Evan start to blush.

"Well, she does sort of —" he was about to say, "fancy me," when Watkins finished the sentence.

"She said you were being so clueless that somebody had to get to the bottom of things." He looked at Glynis and they started laughing. He pulled up a chair and sat beside Evan. "But I think I'll keep that remark to myself when I put in my recommendation to Colwyn Bay."

"What recommendation?" Evan asked.

"For you to fill the vacancy in the department. Now that I'm being promoted, I'm hopeful we can take on an extra trainee."

"I hope you get it," Glynis said. "I really

like working with you."

"That's great." Evan nodded as he got to his feet, digesting this information. "Thanks, Sarge — oh, and I can't call you Sarge anymore now, can I? What do I call you instead?"

"God will do," Watkins said. "Or sir. Your honor. Your worshipfulness . . ." He laughed as Evan gave a mock bow.

"I've got to go," he said.

"Yes, you were told to stay home and rest, not shred your hands to pieces out in the ocean. Now go home and stay there, or I'll tear up my recommendation."

"I've got to see Bronwen first. I haven't been able to see her since they took her into hospital. I don't even know how she's doing. She'll think I don't care."

"Go on then. Off you go," Watkins said.

"Good luck, Evan," Glynis called after him. "And if she thinks you've been ignoring her, I'll come and tell her that you've been heroic again."

"No, don't do that!" Evan could just picture Bronwen's reaction to the gorgeous Glynis. If he got the transfer to CID, Bron would have to get used to his working with Glynis, but she'd have to get her strength back first.

The ward sister was nowhere to be seen when Evan arrived at the hospital. He went down the ward, looking for Bronwen, then stopped when he came to an empty, made-up bed. It had Bronwen's chart at the end of it. His heart did a complete flip-flop.

"What happened to this patient?" he yelled at a nurse who passed the ward.

"Miss Price? She's getting ready to go home," the nurse called back, "and don't yell. You'll have Sister in here."

He turned around and there was Bronwen, still looking very frail and white, coming into the ward in her street clothes.

"Bron, you're okay!" He ran to embrace her.

"More than I can say for you," she said, turning her cheek as he went to kiss her. "What happened to you?"

"I got my hands burned yesterday and I fell into the ocean today. Apart from that I'm fine."

"I leave you alone for two days and you nearly destroy yourself," she said. She looked up at him tenderly and she was smiling.

"Bron, I'm so sorry about what happened. I've been going out of my mind with worry. I tried to see you but they wouldn't let me."

"I know. The nurses told me. And it's I who should be sorry. I suppose it was because I was so weak and dehydrated that I flew off the handle like that. I should have known better. As if you would have jumped straight into bed with Betsy the moment I wasn't around."

"I did spend the night with Betsy," he said, watching the reaction on her face. "She came to me in a terrible state. I couldn't send her home again in the middle of that storm, could I? But you don't have to worry. Nothing happened." *Almost nothing,* he corrected himself mentally. He had kissed Betsy, after all, and he had been tempted. Still, he was only human. . . .

"I'm really sorry, Evan," Bronwen said again.

Evan slipped his arms tightly around her. "We have to trust each other if we're going to have any kind of life together."

"Who said anything about life together?" Bronwen asked, looking up at him with serious blue eyes.

"It's about time we started thinking about it," Evan said.

"So what exactly are you suggesting?"

"I want you to marry me. You know that."

"No," she said shakily. "I never really knew that before. You never asked me."

"I'm asking you now." He took her hands tenderly into his and was about to drop to one knee.

"Bedpan, nurse," came a petulant voice from the far end of the ward.

Bronwen looked at Evan and laughed. "Hardly the most romantic proposal I've had in my life."

"Let us both get better and then I'll do it

properly, all right?"

"I don't need it done properly. I've wanted to marry you since the first moment I set eyes on you," she said. "Which is more than you can say for me, I think."

"Miss Price, haven't you gone yet?" The ward sister appeared at the door. "The ambulance is waiting to take you home."

"Miss Price is coming with me," Evan said firmly. He put his arm around Bronwen and led her out of the door.

"You don't have your motorbike, do you? I don't think I'm up to riding pillion yet."

"No, just the old bone-shaker, but I think it will get us back up the hill."

"Talking of hills," Bronwen said as he opened the car door and helped her in. "They found out what was wrong with me at last. It was *Giardia* — you know, a microbe you can pick up through drinking in mountain streams. I must have picked it up on that hike I did the weekend you were working."

"That will serve you right for going hiking without me." He grinned, then grew serious again. "Thank heavens they found that out. I was so worried." He climbed in beside her. "I thought all kinds of things, ranging from terminal illnesses to Betsy poisoning you."

"Betsy poisoning me?" She looked amused. "Well, I suppose she is resourceful."

"You have no idea how resourceful," Evan

said and told her of the last few days.

"She sounds like an ideal policeman's wife," Bronwen said. "Maybe you'd better marry her instead."

"Oh, no." He smiled at her. "I couldn't risk having a psychic wife. She'd be able to spy on me when I was out interviewing beautiful women and — ow, don't hit me, I'm wounded!"

Bronwen laughed as Evan swung the car up the mountain pass that led home.

The next week a large banner appeared outside the Red Dragon. "Grand Celebration of Kitchen Reopening. Welcome Back Betsy Party. Free beer to all locals on Friday Night."

"Harry must be very glad to get her back," Roberts-the-Pump commented to Evan, "to make that old skinflint give away more than one pint of beer."

"Perhaps it's South Wales beer," Evans-the-Meat commented, "and he can't find a way to get rid of it!"

Evan was about to continue up the street on his evening beat when he heard his name and Mrs. Powell-Jones came running toward him. "Good news, Constable Evans," she called. "That heathen establishment has been closed down. I read it in the paper. We have taken on the devil and we have won." She beamed at him. "Now do you believe in the power of the righteous?"

She strode up the middle of the street, back toward Capel Beulah, singing, "Fight the good fight with all thy might" at the top of her voice. Suddenly there was a loud pop-popping noise and a motorbike came speeding down the hill at great speed, with Evans-the-Post hanging on for dear life.

"Out of the way!" he yelled.

Mrs. Powell-Jones gave a high-pitched scream that echoed from the hilltops as she flung herself to one side and the bike passed her by inches.